AND GO TO INNISFREE

THREE NOVELLAS AND TWO STORIES

DON ERON

CONTINGENCY STREET PRESS

ISBN: 978-1-958015-01-8 (pb)

ISBN: 978-1-958015-00-1 (eb)

Logo art: Janet Glovinsky

Cover design: Suzanne Hudson

The author gratefully acknowledges *Natural Bridge* #5, where "The Legend of Elk Avenue" previosuly appeared.

CONTENTS

I will arise and go now, and go to Innisfree . . .

And I shall have some peace there.

— W.B. Yeats

GISELLE'S TEARS

G ISELLE'S TEARS ARE HUGE and slow. They descend her face with all due deliberation, accelerating as they reach her chin. Were I a surrealist, I'd talk about the puddles at her feet, for her tears don't dissolve but accumulate, the small lake expanding across the room, the flood of tears wading across fields with tears ebbing at her knees. When we were little, she cried every day, every hour. Time wouldn't move unless her tears pulled it downstream. She cried because I hit her, or Rachel was allowed to go down the street and swim in Montgomery's pond with Suzy Montgomery and Giselle wasn't. She cried because she didn't want to wash her hair, because I broke my favorite glass, the one in which I liked to drink my favorite milkshake concoction. ("I loved that glass so much," I told her, and then the tears rushed forth.) Giselle was sensitive, I'll admit, even for a kid; it didn't take much to set her off. When she was older and had plenty of stuff worth crying about, she cried about that, too.

Picture her room. More specifically, Giselle's bed and the dolls atop her bed. Because I had to pass through her room to go downstairs, I got to know that bed. Giselle's dolls were piled halfway to the ceiling. Dolls crowded out of the windows onto the lawn. Here goes the surrealist in me. Wherever she went, she found her way home by the trail of dolls. Sometimes travelers would report a giant doll-like spacecraft in rural New York. Experts dismissed these reports as illusions, as tricks of light and the standard distortions of perception and memory, but we knew of what they saw and where. They saw Giselle's bed through the window.

To go to bed, she had to clear off the dolls—fortunately Mom didn't compel her to arrange them neatly, for there was more to be done in childhood than to spend it stacking dolls—except for a favorite half dozen that protected Giselle under the covers. Perhaps her dolls cried with her to sleep as she recalled the day's laundry list of grievous slights.

It was tough enough being Rachel's little sister, but Giselle wasn't satisfied with being second best: she wanted to *be* Rachel. That's a lot to expect when your sister's the knockout, the charmer, the brain who tests so high it's suggested she audition for the TV quiz shows; as well as being, to hear Rachel tell it (her stance on the issue fashioned in the days before she had competition for the post), Mom and Dad's *favorite*. Once the favorite always the favorite, went Rachel's theory. Within two years of my clouding the picture, she'd pushed me off a highchair, breaking my femur (in the process furnishing me with my earliest distinct—if fleeting—memory), and slammed a car door on my fingers, tearing off the chunk of finger above the bone. I guess Rachel was telling me things were swell when it was just she and Mom and Dad. Four's a crowd, Bart, so go back where you came from. By the time Giselle got into the game a year and a half later, Rachel was sufficiently sophisticated to understand that it was unrealistic to expect us, despite a little urging as she danced us on highchairs or helped us into cars, to disappear into thin air. Rachel's sense of entitlement Giselle would always covet. Along with the beauty, the charm, the smarts.

Me Too was our name for Giselle. Rachel and I were going swimming. "Me too." We rode our bikes into town for pop and candy. "Me too." We ordered fried chicken in a basket at Nitzchke's Diner. "Me too." You couldn't blame her for wanting to be included. Not that Giselle didn't have friends of her own to involve her, but that didn't matter. Even if she spent all her time with her friends, it couldn't begin to compare. Me too. Me too. She would have been content to spend her life as the tag-along runt kid sister, so long as we let her tag along. If we didn't, she would cry about it to Mom.

We had to take Me Too along, we had no choice in the matter, yet if we lost her there'd be hell to pay. Call it a series of early lessons in reality. And she was harder to keep track of than she was to lose. Giselle couldn't focus in those days. We'd be walking into town for candy and pop, and the ducks would be out in Darrington's yard down the block. Suddenly Giselle wasn't out of the house to go into town for candy and pop with her sister and brother, she was out of the house to watch the ducks in Darrington's yard. Rachel and I still followed the original plan. We couldn't care less about the ducks in Darrington's yard. They didn't correlate with reality as we knew it. Giselle didn't correlate. We'd be drinking our pop bottles before we'd remember Giselle. Sometimes she'd be curled up by the picket fence another house down, by Mr. and Mrs. Foster's, crying, at home within her tears.

Whereas Giselle was jealous of Rachel, and jealous of me, if only because as a boy I got to do all the athletic boy things that back in those days it was unseemly for a girl to be obsessed with, at the price of being labeled a tomboy (which Giselle was, though she would have preferred to serve the office without the stigma), I wasn't jealous at all of Rachel. I had my own little sports world that could hardly admit her entrance, even were she inclined. I think she still hadn't forgiven me for intruding on her turf. Maybe it was because she was two years older, and whatever stage of development she was in, I was in the awkward, embarrassing stage she'd just grown out of. To Rachel I was always awkward and embarrassing. In fact, I *was* awkward and embarrassing, a strange kid. Who wanted a kid brother who couldn't walk down the halls at school without falling, usually taking two or three innocent bystanders down with him? People learned to give me a wide berth as I walked the halls. Who wanted a kid brother everyone gave a wide berth to? For that matter, who wanted a kid brother who was so superstitious, so compulsive, he couldn't leave a room without touching the floor and walls twelve times, fourteen times, or else his mom and dad, or Warren Spahn (his favorite baseball pitcher), would die? Who wanted a kid brother with so much responsibility—who couldn't walk into his house after school without yelling, "I'm home!" exactly thirteen times at the top of his lungs or something terrible would happen to somebody he loved?

Not Rachel.

I can't remember a single thing Rachel said to me between the time she pushed me off the highchair and when we were in college. I'm sure we had a lot of normal conversations during those fifteen years and talked about the usual things and had our share of fights and conspired to torment Giselle—certainly in town, as we drank our pops, oblivious to Giselle lagging behind, crying, curled in the fetal position by the Fosters' picket fence, words must have been exchanged—but I can't remember any of it, except for one day in high school when we passed each other in the halls. By now she was the prettiest girl in school, a senior, and I doubt anybody who didn't happen to grow up with us had any idea I was Rachel's brother. It didn't correlate. I was a football player, a wrestler, a track man, a muscle-bound, friendless mute, and as I passed Rachel in the hall, she quickly said hello. I remember I looked over my shoulder and didn't see anybody; we were the only two in the hall. I was a wiseass. But

I wasn't being a wiseass when I looked over my shoulder to see who Rachel was saying hello to.

And one other time. I was in fifth grade and Rachel in seventh, junior high. Junior high was a different world, different teachers for each subject, walking the halls with ninth graders, *high school* freshman tall as adults, while in fifth grade you walked the same halls as kindergartners. The idea of participating in a process as elaborate as junior high was beyond my comprehension, terrifying and foreign, though at nights I'd dream of playing junior high ball. I'd heard rumors of popular kids at our school who went to junior high and were *outcasts*. I'd heard that kids who wore blue jeans were ostracized, that ninth graders yanked the hanging loops, the fruit loops, the *chaddy rinks*, off the backs of kids' shirts as they walked down the halls. And there were the fights, too. If you made the mistake of buttoning the top button on the collar of your button-down shirt, you not only risked ridicule, but a ninth grader was liable to beat the living daylights out of you after school, if not right then in the hallways. I'd heard rumors that squads of ninth graders publicly descended on seventh graders who struck them as in the least way odd, and pulled off the victim's pants, gave him pink belly, strung his trousers up the flagpole, all in front of a crowd of people they'd known all their life. There were endless social gradations and nuances and rituals to junior high that I already knew I'd never understand, even if I survived into the ninth grade.

Rachel, on the other hand, *was* junior high, she was born to it, her entire life until junior high was treading water; now she had permission to swim. Giselle, at least, she still had use for. They could talk their girl language, and Rachel could put curlers in Giselle's hair and show her cheerleader moves and teach her the social nuances and gradations. Giselle was an opportunity for Rachel to be the sophisticated junior high woman she was, on display at home and not only in the halls of Central Junior High.

We'd had a Schipperke, Mitty, for a year. Rachel had already outgrown the need for pets, but both my world and Giselle's revolved around Mitty. I could spend hours giving him body massages, rubbing his thick black fur, taking him for long walks down River Street. When you're ten years old there's not much more fun than taking your dog for a walk, if you like your dog. I liked Mitty. Though I doubt I had the perspicacity to take this for an early object lesson, as much as I liked my dog, Mitty turned on me regularly. Maybe I was too aggressive with the body massages? Maybe I'd force him on walks he didn't want to take? I'd walk into a room, and he would bare his teeth, growl alarmingly, lunge at me until Giselle or Rachel, if she wasn't in her room fashioning lipstick and eyeliner, calmed him. "Good dog, Mitty, good dog. We won't let Bart hurt you."

Three dogs in our neighborhood had been poisoned in the weeks before I came home from school one afternoon and found Mitty in our driveway, teeth gritted, stiffened, legs fixed in the air. Because of the poisonings, we'd kept him on a long leash at the end of our driveway, fifty feet downhill from River Street. That morning as I left for school, I noticed an open can in our front yard, and I think I supposed it belonged there. I can't say I didn't think anything of it—certainly I thought a lot of it after I found Mitty, and for months afterward—but I'd always envisioned the poisoner-walking up to the dogs and feeding them from his hand, the way old strangers in parks were supposed to offer candy to trusting kids. As soon as I saw Mitty I knew instinctively how naive I'd been, how much a grade-schooler, for anybody serious about poisoning a dog wouldn't go up to the dog in broad daylight and feed him the poison where everyone could see, the poisoner would drive by at night and quietly toss a poisoned candy bar maybe, or a poisoned sugar cube, through an open window onto the lawn.

When I saw Mitty, I was anaesthetized, the shock narcotic putting me at one remove where I could observe, where I could evaluate. I thought—I didn't think this was likely, but I wasn't a veterinarian, I wasn't a doctor; I was, as was profoundly apparent, a naive grade-schooler—that Mitty might be alive. I walked inside our house. I went upstairs and knocked on Rachel's door. I could hear music behind her door. Chad and Jeremy, or Peter and Gordon. The Dave Clark Five. Those were the groups I'd heard of. Rachel already owned a lot of records. I wouldn't have known where to buy a record even if I wanted to own one. I don't want to sound disingenuous, but it had just been a few weeks since the Beatles were on Ed Sullivan. Music didn't seem like much of a thing worth having an interest in. I'm sure they had record stores in Iowa in 1964, where Dad's job brought us from upstate New York, but I didn't know where they were.

"What do you want?"

"Rachel, Mitty's hurt."

Rachel turned and went back to her music.

"Please go out there with me."

Rachel sighed. If she'd been doing anything else but her homework while playing the music, I know she would have told me to get lost. Rachel followed me out. Mitty was still at the end of the driveway, his legs still petrified in the air. I kneeled over and massaged his belly.

"Do you think he's alive?"

"The dog is dead," Rachel announced, turned around, and walked back inside.

I continued massaging his belly. I don't think I was mad at Rachel. I doubt I expected her to be much help. Mitty had been crazy about her, but she never had much use for him, perhaps because she sensed he so captured Giselle's and my imaginations. I'm sure she didn't feel good about it, but the dog was dead, and none of it had much to do with her. Later in her life she became a lover of animals, she had dogs she loved almost as much as she would have loved her children, but this was still 1964 and I was leaning over Mitty and massaging his belly, anaesthetized, without a clue as to what to do. I knew it would be an hour before Mom and Dad got home. Giselle was off at Brownies. Then I took a breath and walked inside and pulled down the telephone book and looked up veterinarian in the yellow pages. I called up the first listed. "I think my dog's been poisoned. Can you come out here and look at him?"

The woman who answered the phone asked what he looked like. "He's very stiff. His legs are in the air."

"I see. I'm sorry. You're very brave." She asked me if I would wait a moment, and a moment later came back to the phone and said they could be there in an hour.

"But he may be dead by then." I told her I'd call back if I couldn't find somebody to come sooner.

I made a note beside the vet's name in the yellow pages. One hour.

The seventh vet heard my voice and agreed to come immediately. Once there, he quietly confirmed Rachel's pronouncement. I told him about the open can I'd seen on our lawn that morning. He looked at me. Well, he said, dogs can die suddenly, and for a lot of reasons. He asked if I'd like him to take Mitty away—in fact, he wanted to send some samples to Ames to verify the poisonings. I thought it over. "I don't think Giselle should see Mitty like that." He nodded and wrapped Mitty in a black wool blanket, then placed him in the trunk. Before the vet drove Mitty away, though, he seemed to hesitate. He may have been on the verge of offering an apology on behalf of human nature. Where could he begin? I wish I could remember the good man's name, if I ever took it in to begin with. He stuck out his hand and I shook it.

I didn't cry until after Giselle got home. My parents had been home for half an hour already. They were proud of me for calling all these veterinarians. They said it was a very brave and responsible thing to do—they couldn't believe I was only ten years old. When Giselle got back from Brownies and they told her Mitty was dead, she thought they were kidding her. Then it struck and she began sobbing. Huge tears slowly descended her face, accelerating at her chin, swamping her blouse.

She buried her sobbing head in my lap, and I remember crying into her hair as upstairs the Dave Clark Five sang to Rachel.

"Giselle would have been much happier if she could have been a wrestler," my dad told me in one of those talks we have periodically in which we encapsulate the past. ("You used to have to scream, 'I'm home! I'm home! I'm home!' thirty times every time you came home," Dad recollected once. "Well, Dad, it was a burden." "A burden? I'd feel like yelling back, 'Who cares! Who cares! Who cares!'") The conversations don't tend to last long, if only because Mom has a way of sensing that some important matters are being discussed and must come into the room from the kitchen or her bedroom where she's riding her exercycle or running in place while watching the soaps—in her late fifties she became a fitness fanatic—and change the subject. Theoretically I'm sure Mom strongly endorses important conversations, but you can't beat mother nature, and her instinct for survival has a way of cutting them off at the pass. Maybe she feels, given the unresolved emotions that dominate any family that risks taking each other seriously, that it won't be long until blame is assigned. Blame makes her uncomfortable. It has a way of suggesting that things might have been different.

Though I never would have said it—when I venture reflections about Giselle, particularly her history of imbroglios and losses, my motives often tend toward the transparent—Dad's right. She would have been happier if she could have been a wrestler. I was a wrestler, and that's been the key to my happiness. But seriously, ladies and gentlemen. If she could have been a boy instead of a tomboy, she would have accomplished a few things that she'd take seriously as accomplishments. And she wouldn't have been her sister's little sister, always a step behind, never measuring up. Boys have measurable things to compete in, on level playing fields. You fight it out on a mat with a referee and afterward they raise your arm if you outscored your man, even if your man happens to be your brother. There may be hard feelings, but you know where you stand. And if you try hard enough and put enough time into it and are lucky enough and have any talent, you can stand over there and not always a step behind, never measuring up. They had girls' sports back in the sixties when Giselle was growing up: swimming, tennis, gymnastics; not basketball yet, like today, courtesy of Title IX, not track and field and cross country and softball. But none of that was Giselle anyway. She was built for power, stocky, low to the ground, a born nose guard like her brother, a wrestler, big on muscle, crude with the finesse. There was no equivalent in girls' sports, no place to develop her nature, to channel her temper, to show her best goods. Instead, she started the Mat Maids at our high school. The Maids ran the PA system during the home meets, worked the scoreboards, made posters during the week that they hung on bulletin boards or held above their heads as they sat in the stands in their Mat Maid section, cheering their heads off on the rare occasions they paid attention. Sometimes they made sandwiches for the team for after the meets and otherwise tried to look like they belonged. A Giselle natural. Mostly freshmen and sophomore girls who had nothing else to do weekend nights signed up when Giselle founded the club her junior year, when I was a senior. While the concept was nice, nobody on the team had any interest in those girls.

Marian Leigh Anberg was Giselle's best friend, or close to it. Giselle always had a lot of friends, as befitting her office as Matron of the Mat Maids. Sometimes she'd claim they had crushes on me. If so, they'd never betray it in our rare conversations. Marian was very thin, almost anorexic before the days of anorexia as a defining cultural symbol, and had huge white teeth when she smiled, which was almost always. She had jet-black hair. Three or four nights a week Marian was at our place, with Giselle and the muffled laughs and rock music playing behind closed doors. By now Rachel was off at college. I had the huge room downstairs, next to the rec room, and every night did jumping jacks or ran tiny laps for hours behind my own closed door, the lights out, as Cat Stevens or the Grass Roots performed on the portable hi-fi. Mom, passing Giselle's door or loading the washing machine on the other side of the rec room, passing my door, must have thought we lived in an entertainment complex with competing rock and roll venues.

What did I think about during those hours in motion? Nobody in the world wanted to know, and I liked it that way. It was good training for wrestling, as I'd punctuate the laps with the occasional set of one hundred six-count burpees, two hundred pushups, then back into motion, then fifty pushups clapping my chest with my hands each repetition, then one thousand jumping jacks, then back to the tiny laps. All this, needless to say, on top of practice after school, on top of my official workouts after practice when I lifted weights. Before my senior year I could bench press three hundred pounds, do three sets of curls with 155 pounds, applying less than strict scrutiny to my form. The weight was the thing, and you can be sure I was going to hoist more weight than I hoisted last week—certainly not *less*, never—more than anybody in my high school. The official workout after practice was competition, was never letting up for a second, was winning. What I did after that with the lights out in my room and the hi-fi set as loud as Mom and Dad upstairs could tolerate, the thousands of tiny laps in place in the dark with the side bars of six-count burpees, pushups, jumping jacks, clapping pushups, then back into motion again, was my time free of the rigors of keeping up and pushing myself harder. It was dreaming. It was glory on the mat, dramatically winning the state championship, and cheerleading girls so in love with me they'd feel a sock catching in their throats as I'd walk by. That's what I would dream in motion during an hour commercial free, twenty in a row on WBBM-FM. My career in rock and roll unfolding before my eyes in a dark room. And if it was all tied together, contingent, conditional, first the glory on the mat before the girls revealed themselves, I wouldn't have wanted it any different. During my time, everything I dreamed was inevitable.

Where were those girls outside my room when the dreams wore thin and shiny by the brunt of infinite repetitions? Sometimes they were upstairs in Giselle's room. As I've mentioned, to hear Giselle say it, there were girls who had crushes on me. She kept me posted. I'd look around for the names she'd mentioned at school. I'd look for them at meets but they all looked the same in their blue Mat Maid outfits. Sometimes I'd go upstairs and look for them in the kitchen, for they were down the hall behind the closed door to Giselle's room, listening to music and doing whatever they did in that room (not six-count burpees, I presumed), giggled about whatever they giggled about, planned Mat Maid strategies for all I knew, and didn't have their ears peeled for my cumbersome machinations in the kitchen. Whatever I burned off during my hours in motion in my room, I'd gain back half afterward in the kitchen.

Marian didn't have a crush on me to my knowledge, or Giselle's evidently. Though sometimes Giselle didn't require knowledge before telling me girls had crushes on me. Sisterly instinct would do. That worked better than knowledge, surer in its urging. Giselle would have an instinct that Robin or Stacy had crushes on me, then report it to me as knowledge, as fact. Luckily, when I looked for them at school, they were never around. I had trouble distinguishing sometimes. It was a big school, the size of a small college, in the town we moved to, outside Chicago, from Iowa, before my junior year. Every girl I saw in the halls was the same girl, the generic girl in my imagination, the same long, frizzy, black hair, and worn, rump-hugging jeans, and the same huge eyes that fixed on you like a favorite song they'd forgotten suddenly coming into focus. And some versions of that girl had crushes on me, according to Giselle. It was dizzying. Outside the girls in my classes, and some of Giselle's friends, I never knew any of them personally.

Marian touched my face once, before a wrestling match. It was a road match, a dual meet at Proviso East in Maywood, and we'd gotten there early to weigh in. After weighing in, once we stopped gorging ourselves with thermoses of hot chocolate, with sandwiches and brownies and cookies, gaining back some of what we'd lost to make weight, our bodies and souls surging back to reality so we could focus on something beyond when we'd be able to eat again, such as our imminent matches, we milled around. The JV teams were already dressing in the locker room. I was full, gorged, bloated during that sweet time before nervousness would hit so hard I was liable to be exhausted before stepping onto the mat for my match. The first few fans were filling the stands, other than the Mat Maids sitting together or running back and forth, and my teammates stretching out in the bleachers, some of whom would sleep before the match, well into the JV meet, bypassing nervousness entirely, until somebody would tap their head with a boot and a wisecrack, and we'd descend together into the bowels of the locker rooms. I always wished I could sleep like that before a meet, though the only time I'd managed to, I awoke so freezing I didn't stop shivering until after my match. This day I was walking across the Proviso East gym for a drink of water. I could never stop filling myself before I'd surge into focus and the nervousness hit full bore. Sometimes while I was making weight, my body decomposing, my muscles atrophied by starvation and lack of fluids, I fantasized long drinks of freezing water from ice-gray water coolers. One night I dreamed I was sweating to death and couldn't find a cooler anywhere, just a white block fountain with its tepid stream of warm moisture—it was demoralizing, a nightmare. I didn't know where I was going to college, but I wouldn't go anywhere where there wasn't a legitimate ice-gray cooler on my dorm floor. Thus I passed my bouts of starvation and thirst. The drink I just had, across the gym floor, was from a fountain, hardly sufficient, not what I required, but what was there. I turned back in my mild disappointment to see Marian walking toward me, or toward the fountain behind me. But she was looking at me and smiling, as always, and I tried to think of something I could say to her, should she stop and wish me luck in my match, something beyond garbling 'Thank you, Marian,' because in that moment, as she walked toward me in the yellow gymnasium light, I understood that Marian was beautiful.

Maybe it was just the way the light hit her face because, although I was forever suddenly realizing that girls I'd thought ordinary were beautiful as they walked toward me in dim hallways and across gymnasiums, I'd never felt that way about Marian. Perhaps that's why I was able to be friendly with her, to establish an easy repartee that was beyond me with some of Giselle's other friends or the girls in my classes. Because she was pale and too thin, almost anorexic, I had nothing at stake around Marian, and though I would have much preferred to impress her, I didn't *care* if I impressed her. And so I could be released from the self-consciousness that entombed me around the others. Around her I was mercilessly awkward, but I was used to that. With awkward I breathed easily. Awkward I wore naturally; I'd spot awkward in the mirror and recognize myself. Until ten seconds ago; when she walked into the light, she carried the light with her into my imagination, and I saw not the pale, thin girl who'd befriended Giselle, but Marian in five years or ten or fifteen, a woman, beautiful, smooth, daring, sophisticated in her whimsy, compassionate, fun.

Ten seconds ago, falling for Marian was so far beyond my comprehension that I'd never considered it—and my scope was large in the girls I'd consider falling for, even if I sometimes couldn't distinguish one from the other. Now Marian was inevitable, for I'd seen her; that's the only way I can put it. Falling for her was the most natural thing in the world.

And she didn't walk past me to the fountain. "Are you growing a beard?"

I looked at my teammates stretched out in the bleachers. None of them were watching us. I looked at the Mat Maids and the crowd of parents and friends and classmates beginning to settle in; none of them noticed us. We were two people having an inevitable conversation in the corner of a high school gym in complete privacy, on a winter evening in 1970.

"I don't shave the day of a meet, Marian."

"Does it make you feel tough?"

Marian was standing six inches away, her black eyes piercing me as if it was only a matter of time before I said something interesting. I couldn't remember anybody standing that close to me before, or looking at me in quite that way. "No, Marian. It makes me *look* tough."

Then she touched my face, running her finger along my two-day beard.

I didn't kiss her. I didn't tell her she was beautiful, that I'd just seen a vision of who she was going to be in five years, ten years; that she would never again be who she was two minutes ago, her transformation already inevitable. But if some men date their sexual practice from the first girl they kissed, I date mine from the evening Marian Leigh Anberg touched my face.

"It feels rough," Marian said, her hand still grazing my face.

"The secret to my success," I told her.

In another ten seconds she was leaning over the fountain, running the tepid stream of water through her mouth, and I was walking up the bleachers toward the guys I wrestled every afternoon. It all made sense.

Thus began my covert affair with Marian Leigh Anberg. Covert because she was Giselle's friend, and it would be too complicated were Giselle to know. Covert because she was a Mat Maid and none of the wrestlers were allowed to take any of the Mat Maids seriously, by unstated immutable agreement. Covert because Marian wasn't yet who she was going to be in five years, ten, fifteen; though I was never to forget the vision I saw as she walked toward me in the gymnasium light, I never saw her that way again; in the trick of reality, she was ever after the bucktoothed, pale girl, startlingly thin, with the black eyes too big, too piercing for their sockets. Covert because I'd never had a girlfriend before, I'd never kissed a girl, never been romantically linked in the eyes of my family and teammates, never gone on record as having a type; I wasn't eager, either, to establish a precedent I wasn't sure I could live with. After all, we're talking about a life. My image embedded in their consciousness. What's evoked at the sound of my name. Nothing to be overt about if I wasn't absolutely certain. Covert because there was no way I could be certain that Marian knew we were having an affair.

It took place in the corners of other people's conversations. In groups we sought each other out, quick to smile after the night she touched my face, quick to ensure we exchanged a few words, made contact— "Hi Bart." "Hi Marian" "Going to class?" "That's why they take attendance, Marian." "Me too." "Yeah, see you at the meet." "Good, I'll see you at the meet"—what we said didn't matter, whether or not anybody could read something into the words beyond the inane sentiment or feel the currents of warmth didn't matter, to the almost physical hunger we felt to say something, anything, to each other every day. We had to have that. Those words assured we were right on target.

For what? Since it—we—never went beyond the corners of conversation, the quick warmth and brief, compulsive contact every day, it's hard to say. Perhaps on target toward being less covert, more like those teenage couples you see whose compulsion is a physical hunger to ferociously suck each other's gums, anywhere, anytime. Toward being typical, regular, talking on the phone two hours every night, taking long drives then swallowing each other in the back seat of my parent's Dodge, if I could borrow the keys. If I could talk her into it. Marian spending a little less time with Giselle mapping out Mat Maid strategies, if such they were doing, a little more time downstairs behind my closed door. Just looking at each other. Just holding each other saying nothing as WBBM-FM played fifty-six minutes of music an hour. I never felt that way around anyone else. Although it wouldn't be long before I was over my head in real affairs, overt, physical contact, complications, jealousies, humiliations, I never would feel so excited, so content and warm to contemplate just looking at somebody, just imagining what it would be like to spend hours with her in a room behind a closed door, not even touching.

Some days I'd walk down the hall saying her name over and over, my secret mantra: Marian Leigh Anberg.

Affairs are by definition finite, aren't they? Interludes. They're not relationships or marriages, friendships, obsessions, though at their best they contain elements of each. Perhaps no affair is more finite than a covert affair, particularly one so understated you can't be certain the other person is aware of her involvement. I said you can't be *certain.* But you can be sure, pretty sure, quite sure that she knows, that in the days or weeks that the hunger crescendos that you're almost as much to her as she is to you. More, for all you know. Perhaps Marian knew she was my mantra. Perhaps she made a point of thinking about me as she fell asleep so that I might be with her as she dreamed, never far from her thoughts, with her as she wakened. Of course, were she so obsessed she would have devised strategies and opportunities, revealed herself, would have, at least, felt out Giselle as to whether I'd mentioned anything about her, conspicuously brought up her name, *anything*, and Giselle would have mentioned her more often to me, felt me out, asked me flat out what I thought about Marian, didn't I think she was pretty?, told me that yes, Marian has a crush on you, Bart. And this one you'd better do something about.

But none of that happened. And I wasn't going to risk saying anything to Giselle. Losing on the mat was all the public humiliation I was willing to bear.

If covert affairs are so covert they have nothing to sustain themselves but themselves, if their only home is in the imagination of a healthy seventeen-year-old wrestler soon to be instructed—ever on the lookout—by real affairs, they are not long for this world. At best, candidates for dim memories. I happened not to see her in the halls for a couple of days. On the third day, I was late for a class I couldn't afford to be late for, didn't stop for the warm, quick smile, the litany of words, the anything that had spoken so much when I needed to hear it. Perhaps she was miffed. Perhaps she was relieved. The other people's conversations, on which our covert affair played out on the edges, soon proved more elusive. Soon the words were in a language I'd lost the fever to learn.

When an affair ends, things can get awkward for a while. I could handle awkward. But when the affair is covert, the transition back to routine is smoother. And so, when the affair ran its course, we had no need to avoid each other or ignore each other as we walked through the halls. We simply stopped noticing each other. And if one day I found myself walking the halls without a mantra, I didn't notice anything was missing. But I've never completely forgotten what I'd seen in the yellow gymnasium light before we wrestled Proviso; or that, unbidden, Marian Leigh Anberg touched my face. It's most of what I remember about her. And the way the light you walk into every night of a wrestling season can turn you completely around if the right girl walks into it. Even if the girl you see isn't precisely the one that's there looking for a drink of water, seeing her friend's brother, noticing his beard, but a version of what she'd do well to become. According to you at seventeen.

And perhaps I wouldn't remember even that if Giselle hadn't blown a red light the next year. I was away at college. My legitimate sexual life had begun two nights before with a townie, as we liked to call them, a high school girl from the small Minnesota town my college was in. I met her at a college dance, and an hour later we were in my dorm room. I liked the way her breasts sagged, though she couldn't have been more than sixteen. I liked the way her dirty blond hair curled around her thin shoulders. Her face was slanted and wise, and I liked that. I liked that she was as hungry for it as I was. I liked a lot of things about her. I knew that after we walked the quarter mile to my friend Rick Potter's room, and I borrowed his car keys and drove her into town and kissed her goodnight in her parent's driveway out past the Maytag factory, that I'd never see her again.

The red light Giselle blew was blinking red, and she didn't so much blow it as fail to register the Cadillac sedan driving through the blinking yellow light at the intersection. Giselle wasn't drunk, wasn't high on grass; she was a kid finishing her last year of high school driving home later than she'd expected to be out. The night was new to her, in a car she could drive whenever she wanted. There's no way to know what she was thinking of or talking about to her friend and passenger. A plastic surgeon would spend most of that night sewing shut the lacerations over Giselle's fractured cheekbones. Giselle wouldn't remember that. The Cadillac hit the Dodge at the passenger's door. Chances are Marian was killed before Giselle's cheekbones hit the steering wheel.

I took the bus into Chicago the next week. By then they'd removed her bandages. Giselle's face was swollen and pale beneath the lines of sutures. From her black and bruised eyes, as she saw me walk through the door of her hospital room, huge tears descended.

WELCOME TO GILGAMESH

O CEAN BARTOK, JR., WAS no relation to the Hungarian composer, though who could say? You go back far enough, there's a common seed. But that's not what people meant when they asked, and to his embarrassment he occasionally claimed a kinship. Often as not, though, he'd add upon being introduced, "No relation." If this clarification inspired a moment of mirth—say a pretty woman smiling—Ocean found grounds for encouragement. (Perhaps he'd found, at last, a lass with a classical approach.) That is, until he found himself in bed one morning with a tinny blond who belched like a smokestack when she told him she'd thought the "no relation" was a reference to the Atlantic and the Specific.

"From the Denver Bartoks," he'd sometimes elaborate. This was not only true, but of no small consequence to those in the know, who were fewer and fewer as Ocean aged. His father, Burt (the Ocean with the Junior was a flourish the son himself added in his thirties), was euphemistically known as a wholesaler. 'You need it, Burt can get it for you,' was the lament of numerous small businessmen in Burt's heyday, Denver in the forties and fifties. 'And you better get it from Burt. And you better need it,' went the unspoken parenthesis.

In the early sixties Burt made the disastrous decision to go clean and run for mayor. (Not that the two considerations were mutually exclusive in Denver, but months before his decision Burt tumbled off a horse on a Sunday outing; when he came to moments later, he found he'd turned idealist.) Like many a thug before him Burt considered the source of his respect coincidental (a little muscle, a little *sachel*, what's the difference?), and was more amazed than humiliated by both his dismal showing in the mayoral— "Forty votes," is what Ocean liked to say. "Burt and thirty-nine others."—and the intransigence of Ocean's Uncle Myron about letting his brother Burt back into the family concern once Burt read the election returns and was thus inspired to another awakening directly canceling the previous. Still, he'd turned philosophical in the interim, and soon thereafter moved to Scottsdale where he still lived forty years later—albeit not with Ocean's mom but the fourth Mrs. Burt—thus both providing Ocean Jr. with—and depriving him of—his legacy. A son of a thug is a son of a thug, and poor is poor.

"Could it be you were eluding the legacy when you changed your name from Burt Jr. to Ocean?" his therapist asked during his one and only session on the couch.

For this he was paying eighty bucks?

"The old shake and bake," Ocean smiled distantly.

The therapist looked at him blankly. She was a haggardly if stylishly dressed middle-aged woman who throughout the session peered forlornly at her desk—in search of a pencil to chew on, was Ocean's guess. Or else—despite professional pretensions—the bloodless counselor found Ocean Jr. as uninteresting as he found himself.

The woman he was seeing at the time had urged—coerced, was Ocean's view—the deposed thug's son to seek counseling, and when Ocean returned from the one and only session bemoaning "trite banalities" and "takes one to know one," the girlfriend confirmed what she'd suspected: that Ocean agreed to the session only to gain extra leverage in his ongoing quest to be, as she saw it, the mayor of their relationship. Within several days, before he had the chance to play the 'I even sought counseling' card, she left him. Forever after, she'd think of Ocean Bartok, Jr., not as an old lover so much as a crazy uncle she'd spent the summer with back when she was young and a little crazy herself. To her surprise it was a good memory, one she turned to over and over as she reached into middle age, even going so far as to call Ocean one night—his name was right there in the Denver book—though she hung up before he could have answered. After all, she reasoned later, when talking about it to friends to whom she'd often mentioned Ocean Bartok, Jr., it would be Ocean and not the memory answering on the other end.

Among his old girlfriends, she wasn't alone in recalling Ocean fondly, though after she left, he made less of an effort. Perhaps he was too consumed raging at his "legacy of poverty" to express much rage at them. There would be words when provoked (though often not), feelings would be hurt, voices raised, but mostly he'd appraise them from a benevolent distance. His yearning for them became of the flesh, not the heart and soul, but enough of the flesh that some would confuse his appraisal with passion in those moments when the distance closed. But as he rocked them in his arms, he'd murmur not sweet nothings but diatribes against the legacy his father left. "I could have been on Easy Street, let me tell you, but Dad had to go clean. Then when Myron squeezes him out, he takes it with a shrug, 'See ya sometime in Scottsdale.' Not that I'd want him to be a bully or a bad guy, a *shtarker,* a *gonif.* That's not the point. You see?"

"Sure," the woman was liable to say, under the impression Ocean Jr. was revealing, for once, tender confidences.

"Every time something good happens I blow it in a fit of conscience, a fit of 'do what's right.' At exactly the wrong time, that's when I decide the time's right to be a *mensch*. Mom—that's Mrs. Burt #2—stenciled Sucker in my BVDs. Should they get misplaced at the laundry, she wanted all to know who they belonged to."

"Are you being funny?" the woman might ask now, without irony.

"Are we laughing?" Ocean might rejoinder.

Eventually the women would leave, believing at the time that nothing about Ocean had anything to do with them, he was too remote; when they stripped it was anyone's guess whose bosom he touched. "He made me feel like a woman, not a commodity," Lucy Miller acknowledged to a friend after leaving Ocean, discussing what went wrong. "But if I *was* a commodity, he made me feel like I'd be off the rack. A nice guy, but after enough of that," Lucy couldn't resist adding, "I needed to put an ocean between us." Her friend got it. "It's not that there's no there there with Ocean," she summed up, echoing Gertrude Stein's appraisal of Oakland. "There's plenty of there. But the there is always elsewhere. See?" The last word gave Lucy a pang, because that's how Ocean ended half his sentences, as if surprised somebody in his arms could possibly understand.

And Ocean when they left? A half glass of ouzo, then another cut with water, a quart of butter brickle, toss in a few hours of sleep, he'd be fresh as new. Later he might grow a beard or shave one. That was Burt's legacy #2—not that the two were unrelated, Ocean knew himself well enough to know that. Right behind 'Fuck things up when the going gets good,' there was 'Women leave.'

So: hit me again.

In fact, Ocean Jr. was shaving his beard when the call came that would change his life.

'Lucy, I'll take you back,' Ocean was thinking when the instrument rang. Lucy was one he smothered. Around her every thought, every fact, every event was relevant material for speculation. A little Ocean went a long way, but too much was too much, somebody could drown there. He knew that but couldn't help himself from unloading on the gal. Ocean's other style was to keep them so far away they'd hardly know—after leaving—they'd ever entered the arcade.

It was his boss, Mr. Wills, saying "Judy" when Ocean answered.

"Mr. Wills," Ocean said.

"Have I mentioned before you could call me Larry?"

"I know I can call you Larry, Mr. Wills."

"Look, Ocean," Mr. Wills began. This meant he wanted Ocean to listen and—if possible—reduce the level of bubbamagumba. Otherwise, he'd call him Judy—for Judith Bunting Pride—or Phyllis—for Phyllis Rose—to indicate what line of card he wanted Ocean to work. While the signal saved them not more than a minute or two a year, both men accepted it as natural. Ocean knew Mr. Wills was trying to be friendly with the jovial shorthand, and after talking to him was often grateful for his boss's efforts. During the conversation, it was a different matter, though.

"Yes?" Ocean said indulgently.

"The latest Judith Bunting Pride." Mr. Wills began reciting in a high-pitched tone that brought to Ocean's mind a starling:

Through all our years together
we've weathered every kind of weather
but to this day, love, when you look at me,
you're everything, everything, everything I see.

"Yes?" Ocean said when Mr. Wills finished. "I don't recall pretending it's Ezra Pound."

Mr. Wills paused. He knew where he could and couldn't go with his authors, and this was cutting thin. "Can we jettison the third 'everything' in the last line? Cross it out? Lose it? Eliminate it, Ocean?"

"I write them, you print them," Ocean said, "and we can stay pals. See?"

"It's just a suggestion," Mr. Wills begged. "Don't blow your lid."

While Ocean knew the *shmaltz* was fluff designed to sell occasional cards to ladies who viewed the world through the prism of romance novels (the sensibility, Mr. Wills liked to claim, of the average American), nonetheless it was carefully rendered fluff. Nobody did Judith Bunting Pride or Phyllis Rose—or Tiffany Lager Bush—like Ocean Bartok, Jr. Ocean knew it was crap, but somebody like Mr. Wills—who couldn't even tell the third "everything" in the last line was Judy Pride's heartfelt signature (an idiosyncrasy Phyllis Rose, say, or Tiff Bush, would never utter)—had better keep similar opinions to himself.

"Tell it to Rosemary Pickleman in Dubuque," Ocean said. "Tell it to LeAnn Lulu in Arlington Heights. Tell it to Jessica Pitchford Blake in Logan City, Oklahoma. Mr. Wills, tell *them* the third 'everything' doesn't belong."

"Now don't get your back up, Ocean."

"And then you know what, Mr. Wills?" Ocean wasn't proud of himself for rising to the bait, but sensed, for all the discord it could generate between them, his boss would be disappointed if he didn't make the half-spirited approximation of a conniption fit, after which Mr. Wills would mutter "artistic temperament," and "can't live with 'em, can't live without 'em," which, given that Mr. Wills' livelihood was the production of greeting cards entirely dependent on the romantic, moody musings of Ocean Bartok, Jr., was literally true. Because both knew this—to the chagrin of each—the exchange in its biweekly permutations took the form of ritual.

"My aching prostate," Mr. Wills groaned. "Don't tell me."

"If you don't like my Judith Bunting Pride, if you don't find her suitable for the special anniversary line of Wills Cards and Sentiment"—when Ocean pronounced this it always sounded to Mr. Wills a lot more like 'sediment'— "you don't have to run Judith Bunting Pride, Mr. Wills. Or better yet, Mr. Wills, you can write them yourself. Then," Ocean's voice was rising now, concluding with a flourish not even Ocean was sure was ironic (once started, he played the role straight, as he did the greeting card verses) "you can use the exact number of 'everythings' your little businessman's heart desires. Do I make myself clear?" This last Ocean felt was crueler than intended, for he considered Mr. Wills—as he did the buying public for his romantic 'sediments'—functionally illiterate.

After nearly half a minute, Mr. Wills said, "Crystal."

"Whew," Ocean sighed.

"Thought I'd mention it, that's all," Mr. Wills said. "Nobody's perfect. 'Nother reason I called though, Judy. I have an idea for another line."

"All kidding aside," Ocean had to interject, "I'm already doing Judy Pride and Phiss Rose and Tiff Bush. I can barely keep them straight. Now you propose another line? My plate's full, Mr. Wills."

Now Mr. Wills paused. Unlike the writings of Judith Bunting Pride and Phyllis Rose and Tiffany Lager Bush, the conversation of Ocean Bartok, Jr., could either be taken at face value or its opposite. Either that or everything Ocean said was a euphemism, though a euphemism for who knew what. Thus, the full plate could mean Ocean was overloaded, or it could mean he only has a spare twenty-three hours to work with once he finished with the holy triumvirate of Wills Cards and Sentiment. Ocean was a kidder; like many others of that disposition in Mr.

Wills' experience, he didn't like it much when you couldn't tell if he was kidding. "Burt, this is different."

Burt. Ocean didn't snap at Mr. Wills for invoking the verboten. Burt. It had taken years to get everyone of his acquaintance to call him Ocean—here and there he'd had to stage a snapping to encourage the recalcitrant—but now that it had been years since anybody had called him his given name, he sort of liked the sound when Mr. Wills said it. That had been him once. Burt Bartok, Jr. It's not something somebody would like to be called on an everyday basis, but as a change of pace Ocean now found the name surprisingly palatable. While this was no time to turn sentimental, maybe Dad and Mom knew what they were doing back then? With Ocean's current view being that they'd agreed on little during their marriage, he briefly wondered if the choice was unanimous. Had the moment presented them with a ray of hope? "Aw," Ocean said, "you ever hear the one about the *shmuck* on the camel?"

"*Ocean Bartok, Jr.* Yes, *Ocean Bartok, Jr.* Now don't hang up, Ocean. We can branch out. Masculine sentiment for masculine men. Macho guys like you, Ocean, the strong silent types, the guy every floozy wakes up beside five years later and discovers she's married. Verse not *by* Judith Bunting Pride but *for* Judith Bunting Pride in the very words the somber hunk would use if he could use words. You don't think that'll fly, Burt? You don't think that dog'll hunt? You don't think that's our ship? Judy Pride's okay, but Judy Pride ain't gonna get us where we're gonna go, pal. Whaddya say, Burt? Naturally, you'll be sole writer for the line. Exclusive. Fuck Judy Pride," Mr. Wills said, then braced himself for the explosion.

"I don't quite know how to take that," Ocean Bartok, Jr., replied softly.

Times like this, Ocean wished he was on speaking terms with Burt Sr. It wasn't that they never talked—Burt Sr. out of guilt for the legacy of poverty he bestowed on the boy, Ocean out of fear of lambasting the old man. Senior called Ocean almost every week, but once they'd covered the respective weathers in Scottsdale and Denver, they always and only talked about the same thing: Ocean's social life. Ocean had been with a lot of women, but Burt Sr. had a way of timing his calls to the exact hours after the woman left Ocean, leaving either because he was stultifyingly possessive or else so remote as to make it unclear to the woman why she was seeing Ocean to begin with. If this wasn't the case for all Burt Sr.'s calls, it was the case for every other, and Ocean dreaded the inevitable inquisition. ("How's it going with Rosemary, Ocean?" "Well, things are ambiguous with Rosemary at the moment, Dad." "No! No! Not again, Ocean. I'm so sorry! I'm so sorry! When are you going to have any luck, son? Is it that I left your mom? I've been one poor example for you, Ocean. I've been no good. I'm so so sorry.") Well, it was touching at first, Pa as feverish apologist, copious with the mea culpas, and if Ocean suspected Burt Sr. was playing the role to preclude any accusations Ocean might levy along these very same lines—the obsessive theme first sounded shortly after Ocean changed his name from Burt Jr., without much explanation why the moniker that had treated Senior right well for over sixty years was no longer quite adequate for Burt Bartok *fils*—Burt Sr. getting a message of disapproval here that Ocean was never quite certain he intended to send—the pity and disappointment in Burt Sr.'s voice sounded genuine, and overwhelming. It would depress Ocean for hours afterward. While at such times of abandonment, in the midst of the second ouzo cut with water, he welcomed diversion, he didn't need the second boot to the *tuckus*. Ocean never considered lying to his Dad—doomed strategy with a shitter like Burt Sr. (as Ocean recalled, his first lesson sitting at Burt's knee was "Don't shit a shitter," followed by "This too will pass.")—but would consider not picking up when Senior called the machine. ("I know you're there, Ocean. Pick up. It's your old dad.") At such moments Ocean half-suspected Burt Sr. knew he was there, so picked up even in moments of highest resolve. And though the tone of pity and disappointment—all for Ocean, though Burt Sr. wouldn't mind a grandkid to climb atop his lap in his old age, for the lessons are eternal—was overwhelming to bear, he often feared each conversation with his dad would be his last. Burt Sr. was in robust health for a guy of eighty-four but had made too many enemies in his prime. Though he was long out of the thug game, the old man was still an avenue toward punishing his brother Myron, who still called the shots in Denver (and whom Ocean himself hadn't seen in the flesh since Burt Sr. was exiled to Scottsdale). Well, on this count alone, Ocean couldn't bear not to pick up.

That's how it went with Dad. Once he got through wailing, it was hard to work in any other topics, such as should he indulge Mr. Wills with the new line. Burt Sr. knew how Ocean made his modest living, but the manner pained him even more than his son's social life. Greeting Card Poetaster! Better Ocean be one of Myron's thugs! "Should I call Myron?" Burt once asked Ocean, though as far as Ocean knew, he hadn't talked to his brother since he'd shrugged philosophically and moved to Scottsdale.

No, Pa won't make much of a sounding board. ("More like a parole board," Ocean once observed to Lucy Miller.)

Had he defamed Burt Sr. when he changed his name? Had he meant to? Ocean didn't consider the question much. At the time he'd been disgruntled with most everything, not just in his life but in the nation, and was convinced by a pretty girl he knew (*she'd* changed her name to Turquoise Rainchild from Jane Smathers) that even a small change could unbolt the windows and let in great rushes of fresh air. Well, he hadn't been

Judith Bunting Pride then, he hadn't been Tiff Bush. What did Ocean Bartok, Jr., mean? Even that was Turquoise Rainchild's suggestion. He remembers changing to Ocean because he didn't want to take himself so seriously anymore; he'd needed to release some of the baggage, to let go of the legacy. Was it possible to do all that and not hurt his dad? Now here he was, full blown. But if the name gave him enough distance from Burt that Judy Pride and Phiss Rose and Tiff Bush were not only his meal tickets but his best inverted jokes, wouldn't Ocean Bartok, Jr., scrawled in perfect reproduced penmanship beneath three stanzas of sediment, go them all one better? ("You don't shit a shitter.")

Ocean called Mr. Wills. "Yes," he said.

"Judy?" Mr. Wills hoped.

"*Ocean Bartok, Jr.*"

2.

In Topeka, Mrs. Robert Bestwick, Lorna to her friends, steered her Voyager into the parking lot of Canfield's RX. It was her secret parking spot (there were always spaces available) and not too inconvenient when she didn't have to carry bundles the extra two blocks coming back from downtown. Once Lorna ran into Brittta Nelson and decided to join her for the matinee—a romantic comedy starring Nick Nolte and Julia Roberts as rival reporters, which Britta found absolutely believable, and both found more plausible than the intimations of romance between the two stars. After the movie they went for cocktails at Mr. Husky's, where Britta filled in Lorna on her own romantic life, which put the movie to shame both as romance and as comedy. Lorna returned to the Canfield's lot not only much dizzier but four hours later than she'd expected, fully braced for the possibility that the Voyager would be towed. But there it was, not even a note on the windshield. Since then, Lorna parked there so long so often they probably assumed the owner worked at Canfield's—not one of the girls at the register, she imagined, with whom she identified, but a pharmacist. Wouldn't it be like a pharmacist to drive a Voyager?

Now Lorna was in a crazy mood. Britta would understand, though Lorna herself wasn't sure *she* did. She'd been short with Robert this morning. Usually Robert made the coffee, and this morning he hadn't. In fact, there wasn't any sort of formal agreement that he'd make the coffee. It wasn't in their marriage contract, as Robert said. In fact, they'd never discussed it. And there were plenty of days he didn't make the coffee in their six years of marriage. It made sense to Lorna that he wouldn't, for all they did all day at the office where Robert worked as a tax attorney was drink coffee, as far as Lorna could tell. They'd look up laws and drink coffee and write up the memo and drink coffee then fill out the invoice with another cup, and Robert would complain all night. Sometimes. Once in a while. He hardly ever drank any before he went to work. He never got to *share* the coffee, which is what he told Lorna after she snapped at him when she walked into the kitchen that morning and Robert was walking out, wiping the crumbs off his mouth, leaning over to kiss her on the ear.

"Gee, that makes my day," she told Robert after the kiss on the ear.

"What is it now?" Robert said, taking a napkin to his mouth, as if to wipe off the kiss. Afterward, there was still a crumb left he didn't get with the napkin. "Honey, I have to get to work, okay?"

Which is when she let him have it about the coffee she just then realized she hadn't smelled when she walked into the kitchen.

"It's not like we have a formal arrangement that I make the coffee, honey. It's not like it's written in our marriage contract. Honey, it's not like I even get to *share* in the coffee," Robert was saying, the preamble to one of the intricate elephantine labyrinths he often launched into when she was being the least bit unreasonable, dismantling the folly of her whimsy with the precision machinery of formal logic. At such times, she would note, Robert forgot he had to get to work, which was supposedly why he hadn't made the coffee (or whatever else Lorna would scream at him about) in the first place.

The truth was, Lorna understood why Robert went on like this and had even found it exciting the few times she'd seen him turn the barrel on somebody other than herself. Robert liked to talk, though seldom about anything that could conceivably matter to anybody in the way she could talk to Britta, for example. But he loved words, especially when they rolled out of his mouth, and when he went on like this she often pitied Robert Bestwick, her consort, imagining he was in the act of reminding himself why he went to law school (K-State) in the first place, those golden reveries where he would cajole skeptical juries with his golden oratory and eviscerate guilty witnesses with the saber-like precision of his relentless intellect, until he met Lorna Dunberry and fell in love and decided tax law was a more prudent route for a family man than the criminal defense bar.

"Fuck you, Robert," Lorna said when Robert paused momentarily—for effect, she assumed—in mid-vituperation.

"You're on the rag, honey," Robert said quietly.

As if that explained everything.

Lorna stood on the porch in her robe watching Robert lurch out of the garage down the driveway in the blue Camry, then back out into the street. "Robert!" she yelled. "Robert!"

Now her husband lowered the window and peered at her expectantly across the lawn. She sensed his insinuating grin as he awaited her standard tearful apology.

"You have a crumb on your cheek!"

"What?" Robert mouthed.

"You have a crumb on your face!" Lorna screamed across the lawn at her husband.

Robert flipped her the bird.

By midmorning she was on her knees in the living room canvassing the job listings in the *Courier*, spread out across the carpet. Robert was the last man in America who didn't want his wife to work. They met when she was a junior at K-State and Robert was in his last year of law school. Before then she'd worked; in high school she'd worked ten hours a week during the school year at a novelty shop, and in college as a teller at a savings bank. That's where she met Robert, in fact. He was a cute, preoccupied guy (you'd never confuse Robert with anyone but a student in those days) who'd migrate toward Lorna Dunbery's line every week, never exchanging more than pleasantries until the day they found themselves next to each other in line at the post office ("You're Lorna?" "You're Robert?"). He was holding a birthday package to mail to his niece. Lorna, with nieces of her own, melted.

A year later, as he held Lorna in his arms during the hours after he asked for her hand in marriage, which is how Robert put it ("Will you marry me?" not for Robert, the phrasing lacking the golden flourish), they expressed their fantasies of the future. "I need to be in love for ever and ever," Lorna told Robert. "I can't take anything less than that. Do you understand?"

"I understand," Robert squeezed her.

"We'll have a family," Lorna said. "We'll be a family."

"I'll always take care of you, Lorna," Robert promised. "You'll never have to work. I know it sounds like a cliché, but you'll be the best mother in the world. That's more important than anything."

Sometimes Lorna thought if she hadn't fallen asleep then—if instead she'd clarified Robert's fantasy with more of her own—their lives might have been much different.

There was nothing in the Want Ads specifying an elementary ed major who'd dropped out of K-State a semester short of graduation in order to get married seven years ago. Lorna circled the ad—adding a star—for Day Care Aid at the Rainbow Pre-School, circled several for clerk positions, and—this was Britta's idea—a post for Human Resource Assistant at a hi-tech company located in one of the massive industrial parks east of Topeka.

On her way into town, she thought of Robert at work. If this was tax season, she knew he wouldn't have the time to give her an extended thought, but there were many times throughout the year when the load was lighter, and the attorneys would actually sit back in the office as they drank their coffee and talk to each other about matters not directly pertaining to tax law and billing strategy. Poor Robert. By now he'd be beside himself; Lorna knew by now there'd also be the best fawning apology Robert could manage on the answering machine at home. ("Look honey, I was out of line. Let's go to Henrici's later. Okay?") For a moment Lorna felt guilty that she hadn't waited around for Robert to call and relieve his burden. Britta thought she was always letting Robert off the hook. ("He gave you the *finger*," she could hear incredulous Britta saying.) But Britta wasn't married, and she certainly wasn't married to Robert.

And wasn't Lorna driving into town now? Wasn't she going to May D&F and Foley's and then to Koch's Jewelry across the street to look at a bracelet Robert might have bought her last year for their fifth anniversary if he hadn't bought her the Camry instead (which he always drove, leaving the Voyager for Lorna, though Robert genuinely loved the Voyager— "My child," he'd boast to acquaintances, the way other childless couples would refer to their cat)? Britta scoffed. ("Oh, he got himself a Camry for your anniversary. *How sweet.*") But Lorna understood such gestures as the very pulse that makes a marriage matter, though out of context—and sometimes Lorna thought you had to be her, married to Robert, to know the context—it might seem so meager. But every morning when Robert made the coffee and kissed her on the lips and took the Camry to work, Lorna knew. Just as Robert would understand quite well when he got the bill for the gown and the bracelet and the shoes. Yes, Lorna thought, that finger Robert flipped her may very well end up costing him more than a prosthesis.

Now Lorna pulled into her space at Canfield's RX and got out. It was the best day yet of the late summer, low eighties with a light breeze fanning the mugginess that so often seemed to cover Topeka like caramel around an apple. Lorna looked forward to the walk into town. She'd gained a good ten pounds in her marriage, and though Robert kidded her about it (*Of course*, as Britta liked to say) they both felt the extra weight became her—she'd been scrawny like a waif, rather than slender like a model, like Britta—and men would look at her as she walked through town with her shopping bags swaying from her wrist like cheap friendship bracelets. Or they'd look at her if there *were* any men on the Topeka streets in the middle of a midweek morning, and today for once she was happy men didn't find her invisible. Yet Lorna discovered herself instead walking into Canfield's.

The huge Black woman at the register (Bernice, according to her nametag) nodded at Lorna as she walked in. Momentarily Lorna expected the woman to apprehend her ("*You're* the one with the Voyager.") but Bernice returned to her magazine after smiling briskly at Lorna.

There were a couple of housewives in the aisle pushing strollers, not one of them, Lorna would bet, on the verge of strolling into May D&F and charging a see-through evening gown with a gold bodice. Still, they had the strollers, and inside the strollers were babies and toddlers, and Lorna's heart leapt at the sight as easily and quickly as it sank.

On a morning like this Lorna wanted to do something good, too. She wanted to tell the ladies with the strollers that their babies were beautiful, that someday—with luck—she'd have a child just like theirs. Who could resist hearing that about their baby? She wanted, too, to thank the huge Black woman Bernice for her indulgence with—her indifference to—the parking space, to confess she was the owner of the Voyager. ('Bernice, do you mind if people use your parking lot for their convenience, as if it's their personal, private, reserved space?') What could she buy here? Mostly the aisles were stacked with stuff—tee shirts here, beach balls there (useful in Topeka) next to a section of shampoos and toothpaste; the next aisle over were sandals and cheap flippers, not so much arranged as dumped into the section. The more Lorna walked the aisles, the stranger the place seemed. Here were plastic garbage sacks and paper plates, beside what looked to be Halloween costumes—a Superman outfit, a tiger suit—next to a pile—as opposed to a display—of magazines and school notebooks, beside a small display of candles and incense. To Lorna it was as if the store didn't place orders, just accepted whatever surplus the suppliers cared to unload. ("Put it where you want it," Bernice might say, not looking up from her magazine.) Well, she had to buy something, not only to do justice to her parking there twice a week; the tawdry goods haphazardly flung through the aisles seemed to summon her maternal instincts almost as much as the kids in the strollers. She felt *sorry* for the store, she pitied the place, she wanted to hold it in her arms. ("Britta," Lorna wanted to tell her friend now, "Britta, I'm falling apart.")

In the corner by a basket of light bulbs was a stand of greeting cards. She thought of buying one, perhaps something for Robert to ease the sting of her purchases. What if she bought one and handed it directly to Bernice, saying, 'Here, this is for you, Bernice'? Would that give her pause from her magazine? Lorna stood there, trying to compose herself. Pregnant women sometimes felt this way, and although the obstetricians had been clear about what was and wasn't possible, sometimes Lorna was convinced she had sympathetic hormones. After a while Lorna picked a pale blue card off the stand and walked toward huge Bernice and into her afternoon spree of indulgence and revenge.

But an hour later she was back on her knees in the living room reviewing the job ads she'd circled. Soon she was on the phone placing her calls. Everyone but the woman at the Rainbow Center—whose voice was warm but harried as she quickly asked Lorna to call back later to set up the appointment—before, Lorna imagined, hanging up and attending to a catastrophe—and the Human Resource Director at BlasTex, sounded as if they'd been waiting since morning for Lorna Dunberry to arrange for an interview. The Human Resource Director, Mrs. Meyerhoff, asked the question Lorna dreaded.

"No, I haven't worked in human resources. In fact, I haven't worked at anything since I got married six years ago," Lorna said. (She'd worked at getting pregnant, but that was more than Mrs. Meyerhoff wanted to hear.) After Mrs. Meyerhoff didn't respond immediately, Lorna added, "Mrs. Meyerhoff, I have a fierce desire. I believe I can make a difference to any company lucky enough to hire me." Did she really say that? Lucky enough to hire me? Lorna wondered if an hour ago she would have had the nerve to announce what now, evidently, came naturally.

Mrs. Meyerhoff wasn't taken aback by the boisterousness. "I'm a single Mom too," she said, and arranged a time—tomorrow at four—before Lorna could correct her impression.

Lorna took the pale blue greeting card out of the envelope, read it again.

Can you forgive somebody who supposedly loves you—who has a message on the machine now apologizing for not making the coffee, in his quiet voice he knows you can't resist—for saying the worst thing ever? Even if at the time you didn't blanch, didn't shudder, just acted as if you didn't hear—she wondered if Robert now believed she didn't hear, perhaps—by now—believes he never said it in the first place, never (knowing Robert's penchant for preserving his good image of himself at all costs) even thought it? So bad she never told Britta, who's the one person she knows who wouldn't be in the least surprised.

In the world Robert imagined he lived in, Robert was an adult who never threw a "temper tantrum," as he'd call his fits; never had to apologize for what he never said in the first place; never remembered, was never accountable for what never happened. Where historical accuracy was an inflatable/deflatable extension of historical necessity. Lorna wondered why it was her necessity to remember. As the guy she went out with at K-State before Robert liked to say, truth was influenced more by perspective than by objectivity, usually written by the winner in the blood of the vanquished. (This from a boy who'd never been north of Des Moines!) Derek had been melodramatic, and after she met Robert, she thought of Derek as she would a child. Perhaps—how necessary was memory?—she communicated that to Derek the last time she saw him. He looked like he wanted to say something back, but couldn't find the breath, and smiled at her remotely before walking away.

Why couldn't she forgive what was in all likelihood—Lorna was almost certain—an instant of impetuousness, instantly regretted (though not acknowledged)? After all, Robert was hurt, too. Or forgive in her husband the necessity of believing he'd never think such a thing (she could envision now the incredulous turn of his mouth), much less say to his wife on the morning after their third obstetrician told her that, though he'll continue to prescribe progesterone and metrodin (as long as you're willing to pay, Lorna heard behind the sincere notes of Dr. Gasser's monotone), and though there's always hope in medicine (Gasser looks at Robert almost jocularly), that her eggs will never be fertile, when she spreads out the want ads on the kitchen table (what was she looking for? Lorna wonders. Bank teller? Clerk in a novelty store?), because she wasn't going to spend the rest of her life waiting around home to be the Mom she'll never be in the family she'll never have, after Robert saw her circling in red ink the bank position, circling the retail opportunity, then jerked the newspaper off the table, tearing it into dozens of tiny pieces dropping like leaves from his hand to the floor, as shuddering Lorna watched him in amazement and alarm, "I'll hold up my end of the bargain. You're not going to work, honey. Okay?" as if he was at last the judge he'd dreamed of being, imposing sentence.

Lorna called Britta to tell her about the job interviews.

"It's about time," Britta said. "What does—" Britta paused here; Lorna thought her friend wanted to say 'the Asshole' before remembering that Lorna not only loved her husband but quite often stood up for him against Britta's blithe indictments, "Robert," Britta says finally, "say about it?"

"He'll understand," Lorna said into the receiver. "That's what I figured out today. If I tell him, he'll understand. Maybe not at first, but eventually. Do you know why?" Now Lorna paused. She wasn't sure herself if the question was rhetorical.

Nor, evidently, was Britta. "Why, Doll?" Britta eventually asked.

"Because he'll have to understand," Lorna said to her friend. "Robert does what he has to."

"Welcome to Gilgamesh," Britta said, as was her wont whenever Lorna "wised up," as Britta would say, though Lorna had known her to apply her stock phrase just as often when Lorna—and Britta's other friends—committed catastrophic errors. Lorna couldn't always tell until later (even then) which was which, and now wondered—marveled even—that Britta apparently thought she could.

"Britta," Lorna said, "I stopped at Canfield's RX today. That place I told you about where I always park? I bought this card."

"A card?"

Lorna held the card in one hand as she cradled the receiver against her shoulder, and her hand shook though the card filled her again with the resolve she'd felt since she'd read it this morning. It surprised her to understand now how badly she wanted Britta to approve of the sentiment expressed in the card, and she wondered if her friend sensed more was at stake than the expression of a momentary enthusiasm. "Listen," Lorna warned Britta, "don't laugh."

You scare me more than fear can say
and I, who know no fear
in your eyes, must scare up reasons
to hold you away. I've said so much
I didn't mean in order

to say what I could bear, such
was my fear before our love
though I'll say it now,
my love,
here, with all my courage,
and hope that you will hear.

"That's a greeting card you bought at—what's it called?—Canfields?" Britta said after Lorna finished.

"The place is so strange," Lorna said. "You can go there and find everything you're not looking for. But sometimes aren't those the pleasant surprises?" She wanted to say more about pleasant surprises, that she thought it was something Robert could learn, a lesson for the man who knew everything. Maybe, in fact, it was something Robert would say to her this evening when they talked and she told Robert about the job interviews, and he'd listen and approve of her plans, because he *must*, claiming the thought as his own.

"You're in a mood," Britta said.

Well, she gave Britta her chance. It occurred to Lorna now she'd never had friends for long. That her friends in junior high, talking about boys and volleyball and Mr. Swanson in Geography class at school and her parents, weren't the same friends she had in high school, talking about boys and volleyball practice and Mr. Rutger in Spanish and Typing, mostly now with Suzy Corin, with whom she worked five hours a week at the novelty shop, whom she hadn't seen since her first summer off from K-State. (She'd heard a rumor, years after the fact (if it was a fact), that Suzy Corin drowned in Lake Cosco, in a boating accident with her husband, whom Lorna remembered as a hood in high school, and whom Suzy never once mentioned.) In college were new friends, whom now she hadn't seen since she met Robert Bestwick. But she'd made others, and now there'd be more after Britta. What would—Lorna glanced at the card

again, for the name was unusual—Ocean Bartok, Jr., say about
that?

"Lorna doll," Britta said, "would you read me that again?"

3.

Dear Ocean Bartok, Jr.,
Are you real?
Melinda Courtney
Bellingham, Washington

This was the first note. It would remain Ocean's favorite
for reasons epistemological and pungent, for the perfume
emanating from the note reminded Ocean of his boyhood
playing touch football in the pasture beyond Hound's Tooth
Lane (a pleasant event, oddly, he couldn't otherwise recall).
The note arrived addressed to Ocean c/o the Wills Cards and
Sentiment Co., Denver, Colorado.

After Mr. Wills himself delivered the card to Ocean he placed
it atop his kitchen table alongside the electric and water bills,
a flier from the Money Store, last Sunday's *Post* sports section,
and the Spiegel Catalogue he kept handy for inspiration. Two
days later Ocean thought of the note while completing a Judith
Bunting Pride couplet (the Pride line was drying out and this
would be, as far as he knew (as far as he could trust Mr. Wills,
who promised) Ocean's last Judy Pride) and looked for the note
on the table, momentarily—inexplicably—panicked when he
couldn't find it, then watched the letter fall from the table as he
lifted the Spiegel Catalogue. Ocean taped it to his refrigerator,
hoping next time Melinda Courtney would enclose a picture.

Ocean never heard from Melinda Courtney again. Still, in certain moods Ocean was stirred to consider that the note meant more to him than to Melinda Courtney, who bothered to write and mail it to Wills Cards and Sediment, and to wonder about Ocean, a stranger, in the first place.

The next card, arriving two weeks later, more loquacious in sentiment, did enclose a picture of the correspondent, Ms. Becca Finkelstein of Macon, Georgia. Ms. Finkelstein appeared robust and big bosomed and, according to the snapshot, large of mouth as well. (Ocean already guessed as much from the copious sentiment.) Though he didn't tape the snapshot to the refrigerator—or ever see it again (swallowed, apparently, by the Spiegel Catalogue beside the stack of bills)—that night Ocean dreamed the full-breasted Ms. Finkelstein lay beside him in his bed, empty the four months since Lucy Miller left. Though clothed, if barely, in the snapshot, Ms. Finkelstein lay naked in the greeting card poet's arms.

As the letters trickled in over the next month, Ocean often dreamed of sleeping with those who enclosed pictures; there were several, of various stripe. It would surprise Ocean that many of the women didn't bother to gussy up in poses like Ms. Finkelstein's, but sent Ocean photos revealing themselves in all their overweight, acne-riddled, doughy-skinned, bent-nosed plainness, as if they expected Ocean Bartok, Jr., Author, to accept them as they were. ("You understand my breath and pulse," was a common theme of the women writing to Ocean.) If the photos revealed a degree of nakedness—some went full bore, while others stopped, modestly, with the blouse unbuttoned a fraction above the protruding nipple—Ocean might spend a night dreaming of making love to them, once, before going on to the next card. After the first month, however, with its surge of surprise and novelty, Ocean never dreamed of sleeping with a woman who sent him a picture (after a while he preferred those of neat-looking women in sweaters and outdated hairstyles, smiling their pearlies at the lens as if for a high school yearbook) enclosed with their perfume-drenched letters.

"They're homely in their pathos," Ocean told Mr. Wills, who'd asked him what the pictures were like after the first surge showed no signs of abating. "Or else they're pathetic in their homeliness," Ocean added.

"Watch it," Mr. Wills cautioned.

"You mean these women are our meal ticket, Mr. Wills?"

"Ocean," Mr. Wills clarified, "they're making us rich."

So it appeared, thus raising the kind of abstract, ethereal question Ocean had considered since the first day he changed his name to Ocean and confronted his father's legacy: What is rich?

At first the Ocean Bartok, Jr., line was like any other, breaking slowly, the standard orders Wills Cards and Sentiment filled whenever they pushed a new card—welcome by some, for Judy Pride and Tiffany Lager Bush (not yet Phyllis Rose) were losing luster, resisted by others, for Tiff and Judy still retained their steady core, and some customers (mostly ladies, as Ocean always envisioned and wrote for, yet a surprising percentage of men as well) would sooner change their brand of diet soft drink than their greeting card.

Thus it remained for several weeks until a Mr. Arthur Babich, a prosperous stationer from Memphis, called Mr. Wills directly ("Wills, my wife can't get enough of this stuff. I hate to do this to you.") and increased the order fivefold for his chain of stores, while cutting back on the Pride and Bush. A week later, the proprietor of the Independent Bookstore in Albuquerque wrote Mr. Wills that she planned a full Ocean Bartok, Jr., display in her accessory section. "I found it in a Mom & Pop grocery store in Albuquerque," she added as postscript, as if it was the damnedest thing. Both Ocean and Mr. Wills soon noticed the need in consumers ('readers,' as Ocean liked to consider them) to talk about where they first encountered Ocean Bartok, Jr. Mr. Wills would talk to long-standing accounts on the other end of the line, with whom he'd always been perfunctory, if genial (as they were doubly toward him), brusque acerbic people he'd met twice or three times at trade shows, and sense they suddenly wanted to swap stories. ("I found Ocean in a cat house," he was tempted to respond.) But independent bookstores were a new market Wills Cards and Sentiment hadn't the product or the distribution and sales mechanism ("Or the imagination," Ocean told Mr. Wills) to enter before Ocean Bartok, Jr., bared his masculine heart.

By the end of the month several more indy stores placed orders, unsolicited. Mr. Wills increased his sales staff by two full-time, one hourly.

By August, Tiff Bush was down to fourteen orders.

What is rich? In September, three months after Ocean received the first love note, as he thought of the yearning missives, Wills Cards and Sentiment released the Ocean Bartok, Jr., Blue series, which differed from the regular line, as far as Ocean could tell (by now Mr. Wills knew better than to offer Ocean editorial suggestions, not with Ocean's own name scrawled in acrylic beneath the sediment), only in that the verse was printed on blue stationary. Though the blue stationary did portray the faintest imprint (subtle to the point of subliminal was the artist's motif) of a man's profile. You couldn't tell much more than that, and so the imprint became the source of debate among many consumers. Some thought it was an eagle, some a mere impressionistic logo. The series was presented to Ocean as a *fait accompli*, for all Ocean knew the model was Abraham Lincoln, but it was clear to Ms. Beatrice Pabst of Tacoma, Washington, that the profile was that of Ocean Bartok, Jr.

Ms. Pabst was having lunch in Tacoma with an acquaintance, Ms. Audrey Tappingham, and Audrey's wayward sister, Cindy Delure. Three nights earlier, Cindy had called Audrey from the downtown bus station; the sisters talked for the first time in seventeen years. Now Cindy Delure accompanied her sister on her lunch with Ms. Pabst, whose husband Frank Pabst owned and operated a glassworks factory in Seattle. The idea, quickly accomplished, was to charm Ms. Pabst sufficiently that the tycoon's wife—as the sisters thought of her—would offer to persuade her husband to hire Cindy, possibly as a receptionist in the retail shop, Cindy hoped, for that would represent both an advancement and an extension of her latest brief employment, almost three years before, as a coffee shop hostess in Medford. It was then, after their luncheon salads were cleared, as Ms. Pabst rifled through her huge purse for her makeup kit, that Audrey noticed the blue-hued stationary. "Beatrice, I see you have the new Ocean Bartok."

Beatrice Pabst lifted the light blue envelope from her purse, removed the card, gingerly handed it across the table to Audrey as if the faint imprint might shatter upon contact if it fell from her hand to the rim of the water glass.

Audrey stared at the imprint. "Who do you think it is? What do you think it is?" she said after a while.

All activities at LaCurley's stopped to overhear Beatrice's answer. That's how it seemed to Beatrice. Wasn't it nice to imagine everyone wanted to know, a roomful of strangers connected by the synapse of a blue card? If she knew Audrey Tappingham better—they'd met through the Chrysanthemum Club; Beatrice was past president, current head of the Entertainment Committee Audrey recently joined (Beatrice made a point of having a private get-acquainted luncheon with each new member)—she thought she might tell Audrey the blue card is what Frank means when he means well.

"Is it a bird? Is it a plane?" Cindy Delure said looking over Audrey's shoulder at the indecipherable blue impression.

"It's Ocean, of course," Beatrice said to the sisters, before adding (she was nothing if not sensitive to the inclusive obligations of leadership), "Don't you think so, Audrey? Cindy?"

Audrey stared thoughtfully at the imprint a moment longer. "I've heard that." Then she turned to her sister and smiled. "It's your next husband, Cindy."

"Fuck you, Audrey," snarled Cindy Delure, though she was staring directly at Beatrice.

The above anecdote was related to Ocean Bartok, Jr., in a letter from Ms. Beatrice Pabst two weeks after the release of the blue series—mid-point, as it turned out, in its limited run. While the anecdote struck Ocean as a non sequitur, he was no longer surprised. Often women would send him what—while Ocean was still reading the notes and letters, after viewing the often modest snapshots, or once after responding to a frantic phone call (this despite his now private listing)—he came to view as fragments of their lives, often including postscript notations such as Ms. Beatrice Pabst's: "I would see to it Frank hired her anyway," as if the postscript was the point of it all, as if Ocean Bartok, Jr., glimpsed through a faint impression on a blue card filtered through their imaginations, knew exactly what they meant.

PPS, added Ms. Beatrice Pabst, "You are the author of my heart."

What is rich? One evening Ocean went to Mularkey's Pub, where he sat beside a striking, bulky woman whose red hair fell past her shoulders in huge ringlets. It was a look familiar to Ocean through the snapshots, women with big hair like hers or women piling their hair in huge beehives, a dated elegance that sometimes moved Ocean, as if their dream lives were both formed and suspended by the early sixties, though their faces and verbose effusions suggested many were much younger. Later Ocean would wonder what drew him to her, if through his brief fame and bounty he'd become like a crafty pervert gravitating automatically toward the most vulnerable and defenseless. Though that evening all he knew was, despite a kitchen table (and blue plastic file cabinet recently purchased) overrun with photos and cards, it was already seven months since Lucy Miller left.

"What are you drinking?" Ocean asked.

During the several seconds before she answered Ocean wished to withdraw the question.

"I'm drinking the moon and the stars and the deep blue sea," the bulky woman hummed eventually.

"Translation: Bug off," Ocean said, relieved.

"I'm impressed," the woman said. "If I had a dollar for every twerp who didn't get the message. And this," she turned the martini-shaped glass in her hand, "is a margarita."

Ocean ordered a round and introduced himself. He remembered how as a youth, when he approached women, he'd often give a phony name, like 'I'm Randy' or 'Hi. I'm Mac,' as if he were free to say or do anything, and as long as he wasn't Burt Jr. it would seem to him he wasn't accountable. Though with prettier girls he usually played it straight. Since he'd changed to Ocean, the subterfuge seemed pointless. "No relation," he added.

The woman honked a loud squawk Ocean took to be a laugh after which, briefly, she giggled uncontrollably before looking directly at Ocean for the first time since he'd sat beside her. For a moment he was struck by the large woman's beauty. He wondered what she saw when she looked at him. "That's too bad, Mister," the woman gushed when she stopped laughing.

"No relation that I know of," Ocean amended. "I don't really know his music. Is that a shame? Of course I've heard the concertos for piano. And my Grandpa was Hungarian. I suppose if you go back far enough," he didn't complete the sentence. In the woman's eyes—now burning directly into Ocean's—Ocean saw a loneliness he could only think of as cavernous. There was a drunken lyricism in her eyes. What man she wanted would ever bridge the loneliness? How could you begin? 'It would be like tackling Everest' he could hear himself telling Mr. Wills, with whom lately he'd talked frankly about this strange phenomenon he feared was overtaking his life. 'Like swimming an Ocean' Mr. Wills might resist adding, fearing Ocean might sock him. But her neediness isn't what moved him.

"You're Ocean Bartok, Jr.!" the woman blurted.

This is the moment Ocean understood that while he'd been in his three-room apartment scrawling wretched verses, quickly looking at snapshots and reading the half-dozen cards and letters Mr. Wills delivered daily, the very earth beneath his feet was shifting. It had seemed to Ocean the writers of the cards were fictional women starring in imaginary narratives featuring preposterous versions of himself ("Ocean Bartok, Jr."). But when the woman—who soon recovered and introduced herself as Suzy Roads—searched his eyes through the sheen of her vulnerability, Ocean understood any joke he could offer in his own defense was hollow. What had he expected?, Ocean considered as the bulky woman stared him down. If it was a business to him, better than lifting boxes in a warehouse or glowering over delinquent accounts as Uncle Myron's muscle, when they bought the cards ("By the dozens," as Ms. Rhonda Winkel of Omaha claimed), it was real to them. They took the shlock seriously, and possibly assumed he was serious, too. Suddenly, in the time it took Suzy Roads to stop laughing and search his eyes, Ocean knew "Ocean Bartok, Jr." meant a lot more to a lot more people than Ocean himself ever would. And these people were real.

What is rich? Wills Cards and Sediment was multiplying accounts daily, moving units as fast as they came in. ("As fast as cotton candy at the county fair," Mr. Wills, prone to overstatement, told Ocean.) Mr. Wills, confessing his fear Ocean might suspect he fudged the numbers, tore up Ocean's contract, doubling his take ("There's plenty to go around."), showing Ocean monthly statements with the affection he would a prize heifer.

But those were numbers.

"People really read that crap," Ocean shook his head at Suzy Roads, in amazement or contempt, who could say?

"You're not what I expected."

"I'm not the moon and the stars and the deep blue sea."

Suzy recoiled, then tentatively gripped Ocean's wrist. "Mr. Bartok," she said softly.

"There ain't no Santa Claus either, Suzy." Ocean shook his wrist free, and fled Mularkey's.

Suzy Roads followed Ocean. Her height matched her bulk, though she was neither as tall nor as large as she looked to Ocean perched on her barstool. With her elongated stride she kept pace several feet behind the greeting card poet, who wasn't trying to shake her anyway.

"Ocean!" she yelled as he turned the corner at 16th and Market.

He stopped finally and turned. Soon Suzy stared into his face from inches away until he couldn't hold her enraptured stare and looked aslant. "Sir, why are you like this?"

"Miss, leave me alone!" Yet for a moment he wondered if her breath teasing his cheek was sweet or sour?

Suzy Roads hugged him; as a man Ocean caved in to the embrace.

It didn't matter what he said or did. Typically a gentleman, that night Ocean pushed the boundaries of decorum. "Screw you. Fuck this," he'd growl at Suzy Roads, once glowering as if he might haul off and wallop her. Ocean sensed she thought he was all bark, and the bark was what she wanted to hear.

The more unforgivable his behavior, the more she forgave him. Her large breasts were firm, her legs, though bulky, long and supple. "Shut up for once, please. I don't want to talk," Ocean said impetuously, rolling away from her futon in her LoDo loft. Suzy Roads rolled with him, tenderly resting her arm on Ocean's hip.

"Do you think I'm pretty?" Suzy wondered.

"I've seen better," Ocean said.

"Thank you, Prince Charming," Suzy said, and appeared sincere.

"What do you want from me?"

"Ocean, talk the language of your soul."

"Get lost."

"C'mon, Ocean. You're the voice of men when they're broken, when they're lost, when they seek salvation not in a bimbo but the same little ol' Mabel they exchanged vows with. You're their voice when they stare her in the eyes as she pours coffee across the breakfast table and expose their jugular as penance."

Ocean stared at Suzy Roads as if she were insane. "Look, that's not me, okay?"

"Sez you, Ocean," Suzy smiled.

When you think you've met every kind of woman, that's when you meet the new kind who fractures every known mold. For a moment Ocean rejoiced that Suzy Roads wasn't his type—he favored the regular molds, preferably leaner of figure, less whimsically boisterous. Though he was almost convinced he could take the boisterousness without the whimsy, or—possibly even—the whimsy shorn of the boisterousness. Ocean knew, as he didn't take her seriously, that this way he needn't take her seriously. She was what she was. That this defeat—and Ocean saw it coming the same way months before he'd sensed, when he opened the door to his apartment on the day Lucy Miller emptied his closet of her dresses and shoes and the toiletries from his bathroom shelf, the rueful note waiting on the table explaining enough was enough—needn't be a personal defeat.

"Suzy, what's the diff? I mean, I don't get it. Put Judy Pride on the bottom and what you get is Judy Pride. Cool, sure, if you go for that kind of *dreck*, but no earthquake. No mass enchantment."

"Who's Judy Pride?" Suzy wondered, flat on her back now under the blanket covering the folds and ridges and peaks of her body like bitter frost.

This proved to be a conversation stopper, Ocean was pleased to note, though he nonetheless added proudly, "Judith Bunting Pride."

When they made love again Suzy squealed out her orgasm, then furiously gazed in Ocean's eyes, smiling ludicrously. "Women have it rough!"

"What do you enjoy best about this?"

"Ocean, tell me the story of your life."

Well, he wasn't going to go heart-to-heart and soul-to-soul with Suzy Roads, but to his surprise Ocean found himself lapsing into his legacy of poverty routine, until Suzy rolled her eyes and cut him off. "That's ridiculous. Where do you come from?"

Sometimes Ocean was reluctant to admit he was local, fearing people would associate his name with his dad's, or now with Uncle Myron, whose thuggery was more clandestine than his dad's operation, and assume the worst.

"Okay," Suzy said when Ocean didn't respond. "I see that's top-secret information. Okay. When did you start writing?"

Ocean stared now at the ceiling. The flashing lights of a patrol car parked down the street revolved through Suzy's bedroom, forming intermittent red streaks on her walls and dresser and bureau, until Ocean had the not unpleasant sensation that he'd been making love to a woman in a disco. "I wouldn't call what I do writing," Ocean found himself reflecting, "so I never began. But I tried my hand at a novel or two, years back." One novel actually, as Ocean recalled; it was about a mobster's son who took over the business and turned the operation into a charitable foundation. Shit. Ocean shuddered at the image. No wonder he'd ended up scribbling greeting cards. Did the son in his story have a legacy of poverty? Ocean couldn't quite remember, though once it was clear that nobody wanted the novel—mob stories are out, several agents wrote him after reading the manuscript, which he eventually took to mean that lousy mob stories were out—he began to see his father's choices differently. That was surprising. At the time he'd been more tolerant and applauded his dad's breaking off with Myron, and had even been inspired by Senior's need to find love, if not by the transparent bimbos he sought it in.

"What became of them?"

"I got the message that it wasn't what they were looking for."

"They?"

"The publishers," Ocean clarified.

"If it's something real, Ocean, what does it matter if it's what they are looking for?"

Ocean thought that in a strange way Suzy Roads was trying to be helpful, though as a policy he resented people trying to set him straight when they didn't know what they were talking about. "You don't understand. Maybe it was real, but we're not talking about *War and Peace*, Suzy. And if it's not what they're looking for, you end up starving with nothing to show for your time."

"That's if you let them make the rules, Ocean," Suzy Roads said. "And that doesn't sound like Ocean Bartok, Jr."

Now it was Ocean's turn to squawk.

When he thought she was asleep, Ocean readied himself for his mute, secret exodus. Suzy Roads was an experience, give her that, and Ocean was willing to grant she'd found him something of an experience herself. For the first time he could remember, when leaving the bed of a woman he felt the lancing pierce of despair and envisioned a future of brief imbroglios like this one with women in whom he had no interest, beyond that they were women, and who had no interest in him, beyond his scam. More immediately, he thought of how he'd muffle the sounds as he furtively slipped out of bed and pulled on his clothes. Given the abominable things he'd said to her, with any luck she'd think him an imposter when she woke to find him gone, or a stand-in for the real Ocean, and Ocean couldn't say she'd be wrong. Still, he thought of mailing Suzy a sampling of his latest—Ocean Bartok, Jr.'s latest—naturally with no return address. He'd sign it "fondly."

As Ocean slipped on his shoes, Suzy said from her bed, in a soft voice he didn't immediately recognize as hers, "*I will arise and go now, and go to Innisfree.*"

He stopped in his tracks. "What's that supposed to mean?"

"Oh, Ocean," Suzy moaned as Ocean stalked away. "Didn't you know? I'm a writer too."

Do people dream because they bleed? Ocean wondered, thinking of Suzy as he passed the panhandlers and hookers and the runaways and Jesus Loves You graffiti scrawled underneath the viaducts he walked out of his way to see on the mile back from Suzy's to his three-room apartment in LoDo.

The one-mile hike became three and then four. He didn't want to get home until he had put tonight behind him, though the more he walked the heavier his burden. Funny to think, well into his forties he couldn't quite believe all these people he hurried by, who hurried by him for one last cigarette or toke to keep the night alive, or end the night in peace, not only had interior lives, but took themselves as seriously as Suzy Roads took herself. Is that what she meant? 'Innisfree.' Her meaning wasn't crystallizing yet. Not that he was going to trudge back and inquire, though that could be her game right there. A strategy to get under his skin. Leave him with a head scratcher, was that her plan? Well, Ocean was the master of such devices himself. ("You don't shit a shitter.") Innisfree?

Suzy, do they dream because they bleed? Or do they bleed because they dream?

What is rich? Five days later Ocean received a package from Suzy Roads, addressed c/o Wills Cards and Sentiment. Enclosed was a volume of poems by W. B. Yeats, a thick sheaf of poems by Suzy Roads, and a note from Suzy thanking him for the other evening (that sentiment Ocean read a dozen ways), asking to meet at his earliest convenience to discuss her manuscript. Might he have some ideas for publication?

Ocean never read the sheaf, nor did he read the four other cards from Suzy Roads before he told Mr. Wills he couldn't read another.

"No more cards from the Roads babe?" Mr. Wills asked.

"No cards from anybody," Ocean said. "No letters. No notes."

"Sure," Mr. Wills said. "No skin off my nose." He'd already hired a gal to answer each and every note, inscribed "fondly" over a facsimile of Ocean Bartok, Jr.'s signature so uncanny Ocean himself found it real, Mr. Wills told his wife.

Ocean did read the Yeats volume.

In an act of historical revisionism, the greeting card poet soon rewrote the climactic scene with Suzy Roads, until he almost—never completely—convinced himself these were the words that transpired as he left the large, beautiful redhead's bed:

Suzy: 'I will arise and go now, and go to Innisfree.' Ocean, that's W.B. Yeats, the Irish poet.

Ocean: 'Fuck you!' Suzy, that's David Mamet, the American playwright.

4.

It was Mr. Wills' idea that they go on tour, though the idea was propitiously confirmed when the proprietor of the Independent Book Store in Albuquerque rang his office—now expanded into the suite next door—on Speer Blvd. "Why don't you come down with Ocean? We could fill the room fast."

"Could you rent a hall?"

"Betty Duserberg in Santa Fe said she'd love to have Ocean down, too. She'll need a hall."

"Sounds good to me. I'll have to run it by the talent."

In fact, for the last month, as sales resembled not the steady rise Mr. Wills hoped for months ago but an earthquake with a series of aftershocks each greater than the original force, the Shlock Maven, as Ocean had come to refer to Mr. Wills (out of affection or cruel mockery was anybody's guess, though the Shlock Maven took to the designation) had thought often of arranging a series of personal appearances for Ocean. "To take this sucker to the next level," he explained to his wife.

"It makes sense," Mrs. Wills said.

Of course, making sense to Gertrude was one thing, but running it by the talent could prove terrifying. 'Ocean, you'll read a few verses, sign some cards, make nice-nice with the ladies.' Even to Mr. Wills these seemed like the three activities Ocean would be least interested in. Knowing Ocean, the Shlock Maven would need to add: "And don't act like it's a fuckin' joke,

Ocean. Don't spit in their faces, pal, or we're done. *Finis*. No more golden egg. Get it?" In the true tradition of talent, Ocean, who'd been edgy for months by now, would be liable to bite their heads off. He'd be liable to do Judy Pride instead, just to make an obscure point.

For every argument to go on tour, there was an equal and opposite argument.

"The tour could generate even more word of mouth," Mr. Wills told Gertrude.

"The next level," she added, looking up from her crochet pattern.

"That's right, Trudy. Of course—here's what I'm gettin' at—with Ocean up there the word of mouth might kill us."

That was true. Perhaps they could hire an actor to play Ocean? "A big rangy guy like—whozit, honey? Fazio?"

"Fabio."

"Fabio, who'd sound sincere and be willin' to kiss a few blasted cheeks."

Actually, hiring an actor to play Ocean was an idea Mr. Wills got almost as soon as he got the idea to go on tour. And it wasn't entirely that he thought Ocean was liable to turn acerbic and mock the ladies lining up breast to back to hear the sentiment straight from the source. (That's how the Maven envisioned the tour; a series of small rooms packed knee to knee with Ocean seated in smoky silhouette like a lounge singer, though not at a piano but a reading table.) While in the six years since he'd hired Ocean—from Amy Lager Bush, precursor of Tiffany Lager Bush, through Ocean Bartok, Jr.—there'd been few conversations in which Larry Wills didn't think Ocean was ridiculing him ("That's the talent," he shook his head at Mrs. Wills. "Can't live with 'em? Try livin' without 'em."); beyond the cheap irony he appeared to embody, they were about the same thing: Business. The almighty scrip. Certainly, thought Mr. Wills, Ocean liked having it both ways; he liked the three-room dump on Cap Hill with the starving *artiste* number and the parade of floozies tiptoeing through the discarded underwear ("What are they like?" Mrs. Wills once wondered. "Too good for Ocean, honey."). Still, Ocean didn't come through the door six years ago at Wills Cards and Sentiment because he was under the impression 'T.S. Eliot' was stamped on his passport. In the limo (for what was a tour without a limo?) Ocean would mercilessly ridicule these ladies who'd line up and fawn, but under the lights where it counted, Ocean Bartok, Jr., would lavish the Ocean Bartok, Jr., as only Ocean Bartok, Jr., could.

The real problem, as Mr. Wills explained to Gertrude, was Ocean's look.

"Ocean has a look?" Mrs. Wills wondered doubtfully. For all she'd heard about Ocean, she'd only met him once, last year, while he was coming out of the post office. He seemed pleasant, that's what she recalled; pleasant but preoccupied, mildly surprised, as if they were the last people on Earth he'd expected to look up and see. But that wasn't what you'd call a look.

Though the Maven was perfectly capable of carrying on a normal conversation, when he talked shop, Mr. Wills preferred to sound like a character out of Damon Runyan. "Sure, everybody's got a look. The gal in the grocery with curlers in her hair? That dame might not know it, she might think her real self's back home, or in what she'll whisper to her honey when he walks through the door, but the dame's got a look. People see her they make assumptions. Yeah, the assumptions are wrong. Deep down she's nothin' like what they see. But in sales what counts are the assumptions. And when people look at the dame with the curlers, enough of 'em see the same thing.

"When people see Ocean, they see a guy with a story to tell. It's not that Ocean's as ugly as the clump of worms on your front step after the morning rain. It's not that he's ugly as the bruise on the banana, or the hair in your spaghetti. It's not that—"

"I get the idea, Larry," Gertrude Wills said.

The Maven continued his explanation. "He looks like a guy, maybe 3AM you're in the bar four sheets to the wind, nothing goin' on, you need a laugh or something to think about on the lonely drive home, you might be willing to listen to the woe which is obviously forthcoming. But that's where the story ends. It ain't what you want to see across the blasted breakfast nook, or when you open your eyes on the pillow.

"Trudy, one look at Ocean, we may never sell another card."

That was the equal and opposite argument.

As convincing as Larry was, what Gertrude didn't mention to her husband as he debated within himself whether to hire an actor, if Ocean agreed, or to go with Ocean himself on the tour (or to leave well enough alone, option #3 that seemed to gradually fade from sight as the debate roiled), is that if you were reading an Ocean Bartok, Jr., card as your eyes closed and your face dropped softly to the pillow, what you'd see when you opened your eyes wasn't Ocean Bartok, Jr., but the picture you dreamed with your heart.

"They're cards," Gertrude reminded Larry. "Not pictures."

"Now now," said the Maven.

The Shlock Maven interviewed four actors before settling on a personal trainer who'd done local commercials, a stint at the Arvada dinner theater (Stanley Kowalski his specialty), and claimed to have once lasted until the second cut at the Broncos training camp up in Greeley. The Shlock Maven lined up the dates—to his mild surprise it soon became apparent it wasn't a matter of where they'd go but where they wouldn't, settling on seventeen cities over three weeks—before calling Ocean with the *fait accompli*.

After Mr. Wills went over the itinerary in the face of dead silence, he told Ocean—Ocean permitting, of course—about the actor hunk he'd hired to play Ocean on tour. "This guy out-Fabios Fabio," Mr. Wills added.

"Are you there, Ocean?" Mr. Wills said after a while.

Ocean made a fart sound over the phone.

"At your pleasure, of course," the Shlock Maven quickly repeated. He wiped his brow and sighed. Shit. Ocean would kill him.

"The burden's all mine," Ocean hummed.

By the end of the conversation Mr. Wills was so relieved Ocean, in the grand tradition of talent, didn't throw a conniption fit ('I have an idea, Mr. Wills. Why don't *you* play Ocean.'), he agreed to give Ocean an extra five points of the gross. ("There's enough to go around," the Maven explained to Gertrude.)

The only actor playing Ocean would be Ocean, said Ocean.

And that's how the Shlock Maven conned Ocean Bartok, Jr., into going on tour, he'd later tell anyone who'd listen.

And Ocean?

If the mark of celebrity is that when somebody writes a newspaper or magazine story about you, you can't envision anything less interesting than reading the story, Ocean knew he was a celebrity, assuming that the cards Mr. Wills no longer delivered and the encounter with Suzy Roads—and a few others, similar fare, before Ocean caught on once and for all—hadn't already convinced him. After all, one's own light is often the hardest to see.

The first stories were mainly notices in the business sections and industry newsletters, likely as not featuring a snapshot not of Ocean but of the Shlock Maven smiling ear to ear holding up a card (often with the verse not showing) to the camera. Soon, though, the focus turned to Ocean himself, and the stories appeared on the feature pages of the *Cedar Rapids Gazette*, the *Toledo Blade*, the ladies page of the *Dysartville Clarion*, and finally full-length spreads on the Arts pages, as if the editors themselves couldn't distinguish the shlock from the bucket. The stories all told the tale of a singular man, a loner who'd never quite managed a family, who'd knocked around through jobs low (convenience store stock boy) to high (campaign advisor), always more interested in the people he met than in the money he made, who fiercely loved his cat Noodles (this the Maven, who read the articles, thought was a stroke of genius on Ocean's part. Indeed, *The Man Who Loved Cats* became one of Ocean's bestselling cards), a romantic throwback sometimes struck with bouts of melancholy, irresistible to women (though he didn't seem to know it, the reporters—all of whom interviewed Ocean over the phone—often added), who turned to verse in middle age, often staying up composing late into the night, sipping tea as classical music softly moaned.

It was the best myth Ocean could think of. ("He likes to keep his past hazy," one reporter commented.) All took Ocean's few revelations uncritically, at face value, and while an occasional letter was written to the editor from readers claiming the biographies bore little relation to the Ocean they knew personally (one letter alluding to a "long weekend in Poughkeepsie" that Ocean, when he was still reading the stuff, wracked his mind to recall), as many came in saying the Ocean they knew was a *mensch*, a good egg, a regular Joe, every inch the man represented in the story, which if anything was understated. None of these names were familiar to Ocean, either. "Everything you need to know is in the verse," he'd eventually answer further inquiries, as if he believed in the canard himself. Most of the articles quoted readers praising Ocean in much the same language and bespeaking much the same yearning inscribed in the notes and letters that still poured in to Wills Cards and Sediment.

The stories that appeared on the Arts pages almost always carried reactions to the Ocean Jr. phenomenon from local poets. These 'real' poets always expressed, often in vituperative terms, the opposing view.

"Lies pure and simple," denounced a poet on the Arts page of the *Cleveland Plain Dealer*. "Junk," decried the *Des Moines Register*. "Exploitative trash." "Cliché upon cliché. And then there are the clichés," said another poet quoted in the *Toledo Blade*. "Sentimental claptrap, really. It's—" here the poet, a professor in the MFA program at Bowling Green, reached for the coup de grace, "greeting card verse." Ocean assumed the slur was intended figuratively.

"They're academics," Ocean always responded when the reporters confronted him with such sentiment. "What do they know?" Strangely, the reporters tended to cluck approvingly when Ocean said this during the telephone interviews, and seldom pressed for further response.

What surprised Ocean the most during his "reign of ascendancy," as he once described it in an imaginary letter to a fan before he stopped reading the letters, is that he enjoyed writing Ocean Bartok, Jr. Back when he was Judy Pride, he'd found the experience stultifying and claustrophobic, wondering that if he couldn't withstand another syllable of writing this *dreck* ("*so much easier to listen | than to be the sparrow's song*" went one line that found its way into three Judy Prides), what would it be like to live the sentiment? To be Judy Pride? And then he'd remember he already was. But Ocean Bartok, Jr.? Writing Ocean, Ocean found he could be somebody else, dimmer but purer, perhaps the Ocean he would have been if he were born Ocean and not labored for thirty years as Burt Jr., son of the thrice-divorced thug, the calamitous would-be politico, now a demented philanderer living out his exile in Scottsdale.

So he'd pass his days of ascendancy. He'd never go out at night, as if a stranger might recognize him and embrace him for dear life. During the days—when burdened with laundry and cleaning, you wouldn't expect to look out your picture window and see Ocean Bartok, Jr., walking by in living color (it was nutso, Ocean knew; nobody knew what he looked like; but that's how he felt)—he'd sometimes walk for miles, through LoDo and by the Platte, circling back through the mall toward the Civic Center. Once—he'd never done this before—Ocean rented a Taurus and drove the hour to Rocky Mountain National Park, took Trail Ridge Road through the Park, past the tree line, then turned around and drove back. He spoke to nobody. That spring, during the record-breaking snowstorm, he pulled a wool cap low over his eyes and went on citizen patrol, helping push cars from snowbanks or off the ice. People would say thank you and smile meaningfully at the wool-capped stranger. It was always like a beautiful one-night stand. Home again, he'd fire up a pot on the stove—seldom sleeping, always exhausted, drinking many cups of coffee a day—and pull out the volume of Yeats Suzy Roads had given him months ago. An hour or two later he'd pull out his notepad, trick his CD boombox with classical, and spend the rest of the night, long into the morning hours—sometimes nodding off, still at his desk—as Ocean Bartok, Jr. Those were the best times of all, Ocean starring as the Ocean he never was but might have been, now spinning the world, now stopping the spin.

He was in this state when the phone rang. Though Ocean often didn't answer the phone (the service taking the messages) it was always Mr. Wills, or occasionally his dad.

"Ocean," Mr. Wills said, "how are the rhymes going?"

"Try this: 'Most women lead lives of quiet desperation.'"

"That's good," Mr. Wills said.

"Here's my most recent. 'In the room the women come and go—'"

"Say Ocean," Mr. Wills broke in, "Why is it you never read your cards and letters anymore? No matter, Ocean, Louise answers them like *she* was Ocean Bartok, Jr., but I was curious."

"Because there's more honesty in any two of those letters than in all the words I've written put together, Mr. Wills."

"I get you, Ocean. I should go fuck myself for asking, right?"

"That's right, Mr. Wills."

"Say, now that I got you on the horn—and thanks for pointing that out about fucking myself; I can always stand a reminder—I have an idea, Ocean, might just take us to the next level."

Well, the man never lacked for ideas. "The next level, Mr. Wills? What's that, the penthouse?"

"Ha ha, Ocean. Right, straight to the penthouse. And the penthouse ain't nothin'. I mean endorsements, maybe a line of sportswear in the mix, picture a book deal, a movie package...." The Maven went on awhile. Ocean tuned him out. Sometimes during these conversations he'd look longingly at the words scrawled on his notepad, and sometimes he'd wonder casually what mix of genetics, environment, and adolescence absorbed with the male bonding offered by dime store novels made Mr. Wills the way he is. None of that ever explained half, any more than Ocean could explain himself, but he knew Mr. Wills had a more prosaic reality—a dour, dowdy wife, an enlarged prostate (Mr. Wills worked it into every conversation, as if Ocean might capitulate on matters of rhythm and phrasing if he invoked agonies Ocean himself might stare at someday), a business he'd kept running for forty years, though barely making ends meet, if that, from month to month (and justifiably proud of it, Ocean acknowledged, though Mr. Wills' memory was long, and he took some pride as well, Ocean thought, in hiring the son of Burt Sr., the legendary *shtarker*), a daughter, Ocean heard, who ran away thirty years ago and was never heard from since—and then one day, with Mr. Wills already an exhausted, sour man in his sixties, comes Ocean Bartok, Jr., and the reign of ascendance, his ship inexplicably come in and, miraculously to Ocean, Mr. Wills is ready, as if lying in wait all these years, as if the codger's been biding his time, plotting his own ascendance, and without pause Mr. Wills becomes the Shlock Maven and gains his second wind.

He wants to say no. But what if he said yes? For a moment Ocean gets the idea their destinies are interwoven, that just as he's invented Ocean Bartok, Jr., he's reinvented Mr. Wills as well; that, perhaps, they're dreaming this dream together for as long as they dream it before the sunlight of harsh reality awakens them again to the detritus of who they were before, naked, unraveled. Though wasn't it for the sake of the dreamer that the dream must end?

"You don't have to do it," Mr. Wills was saying. "I got this guy lined up, an actor—this fella, he *is* your words—he can play you on the road, Ocean, while you stay here and write the sentiment. You should see this guy, the gals are gonna cream their panties, they're gonna moan bejesus—"

Ocean, betrayed, says, "Fuck you, Mr. Wills. It's me or nobody. The burden's all mine."

And so Ocean Bartok, Jr., himself signed on as Ocean Bartok, Jr., for the Ocean Bartok, Jr., tour.

No *shmuck*, Ocean worked his riffs.

Though for each line of patter—'Thank you for coming tonight. I stand before you humbly. I mean that sincerely'—Ocean could envision himself coughing tentatively here, perhaps evoking the hint of a stammer as the sentiment catches in his throat—'It humbles me to stand before you tonight in a forum where the heart still matters, against the grain of today's fast-paced society'—adding here, perhaps, if the mood struck Ocean right for going over the top—'Society is just a state of mind. You all know that, I know that, that's why we're here'—for each riff Ocean prepared, the greeting card poet worked an equal and opposite anti-riff: 'Don't you believe a word of this bubbamagumba, gals. See? I'm just saying this stuff to get rich. I'm lying to you because I know you want to believe in a benevolent world. You want to believe your guy means well, that he's just hurt and scared to love—because if he fails at love what does he have left? Because it's tough to lie naked in front of another, stripped of defenses, at their mercy—that's why he turns away, ladies—I know you want to believe you're still his core, though in his fear he'll snarl and turn sullen and read the newspaper while you blabber, and work long hours—no, it's not—never—that he's been changed by the oppressive tedium, and not—no sir—that you've been changed. '*Changed utterly: | A terrible beauty is born.*'

After quoting the Yeats to the hushed crowd, Ocean continues. 'You lie to yourself so you can get out of bed in the morning and fix the coffee. This way you don't have to stare all day into the abyss. How much do we matter? How much don't we matter? And I lie to you with this crap, the lie you want to hear, the one you tell yourself—put Judy Pride on the bottom you'd see it for what it is—so we are in this together, ladies, a conspiracy of the blind, pretending we don't see.

'I mean, you know the joke? Why do Jewish men die before their wives? Because they want to! See? You won't find that one in the cards. The only question, gals, is who lied first, which reminds me of another joke, about the chicken and the egg.'

And endless variations.

'You're selling yourself a bill of goods, ladies. You buy these cards, you buy the chaff. And at what cost? Thanks for coming tonight,' Ocean adds, ever the gentleman with the eye on sales.

So went the anti-riff.

Then the greeting card poet, no *shmuck*, practices the riff again.

But when he practiced reading the verses, Ocean found the words, perhaps palatable on the page given the greeting card fare they were, emerged from his mouth stripped of their innocence. It was as if as he read, he raised a placard overhead: THIS IS A JOKE. WHY DON'T YOU GET IT? With the riffs he'd found he could manage a certain cornball sincerity, studied but convincing (were you inclined), by pretending to be—by being, it seemed as he practiced—the Ocean he never was. But the subterfuge was too transparent a mechanism now as he read the verses themselves aloud off the cards.

Worst of all, Ocean discovered, was the blue series, which he had come to think of lately as *dreck*, perhaps, as *shtus*, as sheer bubbamagumba, but it was highly polished *dreck*, a refined *shtus*, a no-holds-barred bubbamagumba full of sediment so sanctimonious as to be stripped of pretension, a singular feat of stacked generalities so platitudinous that each equally meant its opposite; no mean feat, Ocean had liked thinking, as if a skillful Victorian had awakened one day a century past his era, alive in the bloom of his bombastic vigor, sporting an almost contemporary idiom.

> *Love, who reveals my soul, intense, clear,*
> *is tonight more than my soul can bear.*

The single couplet was sufficient to seal his judgment, now that he read the stuff in view of the tour. The subtle satisfaction he'd often felt about the series evaporated. Bad, but of a certain rarified kind? Dishonest, yet efficacious? His heart sank. Even at being a phony he was a phony, and for several moments Ocean wondered what humiliations remained.

Anti-riff: 'When bad's bad, does anybody notice the asterisk?'

Anti-riff: 'Even what I thought I was, I wasn't.'

Oddly, knowing this, the words began to sound better as disconsolate Ocean again read them aloud. It was as if a lid had lifted, and in the gust of fresh air Ocean felt a freedom. He arranged several cards he'd read—it would be the same show night in and night out—and surprisingly sensed a coherence to the order. There was, was there not, Ocean wondered, a touching pathos to the cloying insistence? The freedom reminded Ocean of getting lost as a kid, wandering away, retracing his tracks the several blocks, knowing, clinging to the belief as he cried and tripped through the dark, that his dad was looking for him, or anyway had sent someone.

According to the Shlock Maven's itinerary, the tour was scheduled for three weeks, seventeen cities with two more tentative. Ocean packed two suitcases and part of a third, then unpacked. Who needed the baggage? He decided to turn the trip into an adventure. He'd wear black jeans on stage, a black dress shirt, a rumpled sports coat. Traveling light, he'd change on the run, a kid blown about by the rush of the wind.

Now he repacked like a college boy hitching south over break, the clothes on his back, an extra jacket, some toiletries, then tossed the Yeats volume into his duffel bag before drawing the string. That night Ocean dreamed he was drowning, clinging for dear life to the duffel bag, which rose and sank with the waves.

The next morning Ocean called his dad. Seldom was his father in when he called. Eventually his dad would call Ocean back when Ocean wasn't in and Ocean would call Senior back, not in, the pattern repeated for days until Ocean was no longer clear what he'd needed Burt Sr. to tell him so badly the several days ago, what dream he'd needed his Pop to soothe. When they finally connected, they'd regard each other with suspicion. But now surprisingly Burt Sr. was home. In the background blaring, Ocean could hear Sam Donaldson coyly upbraiding Cokie Roberts and, above the din, Loretta, wife #4, yelling that they were late, could you call your boy back later?

Burt Sr. was unphased. "Ocean, thanks for calling. How's the social life?"

"It's good, Dad. Good."

"How's—what's her name?—Lucy? You're calling to tell me good news? Are you two getting married? After all you've been through!"

"I'm not seeing Lucy anymore. You know how it goes." The understatement of the decade, Ocean thought. "Different ideas. Look, Dad, I'm going on tour. You remember those greeting cards I write? I sent you some."

"When are you getting a real job, Ocean?"

That was Burt Sr. to the core, as far as Ocean was concerned. Just when Ocean finds a gig where he sheds the legacy of poverty and can finally move closer to the old man, heart to soul, his dad asks him when he's going to find a real job. "This is my job," Ocean declared.

"I know, I know. I'm just being a dad. Fuck it, Ocean."

This startled Ocean, too. Sometimes he had the impression his dad barely placed him, that when a few days passed and the calls went unreturned, it was because his priority number was low. Then Burt Sr. would surprise him with an intimation of parental devotion. "Sure, that's good," Ocean said.

"Yeah. I'm happy you called, Ocean. I need to tell you something. This is hard to say. Myron called from Denver. Things aren't going well there."

"You're not going back into the business, Dad?" This was impossible. Still, if Ocean remembered Burt Sr. as a thug, he sometimes thought by now his dad remembered himself as legit. Tough, perhaps. Certainly two-fisted and scrappy. ("Nobody's going to give you *bubkes*," were among the first words Ocean recalled his father saying to him.) That's what happens when you have a catastrophic break with your brother and partner, who's an even bigger thug, Ocean thought. Your mind teases you with images of Father Knows Best.

"That'll be the day Myron takes me back, Burty. And that day ain't neither of us going to see. Burty, Myron don't know from trouble. But there's been some trouble."

"Trouble? I haven't read anything in the papers." Though Myron's maneuverings were clandestine, he'd often see his uncle on the Society page, shoulders always squared above his stout belly, though the gravity they strained against now showed in his face. In the flesh, he hadn't seen his uncle since the day thirty years ago Burt Sr. left for Scottsdale.

"It ain't in the Sports," Burt Sr. cracked.

That wasn't fair, Ocean thought. He'd even sent Burt a packet of clippings, never acknowledged. It amazed Ocean how he could swagger atop the world, the lid lifted, if momentarily (the euphoria he'd felt yesterday diminished by his dream), but one sour word from his dad sent him into a frenzy of sulking.

"This is internal, Ocean," his dad was saying, oblivious as always to his slights. "It's nothing to worry about, but I want you to know. There have been threats. A lot of people are trying to get at Myron. Maybe through me? That's possible. The life of a *shtarker, nu*? Once a *shmuck* always a *shmuck*, that's Myron. Maybe me too. I made some enemies long ago, Ocean. I never told you about that. Maybe I should have. Fuck 'em. Maybe if I sat you down and explained a few things back then you wouldn't be walking around today with your head in the clouds, a *luftmensch*. You always had other interests, your own stuff you liked doing. Anyway, Ocean, Myron's made enemies, I made some enemies, memories are long. Sometimes the chickens come home to roost. What am I saying? I'll be okay, Ocean. I promise. Don't worry."

"Dad, I'm going to Scottsdale," Ocean said.

To Ocean's relief his dad didn't chuckle at the offer. In fact, he seemed touched. "Ocean, please. You go on tour. Sounds swell. I'm proud of you. Myron's been getting this shit for years. The *gonif* probably makes half the threats himself. You remember when I ran for mayor, *bubbeleh*? Myron thought I was a *meshuggener*, but you were behind me, Ocean. I always remember that. Myron don't want me to enjoy my old age in peace, now he's up to his elbows, so he hears something now he lets me know. So I'm letting you know. It's nothing, though, *boychik.*"

It was true, Ocean thought. Beneath his father's disclaimers he'd heard stuff like this for years. Even as a kid, when his father left the house, he would never be quite certain Burt Sr. would return. What would it be like to live like that, never sure when the other shoe would fall? Never certain the next sound you hear might not be the blast of your assassin's Uzi? The burden must have been overwhelming, though it was hard to imagine Burt Sr., a thug, labored under premonitions of doom. His dad had an imagination (give him a minute and he'll hatch a scheme) but not the kind that permitted dread. Well, Ocean had an imagination for disaster. Even now; he couldn't go on tour without dreaming of drowning. Was that why he'd never shown any interest in following in Burt Sr.'s footsteps? He'd always assumed it was because his dad considered him soft, a fool. Now Ocean was amazed his dad remembered him being behind his preposterous mayoral campaign, and not—family lore—the fall off the horse. At odds with reality as always. Perhaps Burt Sr. meant he was the only one—other than the abundant *nuchshleppers*—who hadn't tried to talk him out of it, though if so, it was only because he'd known any advice from Ocean would have less impact on his dad than the romantic musings of Amy Lager Bush. Well, now he was marked down as the sole supporter, though Ocean couldn't be certain Burt Sr. didn't hold that against him. "Dad," Ocean asked. "How come you never wanted me to join the business? Ever since I was a kid all Uncle Myron could talk about was cousin Morty taking over. How come you never wanted me involved?"

Ocean was sure Burt Sr. would demur: 'Sure I wanted you, kid. You just had other interests.'

"What can I say, Ocean. Hell, you were a kid couldn't wipe his ass."

"I see," Ocean sulked.

"Don't take it that way. I'm going now, Ocean. You hear Loretta screaming at me? Don't worry about the *bubbamyses* I mentioned. Have a happy tour."

"Dad," Ocean said, "when I changed my name, I know it hurt you. It had to." Though at the time Ocean thought Burt Sr. was secretly relieved; still his father had accepted the news calmly and never asked why. After all, Ocean supposed now, what reason could be good enough? (Of course, Ocean offered an explanation, fatuous on the face of it, which Burt Sr. accepted mutely.) After that he never seriously blamed his father for being slow to return his calls. Touché. Ocean knew.

"But I like Ocean," Burt Sr. said. "I like the sound. Reminds me of the seashore."

Ocean heard Loretta roar in the background, and it took him a moment to realize she was laughing at Burt Sr.'s quip.

"Dad, when I kept the Junior it was a kind of tribute."

Ocean could imagine what his father was thinking: Fuck this. "Be careful, Dad, okay?"

"Yeah, I'll drive carefully. Have a happy tour, Ocean," Burt Sr. said after a while. "You can call me from the road, you know."

"Yeah, I will," Ocean promised, fearing, as ever lately when he hung up after talking with his dad, they'd never talk again.

That night Ocean dreamed he was delivering the eulogy at his father's funeral. Nobody's there, not Myron, not Loretta, not Gail, the only one of Burt's wives other than his mom that he'd met; just Ocean. "We had other interests," Ocean laments to the empty expanse, and wonders if he can manage another word. Should he mention the dual legacies? "Well, I guess I took my pound of flesh. I changed my name, his name," he finds himself blurting to the hall full of Nobody. "But I kept the Junior as a kind of tribute!"

"That's a good boy," he hears his dad whisper from the grave.

NOTES FROM THE ROAD

It didn't take long, Ocean noticed, for the Shlock Maven to become the Shmooze King.

More than Ocean was on tour, Mr. Wills was on tour. Invariably, when they entered a store, Mr. Wills monopolized the proprietor, clutching her in a bear hug, smooching both her cheeks, asking general questions in a cloying, intimate tone. ("So how's Indianapolis?" Mr. Wills gushed, as if inquiring after a long-lost love.) The proprietor would nervously eye Ocean over the Shmooze King's shoulder, sometimes moving her gaze on in search of Ocean Bartok, Jr. Usually, though, they knew exactly who he was. Though Ocean liked thinking it was because he embodied the fair image of the Romantic Star—a quality he remembered in Burt Sr. from his boyhood, the distinction more of carriage than of looks; when his dad walked into a room the room enlivened, everyone knew he was a *macher*, walking as if the light he walked through was cinemascope, swaggering like a surgeon—it was quite likely they pegged him as Ocean because he was usually the only one standing within twenty feet of Mr. Wills, the Shmooze King.

Almost always, ladies ran the gift shops and indy bookstores. Occasionally they'd hug Ocean after Mr. Wills worked them over; more often they'd extend a hand when Ocean made no move to embrace them. He'd sense they'd want to tell him something personal, but the celebrity greeting card poet at just that moment would lean back, grinning defensively. ("It's an honor to meet you!" they'd say. "Business is good?" Ocean asked briskly.) After that he'd sense, if not a cooling of the general atmosphere, an acknowledgment that lines were clearly drawn: The *shmooze* ended with the lugubrious King. Often there were sandwiches in the storeroom, stale slabs of roast beef on sour mustard, a box of crackers, lemonade, over which Ocean sat smiling and the proprietors and Mr. Wills indifferently discussed sales trajectories. Still, they spoke warmly and gushed when introducing Ocean to the crowd before the appearances.

He'd wear his black jeans, his black shirts usually unbuttoned to reveal a thrush of graying chest hair, his sports coat usually folded over the chair as he stood and spoke, his hair uncombed—Mr. Wills' sole suggestion about Ocean's appearance ("The unkempt look. The gals eat that stuff up. You gotta look like you don't care about bullshit like that. Your mind's on spirit and heart."), though he couldn't remember when Mr. Wills ever saw him when his hair was combed. If he didn't cut a Byronic figure, if he wasn't Fabio at first glance, they'd go with what he had.

The rooms, sometimes the size of a moderate master bedroom, sometimes the floor of a dancehall, were usually jammed from wall to wall; ladies sitting in the aisles, against the back walls, often holding small children aloft on their shoulders. It was the small children Ocean fixed on as he spoke and read, his voice soft, emphasizing the nuances of rhythms in his verse when he could locate rhythms. Sometimes a lady in the front row would cry, and Ocean, despite himself, would square his shoulders and belt out the verses like a torch singer.

In large halls in Indianapolis and Blacksburg, Virginia, ladies called out during the verses for Ocean to speak up. "Is this better?" he'd ask, after projecting his voice in Indianapolis, but not in Blacksburg. Both times they warmly smiled *yes, yes* at the celebrity greeting card poet.

Between verses he'd deliver the riffs—"Sincerely, it humbles me to stand before you tonight in a forum where the heart still matters." "Society is just a state of mind. That's why we're here tonight"—while thinking the anti-riffs—"How about a flash of pudenda there in the front row, please"—and that's what kept him sane. Sometimes after finishing, invariably to extended, standing applause, the greeting card poet remembered (Burt Sr. told him this when he was a boy) the popular radio personality known as Uncle Don, who—in an inspired moment of self-destruction—believing he was off the air after concluding his popular kid's program with his signature, "Goodnight little children, goodnight," added with a flourish what was certainly his anti-signature, *"you bastards."*

He'd pause diffidently, take a long sip of water from the pitcher on the reading table, smile tentatively, and answer a few questions not with the anti-answers ("you bastards") but with old-fashioned sentiment straight from the heart, until the proprietor stepped forward to announce Mr. Bartok, Jr., would be willing to sign their cards. And no photographs, please.

It was these signings Ocean feared more than the readings of the verses themselves, for hunched over on the card tables or the long mahogany reading tables, looking up at the ladies as they peered down at Ocean, whatever coy illusions he'd managed with tricks of the voice and robust posture swaggering before the crowd evaporated. ("Charismatic from a distance," his old love Lucy Miller once said, a phrase Ocean still teased for accuracy. Did she mean twenty paces? Did Lucy mean before you got to know me?) In the harsh light Ocean imagined himself as before an unforgiving mirror, aging and shriveled, pock-faced, his hair thinning by the minute, his mouth sagging, a feral sneer surrounding yellowy, pointy teeth. It was Kirksville, Missouri, before Ocean realized that when he pictured himself in the unforgiving light, the image he saw was Burt Sr.'s.

No matter. Flanked on one side by the proprietor who sponsored the evening's appearance and paid a portion of Ocean's fare, on the other by Mr. Wills, preening, smiling, interrupting all personal inquires toward Ocean with spasms of lugubrious *shlock*. ("Why don't you let me fend for myself?" Ocean asked after the humiliating signing session in Kirksville. Mr. Wills looked at Ocean as if that hadn't occurred to him as a possibility. "Because you're Ocean," his boss said. "There's no telling what you'll say. You'll tell them a joke that's not a joke, believe me, pal.") So Ocean stuck with his sincere "pleased to meet you"s and "the pleasure's all mine"s, gazing deeply into two thousand pairs of eyes, one set at a time, with a studied focus, as if he was peering into a television camera. They gazed back at Ocean and sighed. He signed thousands of personalized inscriptions. ("You are the author of my soul," more than a few told the greeting card poet. "You're what Ocean's all about," Mr. Wills always shot in. "Thank you," Ocean would say, though to Mr. Wills or the lady he was never quite sure.) Far from levying judgment on any perceived discrepancy between the Ocean in flesh and blood and the Ocean they'd painted from the sentiment of his verses, the women extended their cards to Ocean like awestruck petitioners, or towered stoutly above the poet, who stared upward through transparent blouses into their beaming, thrilled faces.

It wasn't at the signings, flanked as he was by the proprietors and Mr. Wills, but at the private receptions which occasionally followed, sometimes desultory, often crowded, catered affairs staged by the proprietor for significant customers and the customer's coteries, that some women got more personal with Ocean. During his first week on tour alone, at least six women directly propositioned the greeting card poet ("Can we get together later and party?"), with another half dozen so drunken at their approach Ocean couldn't tell if their slurring advances were direct propositions, or subtle, considering the state of inebriation. Though drunk, each of the six took the rejection in stride and seemed to shrug imperceptibly, satisfied to have given it the college try. Somebody has to win the raffle, why not them? It was an expression Ocean had felt on his own face often before this latest strange turn of fate. They'd walk away with their desperation intact but not revealed for one and all, and Ocean liked believing he'd handled the situation well, too. Only one, in Tuscaloosa, Alabama, persisted, asking Ocean, "Why not?" after the celebrity greeting card poet rebuffed her advances.

"Because I've been around enough to know a drunken gal I've never met before who wants to sleep with me isn't all that interested in me, if you know what I mean. And I wouldn't be interested in her, Miss Pollybarren," Ocean read off her name badge.

"Even if it's not precisely you, why not give her what she's looking for?"

Ocean was stuck for a response, the proposition suddenly turned hypothetical. Maybe he was wrong about Miss Pollybarren's intentions? She was petite, with thick dark bangs. a large nose, glassy eyes that took on a glint of candor in the dining hall light. Her elegant black dress spoke of delicacy and a wonder so matter-of-fact Ocean was momentarily shaken; he'd wanted her to proposition him, wanted to turn her down. For a second, he was tempted to turn course, as if she really addressed the Ocean he never was. "Because there's never enough in that well, Miss, and all you'll ever want is more."

"You're 110% like your cards," the woman said (approvingly?) before walking back to the punch bowl.

While most of these women were attractive, none were young. (Though many younger than Ocean, he was well aware.) It was two weeks into the tour, in flight from Tuscaloosa to Kansas City, the Shlock Maven beside him *shmoozing* the stewardess ("I'd like you to meet Ocean Bartok," he says to the mystified young attendant. "I'm sorry?" she says, baffled, nervously eyeing Ocean as if she should know him from the magazines), that Ocean wised up to the situation. These women who bought the myth, not young anymore? They were pleased, relieved even, to find Ocean as he was. They didn't want Fabio. ("Fabio ain't the guy they married," Mr. Wills said after the young stewardess broke free and Ocean made the mistake of broaching the topic. "Fabio ain't the guy they met and lost. Who the fuck's Fabio?" the Shlock Maven added, applying his own historical revision. "Fabio ain't practical. That's why we didn't hire the bozo.") Well, it made sense to Ocean, thinking about the evening in Tuscaloosa before the black-dressed woman propositioned him and, briefly, shook his heart. Taking a swig of fruit punch, Ocean Bartok, Jr., a regular Joe if not more, muffled a belch not quite successfully. Mr. Wills beamed at the proprietor through the billow of onion-chipped, sour-creamed stink, who smiled back through the gaps in her pearly teeth, as if cooing, "Ain't he great," Ocean's very belch the fruit of marketing savvy.

Ocean called Burt Sr. every few days on tour. From the outposts of Kirksville, Tuscaloosa, Blacksburg, from Grand Island, from Kansas City. Was Burt Sr. pleased? "Look, Ocean, don't feel you have to call so often."

This was after Ocean's fifth call in a little over a week. A year's worth of sentiment packed in, though his dad was getting bored. Burt Sr., a Depression child, was nothing if not practical, especially when the pattern of the conversations didn't vary much from the biweeklies. "You lonely, Ocean?" Burt Sr. wondered. "There must be some broads lined up when you read that *shmatte*. You don't have to call your old man every ten minutes." Burt Sr. paused. "You're not worried about the nonsense I shouldn't have mentioned to you?"

Worried about Burt getting gunned down by a crony trying to get back at Myron, a bigger crook? Ocean had the impression he was insulting his dad by calling so often, as if implying Burt Sr., the classy thug, at eighty-four couldn't fend for himself. "Dad, I need to keep tethered. You bring me down to earth."

"What's the problem, Ocean?"

"I'm everybody's puppet. I'm a cash cow for Mr. Wills, but he has to keep jerking me so I'll mind my Ps and Qs and not shoot off at the mouth and blow the scam. Like I'll stick them with a shiv. Yeah, the gals are lining up, Dad, but it doesn't have much to do with me. They don't want to dicker with the *shmatte*. Nobody wants candor. You think they want to hear they're shallow idiots? They're after the scalp and the memory, not the grief. Which isn't to say I'm complaining, Dad."

"What are you getting for this gig, Ocean? A hundred grand? Ladies crawling all over you?"

"Touché."

"So you need to keep your lip buttoned and not tell everybody off like a snot-nosed hothead? Is that the problem? Join the club, *pisher*. You don't get it both ways. Ask a guy for a fin you don't question his politics."

"Dad, it's not what I'm not saying, it's what I'm saying. They're buying it. They think the *shmatte's* real."

"And you're the world's expert on what people want to believe, Ocean?"

Well, this wasn't the turn in the conversation Ocean was looking for. He knew his dad couldn't relate. Such meditations he'd find dubious; if you had an angle, you worked it dry. Not that Burt Sr. was unprincipled. There were things he wouldn't do for a hundred grand. He wouldn't pose as the Lothario of Middle-Aged Love, Ocean was certain. You didn't back off your scam just because it was working. To his dad, that may as well be handed down from the Sanhedrin. Second thoughts and cold feet were for *pishers*. Some guys gotta have it both ways, Ocean remembered his father saying about a vicious-looking man named Ike Croft when he was younger. (Was Croft one of the enemies now?) To his dad that wasn't moral questing, that was duplicity, cowardice. As often as it happened, it still disappointed Ocean to think that his dad faintly disapproved of him, that somehow he'd grown into a man his dad wouldn't care for in other circumstances. "Dad, you never made me your puppet. Sometimes I thought you didn't care, but you never wanted me to be your puppet. You never thought I was around for your convenience. I appreciate that."

"You're nobody's puppet, Ocean."

Ocean, surprised by the sentiment, wondered if his dad meant that.

"Plus, we go back a long way. Who knows what I had in mind with you? You were always off by yourself."

"Oh," Ocean said.

"Where are you going next, Ocean?"

"St. Joseph, Missouri. Then Tacoma."

"Say hi to Joe Hardy in St. Joe," Burt Sr. cracked.

In the background Loretta guffawed. "That's from *Damn Yankees*," she yelled at Burt Sr.

"That's funny," Ocean said.

"Ocean, you're a card."

"Hah!" Loretta shrieked.

Like father like son, neither thought to say.

"Call me after Tacoma," Burt Sr. said, though Ocean wondered if it was the only way his dad could think of to get him off the phone.

St. Joe went smoothly. After the reading—for once there was no reception, no interview—Ocean bought a postcard of the Missouri capital building submerged in long shadows and mailed it to Burt Sr. in Scottsdale. "No sign of Joe Hardy anywhere." The small gesture made him feel better about his dad. Why didn't he do things like that more often? His dad would read it and think well of Ocean, the vision not perturbed by the verbal inanities his son was liable to perpetrate over the phone—and that Burt Sr. would be called upon to correct. He thought of mailing one to Lucy Miller, his old flame. "Wish you were here," scrawled across the back of the card. Lucy. Had Lucy heard of his strange success? Did she imagine a new Ocean, not the bumbler she'd left in a huff (after a series of huffs, now he recalled), but a true Lothario of middle-aged love? It was amusing to contemplate. Now Ocean wondered if he accepted her appraisals too readily when she left. But over was over, he'd accepted that. Though pride wasn't his long suit, he wasn't a guy to stalk a woman just to make sure she really meant it. (Though he'd known some gals who'd played that game—abandonment as a wakeup call—just to make the guy angry, passionate in their fury, their possessiveness, as if that meant they really cared. Those were never the ones he envisioned when he envisioned the Ocean he never was and wrote the cards.) Still, he felt a moment's euphoria in thinking Lucy might read the card and wonder. Was she so different from the gal in Tuscaloosa? From Suzy Roads? Where was the harm? ('Lucy, wish you were here—Ocean Bartok, Jr., the King of Crap, the Duke of *Dreck*, the Lothario of Love, the—perhaps pressing here—Frankenstein of Fluff.") The idea was so enticing the celebrity greeting card poet bought several more postcards from the clerk, who didn't appear to know Ocean from the Baltic Sea.

He scribbled one and mailed it to Lucy before he changed his mind. "Lucy, wish you were here." When you stripped it of the numerous layers of irony, the sentiment said a lot. And you could always hide behind the irony if (when?) the message turned unbearable. He mailed one, while he was at it, to Suzy Roads, also in Denver, wishing she were in St. Joe. He mailed one to W. B. Yeats, c/o Ireland. He mailed one—this surprised Ocean the most, he didn't see it coming—to Melinda Courtney in Bellingham, Washington, the woman who'd first mailed him a card with the cryptic note of her own that'd haunted him ever since, "Are you real?"

En route from St. Joe, Ocean scribbled a new Ocean Bartok, Jr., he'd debut in Tacoma. He already knew it would be his last. That's what he'd wanted to tell Burt Sr. the night before, before they got sidetracked, before he backed off in the face of his dad's disapproval. A punk, abandoning the working scam. But it was time to put behind him—or else to become, who knew which before jumping in?—the Ocean he never was. He'd discover which was real. Maybe his mistake had been listening to Suzy Roads? Certainly Mr. Wills would call it a mistake, and probably his dad, too, though in the end his dad would back him. Respect him? No. But back him. Was there anybody else he could say that about? For a moment Ocean flashed on the image of Burt Sr. struck by an assassin's bullet, curled by the side of a Scottsdale road, but bucked the thought.

It was the respect he wouldn't get that Ocean wanted, and he wondered for a while what Innisfree was like. That was from the Yeats poem Suzy Roads had quoted when Ocean tried to steal away from her bed, scot-free. *"I will arise and go now, and go to Innisfree."* Had his father gone to Innisfree? Is that what running in the mayoral was about? That's what occurred to Ocean as the plane circled Tacoma, after he finished scribbling the new Ocean Bartok, Jr.; his last, he decided he'd read it first tonight; a suitable symmetry. Had his dad found peace there? He'd tried to return quickly enough, only to be banished by Uncle Myron to Scottsdale. But had he heard it in his heart's core, for a while anyway? Was Innisfree real, or just a place in your heart? As real as the Ocean he never was? Was it someplace you had to go, once you heard the lake water rushing against the shore? And when you got there, could you return?

Telling Mr. Wills and the 24,000 customers who carried the line wouldn't be easy (he'd tell him after Tacoma, disappointed in himself for putting it off, but he'd changed his mind before), though he thought the Shlock Maven—who'd all but stopped talking to Ocean except when in the presence of others—would be secretly relieved to call off the game. Enough was enough. Was this enough? Mr. Wills had a good year of being the Shlock Maven, the toast of the greeting card industry, and 2½ weeks as the Shmooze King on tour, but sometimes Ocean thought of himself and Mr. Wills as playing chicken. Now Ocean would be the one to blink, and Mr. Wills could go back to being the *shlub* he'd been for sixty years—but more, Ocean thought, playing the grand old man, comfortable again, replaying to anyone who'd listen the surprising year he'd turned the industry on end. That would be the story the old man told. Perhaps Mr. Wills would be in Innisfree himself then, or was there now as he sat beside Ocean on the plane circling over Tacoma, furiously chewing gum to save his ears, scanning the itinerary for the thousandth time.

Nobody had to believe him.

Ocean? If it was the best of both worlds for Mr. Wills, Ocean, too, could begin anew.

A fresh scam that cost him less.

TACOMA

Ms. Beatrice Pabst excused herself half a dozen times before finding an empty chair in the middle of the third row at the American Legion Hall. The Hall was already packed. For a moment Beatrice fretted that Louise Philcox would never find her here: But wasn't that Louise's fault? Beatrice told her they'd need to arrive early to find a good seat and Louise laughed, "After all, Beatrice, he's not the Beatles. Save me a seat."

Though it served Louise right to be consigned to a seat far in the back—and even those chairs were mostly filled by now, though the reading wasn't scheduled to begin for another half hour—it annoyed Beatrice that her best friend (indeed, her successor at the Chrysanthemum Club) wouldn't be able to really see Ocean. While Beatrice had all twenty-seven cards in her purse, several of most, Louise really didn't care. "You're right, he's not the Beatles," Beatrice told Louise. "That's the point."

"Beatrice Moss," Louise Philcox said, "you sound like you're in love."

Beatrice ignored her. Louise always used Beatrice's maiden name when her best friend perplexed her. "I'll save you a seat."

Was she in love with Ocean Bartok, Jr.? Could you be an adult and fall for a person you'd never met or seen? She'd read about women who fell in love with convicts, swooning sight unseen, seemingly normal women who'd turn their lives upside down, relocating, as Frank would say, to live within miles of the prison, to marry a man they'd never touch. Although what Beatrice thought about Ocean was nothing like that, wasn't reading his cards something like getting a letter from a man who had nothing left to lose? Beatrice wondered how many of the women packed tonight in the Legion Hall were wondering the same thing about themselves. Had they fallen? Of course, this wasn't love like she'd ever felt for Frank Pabst, to whom she'd been married thirty years next week, or even like what she felt as a girl for Paul, speaking of the Beatles. Louise was in love with Ringo when they met in junior high, and suddenly Beatrice wondered if their lives would have been different if Beatrice herself had fallen for Ringo instead, and Louise for Paul. Ocean—reading Ocean's cards—made you feel like they would be different, that all these little events you hadn't thought of for years mattered. That's why it was frustrating that Louise didn't get Ocean. It was just the sort of thing Louise—and where is she? Beatrice turned around; the Hall seemed completely full—would understand better than anybody Beatrice knew.

"Beatrice!"

"Audrey Tappingham!" The pretty young woman was sitting in the row behind Beatrice, off to the right, next to her horrid sister, Cindy Delure, whom Frank had hired in the retail shop of his glassworks factory three months ago; she'd lasted one week, then didn't show up—to the relief of everyone, according to Frank's steward, for the week Cindy did show up was hellish for all concerned. They were an unlikely pair of sisters. Audrey plump, well-heeled tonight in a beige velour dress, her long hair black and shiny, and Cindy haggard, her face mostly raw cheekbone, with short limp hair it looked like she'd hacked off with a kitchen knife, and with eyes striking, darting, a gaunt woman wearing spandex tights and an ill-fitting green frayed pullover which somehow made her look scrawnier—not slimmer—to Beatrice. During their interview Cindy told Frank she was bi-polar. Since then, Beatrice had made an effort to give Audrey more responsibilities on the Entertainment Committee. While Audrey hadn't become a friend—the younger woman was a good decade younger, with a cultural frame of reference and values Beatrice found interesting—almost bohemian—but unfathomable, Beatrice did view her as an acquaintance for whom she felt a great deal of warmth and would be surprised to learn that the sentiment was not reciprocated.

"Cindy, you look pretty tonight," Beatrice said.

"I'll go to any length for Ocean Bartok, Jr.," Cindy announced across the aisle to Beatrice.

Deadpan, that was Cindy's rhetorical style, Frank had told Beatrice after he'd fired Cindy—or Cindy fired herself, as Frank put it, when she finally showed up after not calling in for a week and acted as if she'd expected the job to be waiting. "Your sister has a very deadpan sense of humor," Beatrice told Audrey.

"That's me," Cindy said. "Buster Keaton as a bag lady."

"I hope you enjoy the reading," Beatrice said.

"Cindy writes poetry," Audrey said.

Beatrice noticed Cindy glare at Audrey and thought that's the problem with individuals like Cindy Delure. They laugh at everyone but themselves.

"It's quite beautiful," Audrey continued.

"But not like Ocean Bartok, Jr.," Cindy said. "Ocean Bartok, Jr., writes beautiful poetry."

"I'm sure Audrey's right," Beatrice said.

"Of course," Cindy said. "Audrey's always right."

"If only I could meet a man with her attitude," Audrey said to Beatrice.

"Frank knows some nice young men," Beatrice said to Audrey. "And so does my friend Louise Philcox."

"But none of them are Ocean Bartok, Jr.," Cindy said.

"Do you know Louise?" Beatrice asked Audrey.

"Yes, Beatrice, of course," Audrey said.

"A wonderful woman," Cindy said.

"Cindy, I'm sorry the job didn't work out," Beatrice said to the sardonic young woman. "I'll talk to Frank if you'd like to try again. I mean that, Cindy. I'm sure Frank would be willing," Beatrice added, thinking she was sure of no such thing and suspected the opposite.

"Oh, I know Frank's willing," Cindy said.

"Cindy," Audrey warned.

"I like your sister," Beatrice said to Audrey. "But she's very insinuating. Do I know you?" Beatrice turned now toward Cindy Delure, trying not to be insinuating herself. "Have I ever been anything but nice to you? Or to your sister?" Beatrice added, immediately feeling badly for including Audrey, who must have enough problems taking care of an adult, bi-polar sibling. Immediately Beatrice smiled apologetically to Audrey, who smiled apologetically back.

"Now," a voice from the podium announced, as it occurred to Beatrice that she hadn't noticed the lights suddenly dimmed, and she wondered if in the expectant silence everybody in the Hall had heard her scold Cindy Delure, who didn't know any better, "reading words of love, please welcome to Tacoma America's greatest poet, Ocean Bartok, Jr."

"Fuck you very much," Cindy said to Beatrice softly, though not before Beatrice had turned back toward the stage, swept away by the eruption of applause which rose as Ocean Bartok, Jr., made his way toward the podium.

And then it stopped.

The rumpled man before them nodded to the audience and strode toward the podium diffidently, slightly edging forward as if, Beatrice expected, he would make one further announcement before Ocean came out. Or perhaps Ocean wasn't here, his plane delayed in Portland, the poet just now de-boarding. Perhaps like—who was that she read about in school?—Dylan Thomas—he was drunk, indisposed, belting back thick black coffee now just enough not to collapse in a stupor at the podium. The rumpled man looked weary and squinted, smiled haltingly, taking in the surge of disappointment from the audience as they slowly understood Ocean wasn't here. The gentleman, shriveled by the silence, seemed to whisper as he leaned into the microphone extending from the podium. Beatrice from the third row lamented that Louise Philcox wouldn't hear, though certainly Ocean Bartok, when he came out, would be more of a showman.

"The philosopher Santayana," the man spoke softly into the mike, "once wrote that the purpose of love is to increase beauty." Now he paused to peer out at the forty rows of folding chairs arching across the Legion Hall. "Tonight Tacoma is beautiful."

A thought Beatrice couldn't reel in—maybe it was a small regret, or an idea she'd had in childhood long forgotten—caught in her memory. She found herself clapping with the others as the realization swept through the Hall: This is Ocean, after all.

Ocean began talking, and it took a while before the industrialist's wife understood these weren't offhand remarks offered in a studied tone, but the first poem of the evening.

Words are cheap. Love, 'sticks and stones
break your bones.' But some words
I've put on the table
I can never take back, and some words
you've said to me. 'A picture's worth a thousand,'

but no picture brings you back
from the several words you made me say,
I think,
until I play words back
ever dreaming what I meant to say.

The applause was sudden and furious. Beatrice turned to look for Louise; she noticed several women in the back had walked out, either because the rumpled man was Ocean Bartok after all, or because they couldn't hear. Behind her Audrey stared enraptured—Beatrice doubted Audrey noticed her smiling at her now—and Cindy Delure abruptly stood, facing Ocean, turning to leave.

"But of course you can take words back," Ocean was saying. "You must." Beatrice again couldn't tell if this was a new poem, or Ocean talking between the poems. He had a puzzled expression, as if he was making a note to himself. "Words of love? Is that truth in advertising? Or should I take these words back? Can you take words back?"

What Beatrice thought was a whisper seemed to come low from the poet's throat, but the words emerged forcefully, and soon Beatrice knew this was the voice of Ocean Bartok, Jr., the voice she'd heard since the day almost a year ago when, enroute to meet Frank in the city, she'd stopped at Dick Post, Stationer, to search for a wedding card for her niece. Though the man twenty feet away from her, leaning into the podium, finding his rhythm now, a look in his eyes now glassy, searching, suddenly alarmed, was not the Ocean she expected or envisioned, she knew it was the Ocean she wanted. This was her Ocean.

A wild idea hit Ocean Bartok Jr. as he peered at the crowd from the podium—*AL* emblazoned across the front (for American Legion, though Ocean preferred to think: American League), reading his latest contribution to the realm of *shlock*, so when he finished, he began probing the very verse he'd finished. ('You can't take words back? Sez you.') Then—here was the idea—he'd turn the reading into an inquisition. ('This stuff is nuts. Sheesh. So, why do you want to believe? Don't say you're nutty, gals. Give me a reason.') Or, better yet, he'd turn the inquisition onto himself; he'd read for the ladies of Tacoma every last Ocean Bartok, Jr., he'd ever committed (And why stop there? Why not the Judy Prides, too? The Amy Lager Bushes?) and announce after each in turn: *I take these words back.*

If it weren't so over the top, he'd start a bonfire with the detritus.

"I take these words back," Ocean says softly into the mike. "You must."

For the first time he could remember (since when? Ocean wondered. Since he'd first made love to Lucy Miller? Since the first time in school a girl he'd thought was cute smiled at him in the hallway outside Spanish class at Horizon Jr. High back in Denver?) Ocean was giddy with possibility.

The formula was simple. He wouldn't verbalize the sentiment anymore, he'd verbalize the anti-sentiment, and keep the sentiment to himself, that's what he thought. And if it killed Ocean Bartok, Jr., as a commercial commodity—though he hadn't the time to consider the matter (thankfully; upon rumination he'd once again keep the anti-sentiment to himself, delivering the standard fare instead, ever the good salesman, saving not just his own skin but that of Mr. Wills and the 24,000 customers)—in that instant he knew it would save his soul.

And then she had to stand up.

Ocean thought the woman was leaving, as often happened when his readings began. Though this always incensed Mr. Wills ("The rudeness!" he'd rail at the proprietor, until you'd think the women had walked out on *him*) Ocean didn't begrudge their leaving. They needed their illusions pure. Words of love spoken by Fabio, yes. But by this guy? For an instant Ocean wondered at their predicament. He was too much like the guy who stared at them across the table in the morning, who would never say these words; or too much like the strange man at the office who sent them the dozen roses but couldn't control his snicker at the office party, or contain his rage after the second drink; not a creep, but odd, and who wasn't when you got to know them?; as if by leaving they admitted they knew too well these were words they'd never hear outside a greeting card, they'd known that all along, why spoil everything now by pretending this was real?

But the woman wouldn't leave. She turned toward Ocean and seemed to extend her arm toward the showman. Her hair was limp, ratty, and she reminded Ocean of a scarecrow. She wore a sweatshirt and spandex tights over her slim, gaunt frame; Ocean remembered that as a kid he'd see women in grocery stores wearing curlers and housedresses, unselfconsciously pushing their carts, though Ocean felt he was intruding upon their privacy by even noticing, as now he felt faintly illegitimate watching this woman decompose before his eyes. Yet so much of his own life, too, he'd dismissed as not who he was; just Ocean in his day clothes biding his time until the emergence of the real Ocean, the one that counted. Always after the next scam would he emerge. The woman pointing at him reminded him of the perpetually bored women in line at the 7-11 for cigarettes who turned tricks on the side (so Ocean assumed), or behind the counter at Quick Trip, their nails chewed to the nub, distracted, who wouldn't meet his eyes or say thank you when they counted his change. "When you're not counting, so much of your life doesn't count," Ocean said into the microphone, unsure if this was the sentiment or the anti-sentiment. "When you don't think you're being yourself, who do you think you're being?" A smattering of women began to applaud.

He wondered if the standing woman beginning to sway in place was Melinda Courtney of Bellingham, Washington, who'd sent him the first card a year ago: "Are you real?"

From the side Ocean noticed—sensed, really—Mr. Wills, over sixty years old, baffled momentarily, looking about, squaring his shoulders, starting his stride into the crowd toward the odd woman pointing at Ocean.

Are you real? One way or another, in whatever words, isn't that what the emaciated gal would ask him, was perhaps asking him now, without words, in the best way she knew how? She was disturbed, of course, a wacko, paranoid, a disjointed series of eccentricities she'd never surmount, and within seconds Mr. Wills would pull her away by the arm and lead her away to the land of marginalia. Already ladies were murmuring, "Down in front!" "Siddown!" "Make up your mind!" A well-dressed, pretty woman seated beside her tugged at the spandexed leg.

"Let her talk," Ocean said into the mike. The women applauded this, too, the applause clamoring, rising, as if these were the words of love they'd come to hear.

For a second Mr. Wills, taken aback by the applause, stopped. Often later, recounting the myth, he'd believe it when he'd tell people this hesitation cost Ocean his life. ("He told the wacko to go ahead," Mr. Wills would say. "You see, that's the way we worked it. Ocean got to be the nice guy. Joe Compassion. I did the dirty work. Me? Sixty years old, I was his muscle and brains. That one second, I believed him. I talked him into going on tour, did I tell you that? My idea.") What he never told anybody—indeed forgot the moment he thought it—was that he hesitated not because Ocean told everybody to let her talk, but that in the instant Ocean spoke he was overcome by the sensation the ragged woman was his long-lost daughter.

But it didn't have to be that way, Ocean thought. Suzy Roads told him that, but he didn't understand back then and wasn't too certain he understood now, as if he was seeing it, but through the prism of his experience he couldn't shake the distortion. Just because there's a system, and the system has rules for good reason, doesn't mean the rules themselves are good; maybe if you lived nine lives; or maybe if you love the rules or the rules love you. Did the rules love Mr. Wills? It seemed unlikely, and for a moment Ocean shivered with tenderness as the old man ambled toward the woman standing in the fourth row. She looked Ocean straight in the eye (the canary, the evil eye, Ocean knows by now, as he knows before seeing that what she points at him is *not* her hand), though Ocean thinks she wants to talk, after all, to let herself be known, to wring out her aria of agony and loss.

And all these women loved the rules, that's what they wrote to him to say in 3,000 letters—according to the Shlock Maven's latest count—they loved the rules and played the game by the rules and bided their time hoping, wanting, trying hard, as if the rules were a formula for success and not a stay against chaos. They loved the rules, they believed in the rules, but the rules didn't love them; their husbands left or strayed or ran out of things to say or lost the urge to touch their faces; the children grew into lives of their own, if not sullen and strangely resentful, then distant, self-absorbed, happy, dull; they worked their jobs and lost their jobs at the phone company or the charity bureau and nobody ever thanked them from the heart; they aged daily in ways nobody else could see; hoping and wanting, knowing fully the rules don't love them, that it was perhaps too late to start over, but believing, wanting to believe, knowing it was a lie—what else could you do? Fire a gun in a packed auditorium at a man speaking words of love, who reaches out his hands toward the crowd, or toward the bullet itself (nobody there knew, though some claimed to have seen the bullet crawling through the air, as if in slow motion, and some felt Ocean calling to them with his arms, calling more loudly than the bark of a .38 caliber revolver, from the hunger of his heart)?—ever dreaming what they meant to say.

THE CHIMERA IN THE PLASTER

S HE LIKED TO THINK she was Assyrian. Not in a big way. She had this way of slipping it in when the focus was elsewhere. (And the focus was always elsewhere around Calla Dakos.) Did she care if you didn't pick up on it? Maybe not. Anyway, she thought of herself in a lot of different ways back then. She had that childlike quality you often see in women who'd been extraordinarily successful little girls and couldn't quite fathom the sea change. Among her group of friends, Calla Dakos was the one everybody talked about when nothing else was pressing. Like all gossip, theirs could turn malicious despite their adoration. She slept around, for one thing, probably more, on a random-selection basis, than most groups of four or five girls put together. Nor, as far as anybody could tell, was she selective about who sampled the treat—it was unclear whether Calla Dakos considered sex with Calla Dakos a treat. She lacked perspective. She didn't consider what the males of the species would consider.

Kal Norbert, a friend of her housemate Wing Terrill, visiting from New Mexico, was making out with her in the kitchen within ten minutes of staggering in from the curb after the twenty-hour drive. Kal barely even recognized Wing. His wavy hair, not quite long, covered his ears and neck, and Wing was raising a beard he looked considerably better with than without. Kal thought Wing looked a lot like the guy he'd gone to high school with, and a lot like a guy who looked like somebody he'd gone to high school with but, upon second glance, wasn't. A group of five (four housemates and Kal) were standing around the kitchen, and Calla crossed the semi-circle, took Kal Norbert's Schlitz from his hand, and stuck her tongue in his mouth. Maybe it was that their names were similar? Calla could always find something like that to condition the moment. It's not that she lacked emotion, she had plenty. Kal Norbert was a stocky guy, a long-haired slob, mostly interested in beer and grass and paperback novels featuring guys like he wanted to be, and smiling at whatever chimera the patterns on the ceiling sparked in his imagination. (They were lifelines of a sort.) He fancied he thought about things nobody else did, and was shrewd enough to understand it was probably for good reason. He wasn't used to presentable, attractive girls he'd never seen before crossing semi-circles to stick their tongues down his mouth.

Kal Norbert never slept with Calla Dakos—though there was an implicit standing offer, as he saw it, after the kiss. It was something he never got around to, given the chimera implicit in the peeling paint he'd consider endlessly, and the grass and the beer, before, one morning, walking out the door to the station wagon parked at the curb and the twenty hours driving back to New Mexico. One imagines he arrived intact; there was that about him, a solidity for all his goofiness. A pleasant young man, at loose ends, somewhat unmotivated. For a few years he'd think about that kiss and wonder what could possibly have possessed him in not taking Calla up on the implicit standing offer. At the time, though, lacking the prescience to embody his later perspective as he stood in the semi-circle after Calla withdrew her tongue and resumed her position—after perhaps a dozen seconds of delightfully willing confusion—Kal Norbert took in that the conversation, in which he'd hardly participated, was resuming without a hitch. Indeed, the conversation had never been interrupted. Indeed, not even Wing Terrill, his oldest friend, appeared to notice the seduction (if that's what it was), as if Wing himself was in on—such was the level of Kal's astonishment—the cosmic conspiracy; pleasant, stocky Kal Norbert the butt of the cosmic joke. Over the next several years, Kal's perspective on the matter would not appreciably sharpen. As with most haunting memories, the symbolism was evasive. After driving back to New Mexico, he'd often think about the kiss and what it promised, and then he didn't think about Calla for years above and beyond the haphazard, intermittent attention one applies to the memories of anyone they knew reasonably well at one time and might have done well to know better. And then one night he was at a party in Santa Fe, New Mexico, and said something to a woman far more beautiful than he ever saw Calla Dakos, a comment mostly for the sake of being charming, and for a moment he was convinced the woman would cross the semi-circle between them to kiss him. For days afterward, Calla Dakos came back.

That moment, however, in the kitchen at the house in Oregon, the conversation humming by as if the kiss never happened—or better, Kal hoped, as if the kiss was so much the status quo around here that it didn't merit acknowledgment—he noticed the pretty girl sticking her hands in her jeans had now turned toward Hank McGill, one of Wing's housemates. Was she going to kiss him? No, as it turned out (though Kal learned that night the two slept together, as they often did). She had short blond hair parted in the middle, was well-breasted, not quite slim. A pale, pretty face. Calla Dakos was part of the scenery, like the peeling paint, like the patterns in the ceiling, the grass, the beer. That's how he'd have to take her.

CALLA DAKOS

Sometimes, as far as Kal Norbert was concerned, she was mostly just another housemate, driving across the city to the "scenic" campus, as the brochure described it with curious restraint, more likely to be found studying in her airy second-floor room than in the kitchen French kissing strangers. She was a laugher, a good audience, yet serious about more things than most of them were serious about, though it took years after he last saw her for Kal Norbert to figure that out. The Assyrian stuff, for example. Kal Norbert wasn't sure if anybody ever asked her what that meant, or what it meant to her. He'd like to think somebody bothered to—that because she slept around, they didn't just see her as so much paint peeling on the bedroom wall. But he couldn't exactly point fingers. (Calla said she was Assyrian. Cool! End of thought.) He'd never exactly turned to Wing Terrill and said, 'Assyria? Wasn't that the ancient capital of Mesopotamia, the cradle of civilization? Mythic proportions, I believe? Renowned for their cruelty and pretty architecture?' He'd never exactly bothered to look it up and process the information, buffing the surface, trimming the edges until it fit the scheme. (Yes, Assyria. Of course.) Much less ask Calla herself. Such wasn't the kind of thing that occurred to you, back in that house. She liked to think of herself as Assyrian. Whatever her intentions, that wasn't necessarily interesting or provocative beyond everything else about her—or anyone—you never asked about. It was just Calla.

During the six weeks Kal Norbert hung out at his old friend Wing Terrill's, she slept with seven different guys. The Magnificent Seven, as Wing liked to say. Some she slept with more than once. There didn't appear to be a formal rotation. Hank McGill was the mainstay, sleeping with Calla whenever he was between girls. All this Kal Norbert didn't notice so much as couldn't help but notice. They didn't have much in common except for age. (Kal was sensitive to age; when you're twenty-one, thirty is a different animal. Though when you're forty—or when he was forty, looking back at his youth—it may as well have been twenty-one.) Some were lean, some bulky. Some were clean cut, square jawed. Others (most) had beards. Some were handsome, others walking mug shots—maggots, Kal Norbert would think later, though back then the term may have had descriptive relevance to himself as well. It seemed so unlikely that Hank McGill might have been jealous of the others that it didn't occur to Kal, and it seemed unlikely it would have occurred to Hank McGill either. Calla Dakos was, after all, mere setting, a girl who'd sleep with anybody, not somebody who'd spin you in your tracks in a dizzy frenzy. Though—this did occur to Kal, often, a chimera in the plaster—if she was somebody else, with the same looks, same emotions, the precise earnestness, the exact way she'd jut her jaw when she heard something she didn't like or was particularly curious, with the slight alteration located deep in her libido, or in the wound she thought of when she thought of herself that compelled her to cross semi-circles in kitchens and French kiss strangers, well, it was possible you'd make a stand for a girl like that, you'd draw a line anybody crossed at their peril.

Much less seven guys in six weeks.

But that wasn't who she was, so Hank McGill took it in stride.

HANK McGILL

Hank McGill took everything in stride. McGill was an inch or two over six feet, slope shouldered, long curly hair always in place, but effortlessly. Not bad looking, a shade or two above average, he looked like a guy who took everything in stride. Nonchalant. He made a play for every woman he'd talk to. In terms of pure ratio (as opposed to quantity) some few of them—one out of three or four—liked what they heard enough that there were many nights Hank didn't return to the house. Kal Norbert knew he lacked a female perspective on the issue, but it was puzzling that so many women, almost every one of whom knew that Hank McGill had said the same words in the same order to the girl in line in front of her, and should she decide to pass on the opportunity, would pose the same words in the same order to the next girl in line, took him up on the offer. When Kal Norbert didn't find it puzzling, he found it pretty inspiring, he wasn't above that; wondering, too, why Hank McGill rated, as if his having slept with so many girls provided a safety net to one out of three or four out there, a certificate of approval. Sometimes, too, Kal wasn't above thinking, 'Poor Hank. All these women sleep with him because they know there's no risk of emotional involvement, there's no chance they'll get hurt sleeping with sleazy Hank.' Though he liked Hank McGill, and to the best of his knowledge begrudged McGill nothing.

Sometimes—when Hank wasn't off catting and nobody else was around the house—the two of them talked far into the night, just two guys, six or seven brews, and a great deal of idle speculation. It was soon pretty apparent to Kal that Hank McGill knew more about the very things, right down the line, that Kal liked to think he knew more than most anybody about. This was surprising. Although they didn't pontificate about the same books, the books Hank read (all of Willa Cather, for example) likely had a cachet that Jack Kerouac or William Goldman or Richard Brautigan didn't. Sometimes as they held these marathon beer sessions, Kal tossed Hemingway into the mix. That got him nowhere. Calla Dakos had read Hemingway. Even Wing Terrill read Hemingway. As for Hank McGill, as far as Kal Norbert could tell, Hank McGill *was* Hemingway. Still, despite some true if guarded affection for the guy, he enjoyed feeling vaguely sorry—more precisely, vaguely superior—to Hank McGill, that though he'd slept with many, none would take him seriously, such was the effect of his certificate. Their bodies may jostle but never their hearts. Poor Hank.

WING TERRILL

Wing Terrill's role in the house was to be everybody's friend. The good guy. That was always Wing's role. It was as if he was appointed to that office before Kal met him and held it for as long as Kal knew him. A career civil servant. A lifer, though the life wasn't long. Nobody ever said a bad word to Kal about Wing Terrill, and Wing never said a bad word about anybody, unless they deserved it. He wasn't perfect. He had this way of being acerbic without seeming acerbic which could get on people's nerves when they figured it out, especially if the joke was on them. Though Wing meant no harm. Sometimes, too, he had a way of seeming acerbic without being acerbic. He was easy to misunderstand if you were determined to. But to those who knew Wing best, he was everybody's confidant. He knew plenty about Calla Dakos that Hank McGill never knew. He knew things about Steve Strumplater, the fourth housemate who was never around, never said much, and later that year—before Kal Norbert drove back to New Mexico—packed his bags one night and disappeared without notice, never to be heard from again (except perhaps, it occurred to Kal, by Wing Terrill, who wouldn't say, Strumplater's plans revealed in confidence).

Wing knew the names of everybody in Steve Strumplater's family, for instance, knew Strumplater's hobbies, the cities he'd passed through, the names of his girlfriends (a vastly shorter list than McGill's, though not, as it turned out—Wing Terrill knew this—entirely exclusive). In fact, it seemed to Kal that Wing Terrill found Steve Strumplater more interesting than Strumplater's mother could possibly have found Steve Strumplater. But that was Wing Terrill—if you knew him at all you were pretty fascinating, by definition. That kind of attention pays dividends. Wing was never at a loss for company. Some people found Kal pretty fascinating merely because he was Wing Terrill's best friend. Kal knew he scored a lot of easy points with people he wouldn't have otherwise. (Perhaps, after all, that was his certificate: Kal Norbert, Wing Terrill's pal.) People cozied up to Kal when they knew.

KAL NORBERT

Kal Norbert could usually be found in a state of half-temptation to take Calla Dakos up on the implicit standing offer. Likely this would have shaded toward full-temptation if the number of guys taking her up on their own implicit standing offers was more modest—possibly two or three rather than seven. Seven made her a curiosity, a circus act. But the kind you wanted to run away and join.

He spent his days at the house not particularly thinking about Calla Dakos. He read more than ever before and often found that the girls in the books, no matter how they were described in body or mien, reminded him of Calla. She was like a girl you read about; maybe not one you went out of your way to sleep with yourself, knowing too well the ongoing story of her intrigues.

He took long walks through Sellwood, the part of Portland where they lived, not thinking about her. Often Kal found himself greeting people sitting on their porches in much the way Wing Terrill always said hello to everybody, and if a brief conversation ensued about the weather or the Blazers or the rhododendrons, he'd do his best to appear interested in the brief conversation before waving heartily and moving on with the walk through Sellwood. It wasn't unusual for Kal Norbert as he walked—sidewalk hiking, Wing called it, a practitioner himself—to glance at his reflection in the windows as he passed. This was a few weeks after he'd staggered in from the curb. Changes you wouldn't believe. Maybe it was the sidewalk hiking, perhaps the jogging he'd begun around the neighborhood or at the college oval two or three times a week (eight laps, two miles), or possibly the very fact that by living in somebody else's house, at their mercy, so to speak, he was also at the mercy of what they ate. (In fairness, they'd been kind enough to designate a cabinet for Kal's own stuff. And sometimes Kal, living in the house rent free, sprung for groceries for all. If he was at their mercy, they were merciful. (But the truth was, Kal Norbert wanted to try on a different life than the life in New Mexico, that was it. That's why one drives the twenty hours from New Mexico to a house in Oregon and a friend's standing offer in the first place.) Kal ate what they ate when they ate. And if the old Kal in New Mexico had the habit of eating around the clock, the new Kal broke the habit. It was clear, as he surreptitiously inspected his form in the windows walking through Sellwood, that he was considerably leaner than when he arrived. Was it possible? A second-string tackle in high school, he assumed it was his fate to always look like a second-string tackle. This was something new.

Sometimes he drove to the campus where everybody but Strumplater went to school. Making himself useful, a chauffeur for the housemates, a caddy free and easy, but with the clear understanding he was expected to be there to drive them back. So Kal killed the time. He'd run the oval. He'd walk the green to the library or the gym or the student union. Though it was a small college where everybody knew everybody, he was pleased to think many likely took him for a student. As it happened, Kal Norbert sometimes took himself for a student, sitting in on Wing Terrill's economics class, or Calla Dakos's sociology class, once in a while going so far as to offer insights (on, say, the plight of the urban underclass) he'd gleaned not from experience or the casual reading he found himself doing most of the day when he wasn't killing time before driving somebody back, but from what he remembered from sociology classes he'd attended back at his own college he'd dropped out of to drive to Oregon and the different life he was trying on.

He liked sitting next to Calla Dakos. Liked the long wool coat she wore to class and the man's fedora she usually wouldn't take off. Liked the warm way the other students greeted her and didn't give a thought to Kal's being beside her. Did anyone assume they belonged to each other? Sometimes Kal liked to think so. Though she was a circus act, not the idealized Kal Norbert Type, here's what happened when you sat beside her: you found Calla Dakos almost unbearably sexy. Though Calla Dakos never formally introduced him to one and all—'Here's Kal Norbert. He's Wing Terrill's friend, staying at the house. I French kissed him once. We have an implicit standing offer'—he liked what (after a couple of classes) the others certainly found self-evident: 'This guy Calla Dakos takes to class.' He was surprised to find he liked that so much, as if it represented a level above sleeping with her. Often, sitting beside her, with the other students openly assessing the Newcomer, he wondered if he meant anything to Calla Dakos. And sometimes he'd think he could do a lot worse than Calla Dakos.

In the Alternative Universe people are as they are but slightly altered. This was a game Kal Norbert himself invented as a strange—by all reports—adolescent. Mostly then he focused on himself: he was precisely as he was, the exact same kid, except the revised Kal could hit the fastball with authority, hold his blocks half-a-second longer, think of answers in class when asked, rather than after the bell as he shambled to the next class. Well, in the Alternative Universe Kal Norbert, the lean version, was pretty much the way he was, and Calla Dakos was pretty much the way she was with the slight alteration of Calla's not fucking any guy of any stripe who had the slightest interest in fucking her. In the Alternative Universe he could really like a girl like her. And though the game never lasted much longer than he could hold his blocks back at school, every time Kal Norbert drove Calla Dakos back from campus, he half expected to tumble into bed with her.

JULIE BUCK

Julie Buck—Wing Terrill's girlfriend—spent most of her day at the theater wing on the edge of campus, studying to officially become what she already was: an actress. Most of her nights she spent at the house. Tall and thin, she had long straight hair and a pointed, open face. All Wing Terrill's girls had open faces. Kal met many of them, and it seemed to him there wasn't a single one you couldn't take at face value. Not a single one who held back her cards or pretended to be something she wasn't.

They weren't pretty by most standards. Wing's girls never matched the idealized version of the Kal Norbert Type. They weren't even girls who it might have occurred to him at twenty-one to ask out or take any real interest in or particularly think about ten minutes after meeting them, though at forty he'd wonder where girls like that went. What could possibly have become of them? What of their open faces that asked nothing more and wanted nothing more than who you took yourself to be at face value? What would Julie Buck be like at forty? Would she look at him the same way, or does she know by now the price is too high, the cost not worth the return? It's not as if Wing's girls were gullible or naive, like the youngest sibling who assumes the best in the face of all the evidence, setting herself up for mean pratfall after mean pratfall, all in the hope of being included in the game—which she knows she's going to lose anyhow. At forty, was Julie Buck a woman who looked into your face and saw the sum of every face she'd looked into? There was no way for Kal Norbert to know, of course, though at forty it occurred to him more than once that he could contact the little college's alumni office, if it really meant that much to him. Likely they'd be helpful—though likely he may need to invent a pretense beyond 'I need to know if she still looks at people the way she used to'—and he could call her up and drive to her house—even if it took twenty hours—or possibly meet her for coffee or a drink. It was the kind of impossible gesture a man like Kal Norbert could contemplate, briefly. But Kal knew there was a reason nobody ever makes calls like that, even guys like him, or drives the twenty hours cross country to find out. He knew he didn't really want to know. Either way the cost was too high. So he'd think at forty.

Wing Terrill's girls were never girls you thought were pretty when you met them. But the time came, not long after, when you got to know them (and they'd make the effort because you were Wing Terrill's best friend—not to please Wing Terrill (though it would) but because that meant you were somebody worth taking the time to get to know), when you couldn't imagine them being or looking any other way. A little while after that it may occur to you that words like pretty didn't apply to Wing Terrill's girls. Julie Buck, for example, was beyond pretty. This occurred to Kal Norbert as the two of them sat Indian style on the floor of the living room at the house two weeks after he met Julie Buck. They were sipping tea, which Julie Buck drank around the clock. ("It helps my voice," she explained.) Strumplater was off in the corner of the living room fidgeting with the stereo. Calla Dakos was upstairs in her bedroom, studying. (They could hear Cat Stevens groaning from the second floor.) Hank McGill was off somewhere providing an emotional safety net for the girls of the small college. Kal couldn't remember where Wing Terrill was. Julie Buck was sitting knee-to-knee with Kal in the middle of the living room, knees two inches apart, sipping tea, talking about *All My Sons*, or the Stanislavski method, or the winds in Tillamook, Oregon, where Julie grew up. (The conversation freely floated from the professional to the personal, it didn't matter; all was germane as Kal Norbert sat across from Julie Buck, knee-to-knee.) That's when it occurred to Kal Norbert that while Julie Buck, with her plainish pointed face and long limp hair and tallish scrawny body wasn't exactly the idealized version of the Kal Norbert Type, the idealized version of the Kal Norbert Type wasn't exactly Julie Buck either. And around Julie Buck—if you had Julie Buck, rather than being, say, the best friend of Wing Terrill, who had Julie Buck—you never bothered to think about the idealized version of the Kal Norbert Type. Why would you want to? Around Julie Buck, the idealized version was another way of playing Alternative Universe: theoretical, pointless, self-defeating. No, it didn't occur to you to play Alternative Universe around Julie Buck. Julie Buck was real. It may have been in this moment that Kal Norbert understood something he probably knew before without giving much thought to: when you're around somebody who's real, it makes you a little more real yourself. And though there'd be times he'd kick around various notions as to what exactly real is, or what real is in one context, perhaps, but not in another, around Julie Buck you never wondered what real is. She was context enough.

Wing Terrill's girls were like that. One minute you were mildly surprised—yet again—that this was the one Wing Terrill raved about. The next minute you knew she was beyond—indeed, left in the dust—idealized version or Alternative Universe. She was Julie Buck, thank you very much.

But she was Wing Terrill's, whatever the position of their knees or their range of conversation. Wing Terrill loved her, too. Still, it was a good deal for Kal. Around Julie Buck, Kal Norbert could feel the world was full of Julie Bucks, an endless procession, it was just a question of finding them, of taking that little longer look, and of being, perhaps, a little more like Wing Terrill yourself, who probably didn't spend a lot of time shuffling the deck in Alternative Universe. Wing could see women as idealized versions of themselves, could see that confluence of who they were and the possibility of who they might become, and if it wasn't always an easy standard to live up to (that's what Julie Buck told Kal once, astonishing him (he had no context to absorb the remark) as they sat together on a curb outside the Bijou, waiting for Wing to show up so they could see a movie), well, Kal would think, sometimes people let themselves down, too. He knew that better than most people, even at twenty-one. After Wing died, he never saw Julie Buck again and, indeed, never met another Julie Buck. Certainly he knew a lot of that was because as he got older the women he knew got older, too, but sometimes he'd think they went out of style after Wing was gone. That after Wing wasn't around to scout them, there was a run on Julie Bucks. Or that you had to be Wing to find them, and with Wing gone—though he would have it otherwise—he became a little less like Wing every day. Anyway, though they were knee-to-knee for hours, Julie Buck was Wing Terrill's. And she never crossed a semi-circle to French kiss Kal Norbert, like Calla Dakos, whom he'd always half expect to tumble into bed with, until the announcement.

THE BEDROOM SITUATION

Seven different guys in six weeks was just Kal Norbert's informal count. Casual. There were plenty of nights he didn't think to check up on Calla Dakos's arrangements. Nobody's perfect. Guys would slink out in the morning running a comb through their hair, that's how he knew. Calla wasn't one to linger by the door with a long kiss goodbye. The night had been the night, perhaps, but morning was morning. For a young woman of such prodigious (Kal didn't want to think promiscuity) sexuality, she wasn't particularly romantic. She wasn't about interminable soulful gazes or idly drawing hearts in her notebook. Not that Calla was on some estrogen power crusade, like a few women Kal did sleep with over the next several years, campaigning to prove girls, too, can be sullen, boorish, mean-spirited, contemptuous with self-hatred the next morning, making it clear guys were nothing but pleasure objects because, after all, that's what the guys made clear. What's good for the goose, etc. She was just a sweet, sexy, busy girl with a day to get on with. And while she had no particular quarrel with romance, she wasn't a billion stars flashing before your eyes driving you dizzy, weak in the knee; that's not what the guys slinking away in the morning running the combs through their hair were for.

There may have been more than the Magnificent Seven. There was a rumor, impossible to fathom, that Steve Strumplater had slept with Calla Dakos. Strumplater was probably thirty, running to fat, listless. On the few occasions Kal Norbert saw him, he'd sleep heavily on the couch, moving only to ponderously change the album on the turntable if nobody objected, then back to the couch, or the kitchen for a beer, or the bathroom—the head, as Strumplater called it. He barely said anything on the few occasions Kal Norbert saw him at the house, other than that he had to go to the head, and Kal couldn't imagine Strumplater saying much on the occasions he was away from the house. If Strumplater had a job, twenty years later Kal Norbert couldn't recall, and may not have known at the time, though it was hard to imagine he didn't inquire. Perhaps there was something about Strumplater that kept you from inquiring. Strumplater had a look on his face that suggested he perpetually viewed the past as better times than these. It was years before it occurred to Kal Norbert, looking back at his six weeks at the house, that Strumplater was depressed.

There was another rumor, that Strumplater recently had long hair, cutting it but a few months before; it was hard to imagine Strumplater making the effort either way. He was a nice guy, unstintingly courteous if not precisely warm, but morose, cumbersome, phlegmatic, not a guy for whom a sweet sexy young woman, even one not known for her particularity, would extend an implicit standing offer. But Strumplater would have made eight, if the incomprehensible rumor proved true.

Sometimes it was a point of pride between Kal Norbert and Wing Terrill that they were the only two guys around—possibly in the entire city of Portland—who hadn't slept with Calla Dakos. Not that the two of them—as best friends from home—cultivated images of themselves as islands of sanity in an insane world, though from that there might be an understated satisfaction, Kal Norbert could see that from the vantage point of twenty years later. Nor was it that Calla Dakos, for all her resplendent proximity, wasn't in their league. After all, Wing Terrill was the plain girl's pipe dream, the guy who'd take that longer look and see their plain girl's idealized self.

As for Kal Norbert, there hadn't been enough girls to determine precisely his league. Walking around Sellwood, the new man with the leaner look, he'd contemplate realistically what league he might be good for. There was the Kal

Norbert Type. That was theory, though he had what from the perspective of twenty-one he saw as his shot at the big time: Sara Sherman. He'd gone out with Sara Sherman a few summers ago, back home in Illinois. Sara Sherman had the look—the olive Sephardic coloring, the curly black hair falling far beneath her shoulders, the translucent doe eyes, the pretty smile that kept you not only guessing, but needing to guess, as if it contained a puzzle the solving of which revealed much about yourself available only through the way she looked at you in that moment. Wing Terrill was nuts about her, and Kal often thought his going out with Sara Sherman—actually visualizing asking her out as realistic possibility, then acting on it—much less Sara Sherman's accepting—somehow cemented his image as a ladies' man in Wing's eyes. As far as the ladies' man image went, it was probably better that they'd gone to different colleges, given Kal's certified record, though come to think of it he'd always done better with girls when Wing Terrill was around. Even at the house, with the French kiss, the implicit standing offer, the sitting knee-to-knee. This was stuff that just didn't happen too often in New Mexico.

Sara Sherman. He'd gone to a movie with Sara Sherman then later kissed her goodnight, just like that, after which she looked into his eyes and smiled before saying goodbye and shutting the door. Sara Sherman. Probably that was the highlight of his life until then. There was the game against Waukegan he'd started due to injuries and ended up springing the key block on the go-ahead touchdown. There were the two—springing the block, and kissing Sara Sherman—which Kal at the time, walking back to his car after the kiss, a boy transfigured, pretty much saw as the classic case of apples and oranges. Two moments in eighteen years when Alternative Universe was irrelevant, that's how he saw it. And walking back to his car he thought you could do a lot worse with your eighteen years. And when you kiss Sara Sherman you're in a different league yourself—you'll never need Alternative Universe again. That's the kind of heady stuff his sole brush with the Kal Norbert Type generated. Probably best for all concerned it turned out as it did.

At some point between the kiss and when Kal picked Sara up a week later for their second date, the romance had deteriorated. She was careful not to brush against him, and both in the movie theater and his car sat as far away from Kal as logistically possible, given that she sat next to him. There were times it seemed she wasn't actually in the car. He almost pitied her the burden. Afterward she paced half a step ahead of Kal to her parents' door. To her credit, Sara did turn to whisper goodnight—Sara Sherman was not only the Kal Norbert Type, but a nice girl too—before ducking inside. Kal halfheartedly called her later that week, but sometime while he'd been enraptured by heady ruminations, the decisions about Kal Norbert were sealed. Nor was there an appeal process of which he was aware, though he called her yet again.

Such was his actual brush with the Kal Nobert Type. Then there were, in fairness to the record, the women he'd slept with in New Mexico—a total of three, none of whom, realistically, were even in Calla Dakos's league, not even on their best day. Not even Wing Terrill would see anything in these girls. In fact, that Kal Norbert hadn't managed any better was a good part of the reason Kal Norbert loaded his station wagon and drove the twenty hours to Oregon to find himself standing in the kitchen, available for Calla Dakos to cross the semi-circle and French kiss. No, that Calla Dakos wasn't in their league—while evidently in the league of the Magnificent Seven—wasn't their particular pretension, Kal Norbert considered years later. He doubted Wing Terrill thought in those terms anyway. It was probably—looking back, because Kal wouldn't have thought in these terms twenty years before, and Wing Terrill, who might have thought in *these* terms—or anyhow may well have possessed the sensitivity—never said anything to Kal along these lines—they didn't sleep with Calla Dakos because they didn't want to take advantage of her. (That was it, Kal thought, that was *it*, with the satisfaction of one figuring out a mystery, though several chapters remained. Still, who ever really knew?) If the sexuality was the expression of a walking wound, you weren't going to help her any by spreading her legs, or by being there poised when Calla spread them for you. After all, just because somebody waves a sign that says HIT ME doesn't mean you have to rear back and let it rip, even if the three times you'd done it before had probably been the same deal. They'd come on to him, or yielded so quickly he'd felt more manipulated than triumphant. (Though he'd felt plenty triumphant, too.) So Kal Norbert wasn't claiming sainthood—not for himself, though sometimes he had the tendency to view Wing Terrill that way, and had even when Wing was alive—he wasn't claiming a degree of kindness and solicitousness positing him above the lustful fray where the likes of the Magnificent Seven enslaved, Kal and Wing of finer cloth. But these three others were not Calla Dakos. They may have been somebody's Calla Dakos, but they were not Kal Norbert's Calla Dakos. And that she was his Calla Dakos meant he couldn't believe it was a matter merely of Calla not accepting the double standard, either, though in the mid-seventies, when he knew her, there was plenty of that sentiment around. If Hank McGill could, why not Calla? Because—and this was as true an insight as Kal would ever have on the issue—she wasn't Hank McGill.

Mostly, though, Kal Norbert didn't gloat over not sleeping with her—taking fear of complication for a virtue—because he did take her up on the implicit standing offer. After a fashion.

The bedroom situation at the house wasn't entirely clear cut. Kal slept in the bedroom off the main entranceway, an alcove everyone used for storage or the coats when they held a party. It had once been Wing Terrill's room, before another roommate moved out of the attic into his own place, and Hank

McGill moved from his second-floor bedroom to the attic, freeing the second floor for Wing. Why Hank moved to the attic wasn't too clear cut either, though Kal later imagined it had something to do with the awkwardness of Calla's sleeping one room over—awkwardness when each was entertaining others, and awkwardness when they weren't but wanted to spend the night alone. Mostly, though, even when Hank wasn't sleeping with Calla, the attic was empty. Wing Terrill and Calla Dakos had the standard bedrooms on the second floor, with often as not Julie Buck, who lived close to campus across the city, staying with Wing.

Where that put Strumplater was never made explicit to Kal. The situation was odd. Strumplater had official status as a housemate—thus he was introduced—but may have been without portfolio, as they'd say in newscasts about incorrigible ministers of the Israeli cabinet. Often Kal would see him walking downstairs, obviously from upstairs, but he may have come from the attic on nights Calla wasn't entertaining McGill, or McGill entertaining at large. Some nights, when Kal turned in, Strumplater was on the couch in the living room, and was still there in the morning when Kal went to the kitchen. Still, everybody in that house could be found crashing on the couch occasionally. Of course, it occurred to Kal Norbert that the alcove off the entranceway where he slept was, in fact, Strumplater's bedroom; that he'd displaced Strumplater—possibly a break in the rent was involved—and that Strumplater slept in whatever room was open—the attic, the living room, or those places he slept when he wasn't at the house, which was most of the time—waiting out Kal Norbert's promised return to New Mexico, when he could get his own room back. This by itself could account for the older man's morose mien, Kal imagined. Roomless, his view of the past as better days made sense. That Strumplater accepted a deal that dispossessed him—the break in the rent, maybe a cut rate in his food share—nonetheless left him dispossessed—and more than a little pathetic. Kal wasn't above thinking that as he watched Strumplater stretched out on the couch, ambling up only to change an album or go to the head. Perhaps he was resting after years of dodging the draft? That was possible, too. Of course, as far as pathetic went, there were reasons he didn't ask a lot of questions trying to pin down the issue, and even from the vantage point of twenty years' hindsight, he was a little ashamed. After all, it must have taken some effort not to know. There must have been moments the question was in the air and Kal was quick to turn away, embarrassed, possibly sullen himself, sending the signals one sends when they don't want a question addressed. ('What elephant? You're nuts. There's no elephant here.') That wasn't Kal Norbert as he liked to think of himself at twenty-one, or, for that matter, forty.

One other issue about the room, if it was Strumplater's room. It was this: Strumplater wasn't such a nice guy that he'd vacate for six weeks out of the goodness of his heart. Not even Wing Terrill was liable to do that for his old friend. If Strumplater was paying reduced fare to accommodate Kal Norbert, somebody was paying extra to balance the ledger. What Kal Norbert knew is that, though he'd occasionally spring for groceries for the house, and was on call to furnish rides in his station wagon to campus and elsewhere—he'd once driven Hank McGill to a bar downtown, then picked him up two hours later with a stunning girl he'd never seen before or since (for whom poor Hank had provided a sudden safety net) then deposited them at the girl's house (they thanked him warmly)—he knew well that the one contributing the extra to balance the ledger was not Kal Norbert.

No word was ever said, though Wing was no better positioned to foot the bill. But he never mentioned it to Kal.

Sometimes in that house when Kal Norbert contemplated the new version of himself, he saw more Strumplater than Wing Terrill.

THE ANNOUNCEMENT

Kal was never certain why it happened then, as opposed to the two dozen other times it could have happened over the six weeks, for the French kiss Calla Dakos crossed the semi-circle to deliver shortly after he staggered in after the twenty-hour drive from New Mexico, was only the first. Though the first is the one that mattered, the one that caught him off guard, from nowhere, elevated him, rocked his imagination, transfigured Kal Norbert from the guy with the dismal certified record in New Mexico to a guy a pretty woman would cross a kitchen to French kiss at first sight—more in line, come to think of it, with the idealized Kal Norbert—similar kisses occurred semi-weekly. There was never a time he didn't welcome Calla Dakos's tongue in his mouth, but—here's what he told himself once he'd sized up the situation, taken the lay of the land—it was mostly a matter of Calla Dakos being Calla Dakos, playing out the drama of her sensuality, whatever its source, and not much at all to do with Kal Norbert. That wasn't lost on him.

Still, an afternoon came when they were in the kitchen—this after driving Calla back from the campus—they were having a beer, talking about Calla's class, Modern Sociology 2. Kal Norbert hadn't attended that day.

He'd gone to the student union, instead, where he waited her out in the grill, reading the *Oregonian*, drinking hot chocolate, watching the drizzle through the huge picture window that comprised one full wall of the cafeteria—and talking in turns to

Jeb Fisher, Stan Dimstetter, even Carol Carter, a sweet-faced, large-hipped, long-blond-haired girl Hank McGill was known to have slept with, and Wing Terrill spoke highly of. Each noticed Kal Norbert at the table with his *Oregonian*, watching the drizzle, working his hot chocolate, and, in turn, came over, as if under the impression Kal had a natural claim to the place. Here's the deal: They didn't know him from Strumplater—who was older and claimed, in a rare loquacious moment, never to have stepped foot on campus—but he was Wing Terrill's best friend, and he sometimes attended class with Calla Dakos. A chauffeur, a caddy, a man-at-large, a guy with something of a certificate himself, a good guy with a hazy past—this Kal liked thinking when he stared at the plaster in the alcove—word gets out. Unless he was mistaken, each was happy to look up, carrying their trays, and find Kal at the corner table, killing time. None asked him for a ride.

Meet Kal Norbert, holding court.

This was new: In New Mexico acquaintances had a way of not noticing Kal Norbert as he manned a table.

This wasn't: Calla Dakos French-kissed Kal as they stood in the kitchen. Nothing unusual there, status quo, a day in the life, welcome, certainly; then they were holding hands walking down the hallway to the alcove where Kal slept, beer cans sloshing in their free hands.

Calla Dakos's body was magnificent. Though she was fine clothed and felt perfectly fine in his arms in the kitchen, he'd always assumed—if he assumed—the Magnificent Seven were getting bargain bin fare. Strictly routine. Not so. That's what occurred to Kal as she pulled off her jeans, slipped down her panties. Calla's rear was much larger than it appeared clothed, her breasts grapefruits, skin soft. He entered her with his fingers. They laughed a lot now, working their hands and tongues but continuing their conversation from the kitchen—as if this ticket was still Calla being Calla, perhaps accelerated, turned a notch, absolutely a shade sharper—as Kal entered again with his fingers and Calla groaned with a sudden start.

"We can fuck if you want," Calla said.

Whazzhat? Huh? What? This brought him down to earth. Struck him as bizarre. If he wanted? Didn't she want? Was she doing him a big favor, nailing him as a guy who'd struck out in New Mexico? Throw the dog a bone. Is that what this was? Wasn't—here's the gist—the implicit standing offer equally—mostly—about her? Of course Kal wanted to fuck her, but the question threw him off alignment. Off-kilter, Kal raised another question. As stupendous as she was, as surprisingly magnificent was her body with the deceptively huge rear and grapefruit breasts, was she so stupendous it was worth diminishing the point of pride he shared with Wing Terrill as the only two guys around who didn't fuck her?

Was she any more stupendous than Carol Carter, for example, whom he'd never before imagined making love to, much less as he was doing now—imagining that the hair falling over his shoulder was long and a darker blond, the thigh over his larger than Calla's—while making love to another woman? Carol Carter he wanted to fuck, now that he thought of her. But that wasn't who Calla was talking about when she told him they could fuck if he wanted, and Calla Dakos didn't seem all that worked up about fucking him.

"Later," Kal Norbert said. Miffed. And he meant it. Absolutely. In a minute or two. Five tops. She made her point. Now he made his point. No harm done. ("Later." He said "Later." It would resonate, the punch line to a joke.) Then they'd fuck. Still, he pulled away his fingers. She looked him over, waited, smiled. Was "Later" fine with Calla if it was good with Kal?

He kisses Calla Dakos. Her large breasts rise to his chest as she pulls him tight.

Hank McGill walks in.

In all Kal Norbert's time at the house Hank McGill never stepped foot in the alcove off the entranceway. Hank McGill may not have known there *was* an alcove off the entranceway. As far as Kal knew, Kal Norbert's sleeping arrangements weren't something for Hank McGill to take an interest in one way or the other. He certainly never had before. (Though Hank McGill's sleeping arrangements—*there* was an issue of endless fascination.) Many—most—nights McGill wasn't around, attending to his sleeping arrangements. When he was around, or Calla Dakos was entertaining—there was some overlapping, once or twice in Kal Norbert's six weeks—Hank McGill never commented about Calla Dakos's sleeping arrangements. Though (this hadn't occurred to Kal Norbert before he looks up to see Hank McGill hovering over his bed in the dark) those were the one or two occasions he'd sat up late with McGill in the living room, idly drinking beers, discussing the nuances of Hank McGill's sleeping arrangements the nights Hank McGill slept elsewhere.

But now McGill walks into the alcove off the entranceway he may not have known existed—as if by homing instinct, Kal would think later—and stares naked Calla Dakos's ample bobbing rear in the face, her legs entwining Kal Norbert.

Kal Norbert watches McGill over Calla Dakos's shoulder. He thinks nothing. Status quo.

McGill appears to think nothing as well, taking the spectacle in stride as he hovers. Within seconds—still taking the spectacle in stride—he tears off his pants. Then he's in bed beside Calla, his clothes in a heap on the floor beside the heap of Kal Norbert's clothes and the heap of Calla Dakos's clothes, stroking Calla Dakos's back.

Within a minute—there's some polite jostling, McGill checking with Kal Norbert if this turn-of-events was okay; Calla Dakos too checking with Kal, in the exact same flat mildly concerned tone she informed him they could fuck if he wanted—Calla Dakos turns toward McGill. McGill, from what Kal can tell, takes her in stride.

Kal notices she didn't point out to McGill they could fuck if he wanted.

Within another minute McGill says over Calla's shoulder, "I'm sorry, Kal. I can't do this here."

Truer word never spoken, Kal Norbert doesn't think to say.

"Is it okay if we go upstairs?"

"Is it okay?" Calla Dakos asks.

"It's okay," Kal Norbert says. He watches Calla Dakos's ample rear as the two are already moving in the dark. It's morning before they return for their clothes heaped on the floor.

How long was it? Kal Norbert would wonder, not peevishly. In circumstances like this, peevish didn't apply. This was beyond peevish. Three minutes? Less than four, certainly. They're in his room, a room McGill's likely unaware of—hell, McGill's not even home—naked, entwined, Kal Norbert and Calla Dakos at last, French-kissing, fingering, Calla says they can fuck later if he wants, they kiss again, her breasts rise to his chest as Calla squeezes him with all her might, and within four minutes, conservatively—realistically three—Calla Dakos and Hank McGill are upstairs in McGill's attic alcove fucking.

"You can't beat city hall," Kal Norbert summed up the story the next morning to Wing Terrill and Julie Buck as the three sat in the living room. As Kal told the story, it occurred to him he didn't absolutely have to tell Wing the story. He wondered if the cachet from his two dates with Sara Sherman could withstand this latest onslaught.

Wing Terrill laughed. He looked to Kal like he wanted to fall off the couch and roll on the floor, laughing. *"You can't beat city hall,"* Wing repeated. His face turned red, and he clutched his gut, a bit histrionically, Kal thought, but the point was made. "You can't beat city hall," Wing repeated Kal's line, as if his friend had delivered the ultimate coup de grace.

Julie Buck rolled her eyes.

The forty-year-old Kal Norbert would consider why at twenty-one he could have a girl snatched out from under him, literally, and be so good-natured about it. After all, who wants to be poor Strumplater? But there would be times he'd find the experience almost quaint. In the future he would lose women to other men, more than a few. And the guy never asked if it was okay with Kal, and the girl never echoed with her own solicitousness in a concerned voice, checking for permission. In fact, in the future they'd pretty much take the view that it was a free country, Kal's interests notwithstanding. But none of them remotely snatched Kal from the saddle, so to speak, and climbed on to finish the ride. There would be no exact parallels in the experience of Kal's youth.

The forty-year-old Kal would think the twenty-one-year-old Kal sensed that if he caused a ruckus by fuming, he'd no longer be entirely welcome by all parties in the house, and being welcome in the house was too important to him to risk. It suited him to take the view they'd asked first. And to reason, as he did, that Calla was mostly Hank McGill's. McGill had squatter's rights. Anyway, it was sort of touching that McGill found him so threatening. You didn't find McGill bursting in on the rest of the Magnificent Seven. Some of this reasoning Kal shared with Wing Terrill and Julie Buck after Wing stopped laughing.

They were sitting in the living room. Julie Buck, beside Wing, had kept oohing and aahing, a little too much like a nurse attending to a sick child, as Kal communicated the turn-of-events. For half the story, she hadn't paid the least attention, fidgeting with the turntable as if she were Strumplater, thumbing through every album in the rack, almost playing it on the turntable before deciding on a different album. Now that his humiliation was made clear she was back in the game, oohing and aahing like Mother Teresa.

Wing Terrill looked Kal over for about the thousandth time in their friendship. "Well, it's not as if he threatened your manhood or stole your princess."

"Sure," Kal Norbert said.

"Of course not," said Julie Buck.

"Kal," Wing Terrill said, "she's a *nymphomaniac*."

Kal almost couldn't believe this. He'd never heard Wing say anything unkind about anybody, and it wasn't for lack of cause. Wing saw complexity. He wouldn't sum you up to a T and reduce you, even if called for. Briefly Kal Norbert wondered what Wing went around saying about *him* when the name came up—'Kal? I know the guy. His certified record's dismal.' But he knew Wing was saying this for his benefit, in the event Kal was taking it all to heart. Truly, it was nice having a friend who took his defeats more seriously than Kal himself.

A nymphomaniac. Calla Dakos was a nymphomaniac. Maybe it really was that simple? In truth, he'd always thought of her as Calla Dakos, and assumed—if he thought about it—that that was how Wing saw her, too. She was who she was. Loose, certainly. Crossing semi-circles to French kiss strangers, yes. The implicit standing offer. The Magnificent Seven. You wouldn't dispute that she was loose in the one area. She slept with damn near every guy of every stripe, but she was interesting to be around. The looseness was just something about her, an interesting element, though, to be certain, now he thought of it in this light, the one element he kept coming back to—indeed, had never left since the day he met her. He'd liked chauffeuring Calla Dakos to and from classes, sitting beside her in Modern Social Theory 2, sizing up everybody's assumptions about the two of them. He liked talking to her in the kitchen even without the French kissing element, one of the guys in the house, which he liked. But she was a nymphomaniac. It hadn't quite occurred to him—perhaps he didn't want it to occur to him—in just that word. But that's what Calla Dakos was. Among other things, yes—and Wing Terrill too valued her as a friend, as did—it wouldn't surprise him—Hank McGill, though it seemed McGill was mostly in it for the convenience. As did, as far as Kal ever observed, most everybody else who knew her—but she was that: A nymphomaniac. Realistically, how upset could you be when you didn't get much more out of your fling with a nymphomaniac than a self-deprecating story, mildly humorous if you told it right? It's not like this was Carol Carter. How deep did you want to get? Did you want to be her boyfriend and look over your shoulder, wondering about every guy she'd ever had a conversation with, or ever would?

Kal knew it was for his benefit Wing pointed out this interesting fact, but he still couldn't help wondering if Wing meant it—not just during this second, when he thought he was helping his friend who'd been hurt, but all the other seconds when they hung out and shot the breeze and Calla would voice opinions and Wing would listen and respond as if it was a normal conversation. He couldn't imagine. Still, when Kal Norbert thought of Calla Dakos's deceptively ample rear and her breasts rising into his chest and his saying "Later," it was nice to have the word in play. She was a nymphomaniac. While there was much to be said for that—he liked thinking he was something of a nymphomaniac himself, in inclination if not habit, though likely the term didn't apply to guys, not as a pejorative—well, what did he expect?

One thinks what one thinks when one must.

It was at this moment that Hank McGill walked into the living room. As someone who lived in the house, he didn't have to slink away in the morning, running a comb through his hair. He didn't even have to comb his hair, as far as Kal could tell. Even now, after a night of making love to Calla Dakos in two different beds, every curl was in place.

"It's the man for all seasons," Wing Terrill said.

"City Hall," Kal muttered.

"Ladies and gentlemen," Hank McGill announced, "at ease." He took a sip of his orange juice and smacked his lips, as if sampling an expensive chardonnay.

"What if somebody took that orange juice out of your hands and drank it for himself," Wing said to McGill.

"She's not a glass of orange juice," Julie Buck said.

"No?" Wing said.

Wing and Julie looked at Kal now, as if, having set the stage verbally, they expected him to fire out from the couch and tackle McGill. Not that Hank looked concerned—though he should be, Kal Norbert thought through the momentary awkwardness. From here on out McGill had best monitor every step for a shadow. At each turn, if he were McGill, he'd watch his back and his front.

But he wasn't Hank McGill, which struck him now as the point of last night's exercise.

"Have fun last night, Hank?" Wing said.

"An interesting evening," Hank McGill allowed.

Kal thought McGill was tempted now to kiss himself on the shoulder. He had to remind himself of all those times he felt vaguely sorry for McGill; that no girl could take him seriously.

Suddenly McGill sank to the floor. If you didn't know any better, you'd think he'd keeled over from a stroke, Kal thought. But they knew better. When McGill wasn't off providing a safety net for half the girls of Portland, or inserting himself, literally, into other guys' plans, or talking about literature with authority and insight exceeding that of other guys who liked to talk about literature, taking it all in stride every step, he was likely as not performing a melodramatic gesture such as collapsing on the floor in a dead heap the second he takes in that his good friend Wing Terrill is mad at him.

"Gone but not forgotten," Wing commented.

"Maybe Calla will perform artificial respiration," Julie Buck suggested.

The heap on the floor gasped artificially. McGill arched his neck, eyeing the three housemates on the couch; one permanent, two conditional.

"The worm has turned," McGill groaned. Then he told the story.

For all his melodramatic gesturing, McGill—or City Hall, as he would forever after be referred to by Wing and Kal—wasn't one to goof around verbally. He could recognize irony, but you could take what City Hall said for what it was worth, even when it was a load of shit. There may be an agenda behind the words, but you could take the words themselves for what they said and not worry too much about what they weren't saying. If you were interested, too, you could contemplate his motivation, but for a guy—this Kal would later think—who oscillated between taking everything in stride and melodramatic slapstick, City Hall was remarkably uncomplicated. Hank McGill, when he was being Hank McGill, the entire Hank McGill routine, wasn't all that different than Hank McGill in the kitchen, for example, when he wasn't doing the Hank McGill routine in order to ensnare the next girl in line into his safety net. City Hall oozed sincerity, and the secret to oozing sincerity, it would occur to Kal Norbert, is meaning every word you ooze. Whether Hank McGill held to the sentiment in another ten minutes was another matter. Now he arched his neck and took in the three housemates on the couch and oozed sincerity. "This morning Calla made the announcement."

"The announcement?"

"She's in love."

"With who?" Julie Buck asked.

Me? Not me? Kal Norbert wondered.

McGill frowned, pained to broach the topic. "She'll tell you."

"With who?" Wing barked.

"Tucker Mason."

Kal Norbert's spirit sank.

"*Tucker Mason*?" Wing Terrill and Julie Buck gasped, as if McGill had announced that Calla's real love was none other than Julie Buck.

It wasn't that they didn't know Tucker Mason, it was that they knew him too well.

"That's what I said," McGill said with a grimace.

TUCKER MASON

There were few people of Kal Norbert's acquaintance who inspired universal responses. Tucker Mason was one of them, though Kal had never personally suffered the misfortune of talking with Tucker Mason at length. Tucker Mason was an asshole. The epithet so consistently accompanied his name it was likely his teachers called it out when they took roll. Kal tried to think back to Social Policy 2, where Mason sat in the front row answering every other question. Sometimes—this happened with Kal once—Tucker Mason would answer the question after somebody else—in the back row, for example—began answering. Though Kal himself took it in stride the one time, would he feel the same if he paid tuition? Thin to the point of disfigurement, bushy hair combed back, abrasive (needless to say), Tucker Mason was known as an asshole outside the classroom as well.

Kal remembered the one time they were introduced—by Calla Dakos, after class. Could he sense any interest on Calla's part? This may be the one guy, other than Strumplater, that it wouldn't have occurred to him that Calla was about to French kiss. They were talking about an assignment and Kal nonchalantly walked up. Calla quickly—formally—introduced him as Kal Norbert.

Tucker Mason raised a brow. "Cal Northridge," he said, laughing to himself. In another person it may have struck Kal as a clever verbal association, but coming from Tucker Mason (who, according to Wing, wasn't even from California) it wasn't clever, but more evidence that Mason was an asshole. It didn't matter to Tucker Mason if Kal had a name or not, or what it might be, or if it meant anything to him if he had one. Of course, even at twenty-one Kal Norbert knew that described most of the world, but most of the world wasn't introduced to him personally. Not by Calla Dakos. Tucker Mason had a way of letting you know he considered himself about a million times as important as he considered you.

Which wouldn't be so bad if Tucker Mason was Hank McGill, for example, who could be obnoxious but managed to do it all with such a graceful stride that it didn't occur to you until later—say about ten minutes, as you lay in bed realizing McGill's fucking the girl you were about to—that he'd crossed the line. Tucker Mason wasn't Hank McGill, either. In fact, as it occurred to Kal Norbert in the several seconds between the time City Hall arched his neck from the floor, revealing that Calla Dakos was in love with Tucker Mason, and when Calla Dakos, wearing her tawny robe, walked into the living room—a conversation stopper, as it turned out—Tucker Mason probably didn't even rate with the rest of the Magnificent Seven, who more accurately, now Kal was in the mood to grouse, could be called the Mutational Seven, and none of whom, to anybody's knowledge, she'd had the least inclination toward falling in love with.

"Yes?" Calla said.

The three times before that Kal had slept with women, he'd left their quarters shortly after he'd performed sufficient non-sleeping activity to qualify as sleeping with them. Calla Dakos, standing in the archway in her tawny robe, was the closest he'd come to seeing a woman he'd made love to bathed in sunlight the next morning, wearing a robe. Of course, in that the woman he'd almost made love to—now glaring at the four housemates—immediately thereafter slept with another guy (not just almost) and still later announced she was in love with yet another (what's more, an asshole), Kal Norbert, though a sentimentalist, didn't especially savor the moment.

Then Calla Dakos did something he didn't expect. Years later Kal would think that it had a great deal to do with why he remembered Calla Dakos the way he did, as a seminal talisman of his youth, with a tenderness he'd never quite managed toward her when he knew her, and not, as he'd been relieved to think but moments before, as a pathetic nymphomaniac it was pointless to get worked up over. He knew (they all knew) that Calla Dakos must have heard Wing call her a nymphomaniac, and then heard the ridicule in their voices as they dismissed her true love—Tucker Mason, Asshole. She was glaring at them, after all, with good cause. McGill, still heaped on the floor, braced for a brutal kick to the ribcage for his betrayal. But Calla instead turned toward the couch, softly excused herself, squeezed in between Kal and the overstuffed arm, turned to Kal Norbert, searched his eyes—he couldn't read Calla's beyond the identical solicitousness he'd observed eight hours before, when she'd checked if it was okay if she fucked Hank McGill instead (Kal with other fish to fry?)—and smiled as warmly at Kal Norbert as she ever would. "Good morning, Kal," Calla Dakos said.

A riddle, wrapped in a mystery, inside an enigma, Winston Churchill once said of Russia, but he may have been thinking of Calla Dakos.

THE AFTERMATH

After the announcement the house changed. When energy evaporates, deterioration occurs. Decay seeps through. Things go downhill, and it doesn't take forever. There was no more Magnificent Seven to sight slinking away, running combs through their hair. There was no more Hank McGill and Calla Dakos claiming home field privilege, indulging the confluence of proximity and hormone. There wasn't much Hank McGill after that—without the prospect of home field privilege, City Hall spent almost every night elsewhere. (Usually, it turned out, on Stan Dimstetter's couch.) McGill later lamented to Kal that without Calla Dakos on standby—word got out fast—the other women didn't see him as such a safety net anymore, his certificate revoked. There was no more Steve Strumplater staying over intermittently to laconically slump on the couch in a study of lethargy. Strumplater was gone for good, as far as anybody knew. (If Wing knew otherwise, he wasn't saying.) There was no more implicit standing offer. What there was, more than Kal Norbert found strictly necessary, was a good deal of Calla Dakos talking about Tucker Mason.

"The guy's an asshole," Kal told her one afternoon. "I don't mean to be insensitive, but there's a reason nobody can stand him. That's the reason."

"He's not an asshole, Kal," Calla Dakos said, which Kal took to mean she knew Tucker Mason was an asshole, but she wasn't going to let it influence her.

The quest for Tucker Mason wasn't going well. This wasn't a case where she could surprise a guy with a quick French kiss until he staggered off dumbfounded at the prospect of a standing offer. Calla Dakos's reputation preceded her, and she wasn't too sure Tucker Mason would like her much even without the albatross of the reputation. Tucker wouldn't give her the chance. To Kal, it seemed Calla Dakos was beginning to perceive there were disadvantages to being widely known as a nymphomaniac. It wasn't something they talked about in so many words. He never said, "Calla, you're the town pump. Some guys don't want that quality in the girl of their dreams." If he did, he could imagine Calla countering with, "Northridge,"—that's another thing he didn't like about Mason. Since Calla fell for him, she'd taken to calling him Northridge— "I pumped them. I pick and choose. I fucked those guys because I wanted to fuck them." While the distinction was real, it wasn't necessarily one Tucker Mason was liable to appreciate.

"Why Tucker Mason?" he asked Calla, knowing the question was futile. It was like asking Crazy Horse, 'Why Little Big Horn?' Because he was there, because she saw the chance—though the chance didn't apparently extend beyond sitting in the same classroom during Social Theory 2—because he made her eyes engorge when she realized what he was doing. And what he was doing was being the guy she went apeshit over.

Like everyone else on the campus—so it seemed to Kal Norbert—Tucker Mason was a rich kid. Unlike the other rich kids, though, Mason couldn't seem to get beyond it, not even while around other rich kids. If you loaned him an album (this example was provided for Kal by Hank McGill) he wouldn't return it. "As if it was understood the album was offered as a gift to nobility," City Hall told Kal. "It was beneath his dignity to return it."

But it wasn't merely material. This Kal observed on his own, though McGill was quick to verify. He'd give you his opinion whether you asked for it or not, and his opinion was always that your opinion wasn't up to his standards. If you didn't like his opinion, you could take it up with his team of lawyers, that's what he communicated. In fact, even if you liked his opinion, you could take it up with his team of lawyers. Such was the level of Tucker Mason's disdain for anything that had to do with you. He really didn't care if you agreed with him or not. Some people say they don't care about the feelings and the thoughts of others, but to Tucker Mason you were a fruit fly. So went the consensus at the house.

Maybe that's what she saw in him. Kal wondered. Calla Dakos was done with being the town pump; now she wanted to be queen. And all those guys who were under the impression that they'd slept with her? They were entitled to their opinions, but they were fruit flies.

"Have you tried asking him out?"

"Yes," Calla Dakos said.

"And he said?"

"No."

She'd asked him out after class for a beer. She'd asked him to join her study group, which—likely Tucker Mason sensed this—consisted of Calla Dakos. She'd asked him to a Trailblazers game and the movies. When she saw him at the student center, she sat at his table until he left. (Sometimes she'd think about following him, but after a while lacked the will. Even Calla could get the message.) The more he rebuffed her ubiquitous advances, the more necessary it was to wear him down, or else she wasn't Calla Dakos, the Indefatigable. That's what Kal Norbert imagined. As for what she felt about the door in the face, it wasn't long before Calla lost color and weight. Her zest was gone. Calla dragged, her body an empty husk containing her empty spirit. Soon it was impossible to imagine that Calla Dakos ever crossed a semi-circle to French kiss a stranger, and that that stranger was Kal Norbert.

THE MISSION

With Calla reduced, humbled, her spirit flattened, and City Hall never around, and Strumplater gone for good, Kal Norbert seized an irony: The house, where once he'd been a privileged guest with a sort of special status as Wing Terrill's friend, visiting on a temporary visa, an enchanted place where McGill stayed up half the night talking about girls he'd maneuvered into bed, and literature, and where Calla Dakos French kissed him and took on the Magnificent Seven, the house where he spent hours talking to Julie Buck wondering where in the world Wing developed the capacity to find girls like this—and how he could be a bit more like Wing himself—was now practically *his*.

He was almost always the only one around. Calla was usually off talking endlessly to her girlfriends about Tucker Mason, or else off futilely pursuing Tucker Mason. At the house she'd sit in her room: Kal Norbert could hear her playing a side of an album, then not bother to turn it over or turn it off. It hardly seemed worth the effort. While Kal didn't suspect she was avoiding him, she didn't go out of her way to talk to him either on the rare occasions their paths crossed in the kitchen. Within two weeks of the announcement, she'd turned civil toward one and all. That was the level of her social engagement. Sometimes, when they passed in the hallway, he sensed Calla Dakos wondered why he was there. Wing Terrill wasn't around much, either, spending more and more time at Julie Buck's. As for why they'd suddenly spend their time at Julie Buck's and not the house, Kal never asked, and Wing never told him. It's possible that proximity to campus emerged as an imperative—Julie's place was closer, after all—but Kal wasn't so obtuse as not to suspect it had something to do with him. What's more, the few times Wing was around, and City Hall was around, their conversation was terse. Even casual salutations between the two ran begrudging. Calla Dakos makes an announcement, and within two weeks everybody's turned inside out. The only similarity Kal could see between the old house bustling with possibility and the flat, stale, diminished infrastructure where he now stayed, usually alone on the premises, is that he didn't pay rent in either.

One evening—Kal could never recall under what confluence of circumstance—Julie Buck, Wing Terrill, and Kal sat in the living room. Just like old times. Harry Chapin—Wing's selection—was playing on the stereo. From upstairs they could hear the faint moaning of Leonard Cohen from Calla Dakos's room.

"Is City Hall around?" Wing scoffed.

How was *he* supposed to know if McGill was around? With no official status, that was the kind of question Kal was supposed to ask in this house.

"Sheryl Poussin dumped him," Julie Buck said.

Sheryl Poussin was McGill's alternate standby, behind Calla Dakos. "You're kidding," Wing scoffed again. Where McGill was concerned, a scoff was built into Wing's voice.

"I'm not kidding," Julie Buck said. "You always think I'm kidding."

"Don't shout at me," Wing said. "You always shout at me."

Julie Buck patted Wing's hand reassuringly, though it seemed to Kal it was mostly in mockery of the sweet, tender gesture couples unconsciously make to smooth the ruffled feathers.

"First Calla Dakos. Now Sheryl Poussin. It looks like City Hall is in a free fall," Wing said.

"He's hitting on Carol Carter again." Julie Buck knew this because Sheryl Poussin was in her acting class and told her all about it that afternoon.

"You think Kal should hit on Carol Carter?" Wing asked.

"Why?" Julie wondered.

"*Why?* Why do you think? Because romance makes the world go round, Julie. Because she always mentions Kal. Tell you the truth, I don't know how the boy does it. Barely leaves the house, yet Carol Carter can't stop bringing him up. How does he manage?" Ever Kal's champion, Wing scratched his head in bewilderment.

"The Master has his tricks," Kal commented.

He could feel Julie Buck looking at him, so he added, "You're right. I should ask her." Ask Carol Carter. That's all he needed at the moment, chasing after another woman Hank McGill was after. Carol Carter had long blond hair and wore long granny dresses when she wasn't wearing jeans. Her hips were somewhat larger than the idealized Kal Norbert Type. She wanted to be a folksinger and often carried around her guitar. Once Kal ran into her in front of the library and made a minor issue of her guitar, so she played a song for him, right there, just a few chords of Joni Mitchell that to Kal's ear could have been Joni Mitchell. When she finished, she smiled at him and Kal asked her a number of questions about how somebody went about becoming a folksinger—not the art of it, but the commerce. Carol Carter answered him the way she'd answer inquiries from a reporter, as if she was practicing for the career she'd one day have. Though she answered the questions in a professional manner, Carol Carter looked directly at Kal and smiled warmly. It wouldn't have taken a huge leap to ask if she'd had dinner yet. But this was a girl Hank McGill had slept with—according to Wing Terrill—and he felt like Wing Terrill and Julie Buck and Hank McGill and Calla Dakos were watching him as he sat in front of the library talking to Carol Carter. He didn't particularly have the impression she wanted to go out with him. Now Kal could envision being in bed with Carol Carter, almost making love to her, and then City Hall bursts through the door to assume responsibilities.

"Do you think she'd go out with me?" Kal asked Julie Buck.

"Wing thinks so."

"That answers my question, Julie. Thank you."

"You're welcome," Julie Buck said.

"I'm getting a beer," Wing said. "Want one?"

It occurred to Kal Norbert he'd had more beers in his six weeks at the house than in the rest of his life combined. And he hardly drank, maybe a beer or two a day. Hank McGill, for example, probably drank more beer in a week than Kal had in the rest of his life combined. He wondered how long it would take Wing Terrill to accumulate enough beers to match his lifetime total. He never thought about it much before, but Wing drank even less than Kal, so it probably took Wing as much as two months to drink more beers than Kal had in the rest of his life combined. This is what Kal Norbert thought about, sitting on the couch next to Julie Buck, when Wing Terrill left for the kitchen to grab a beer.

He didn't turn toward Julie Buck and say anything. Nor did she say anything to Kal. Kal was—he didn't want to acknowledge this, even to himself—suddenly nervous beside Julie Buck. Maybe it was his imagination, but lately she'd emitted an extra wave of energy Kal didn't know what to do with. Wing Terrill was his best friend, and he'd had dozens of conversations with Julie Buck, the two of them squeezed knee-to-knee on the living room floor, and wondered how in the world Wing Terrill managed to search the ends of the earth and find girls like Julie Buck, an accomplishment a thousand miles beyond Sara Sherman going out with you twice (even if she did kiss you after the first date and smile into your eyes) but it was always in the context of Julie Buck being the greatest girl Kal knew, but Wing Terrill's girlfriend. Lately, though, when he looked at her, he felt Julie's edgy gaze meeting his eyes as if they were kids and Julie Buck was challenging him to a dare, or—and Kal didn't know which—Kal himself was challenging Julie Buck. Even if she was challenging Kal, he knew it was mostly because she knew that as Wing's best friend, he'd never take her up on the dare. She could practice spreading her wings risk free—Kal her safety net, always a poor man's City Hall. But—this was Kal

Norbert's point of reference—though it was assured he'd never take Julie Buck up on the dare, he'd *feel* like taking her up on the dare. And there were times, lying in his bed in the storage alcove off the entranceway, often as not the only one left in the house, he contemplated, were Julie Buck not, in fact, Wing Terrill's girl, should the dare be posed in the new context, taking her up on it with every shred of hope and desire he could muster. And though he never said anything to either Wing or Julie Buck toward which they weren't instantly sympathetic, this wasn't exactly the kind of thing you could go out of your way to discuss with them without risking both their friendships. To Kal, it was all a lot easier when a strange girl crossed a semi-circle to French kiss you.

"When do you start rehearsals?" Kal asked her. He knew damn well she started rehearsals on Thursday—Julie Buck was slated to play Ophelia in a campus production, her biggest role ever (which, now he thinks of it, may account for the sudden wave of energy he's been feeling from her and selfishly taking as sexual)—but he had to say something fast to ward off his mood. Or else give it focus.

"Thursday," Julie Buck said. "I believe I've told you that before."

"I thought maybe there was a change."

"No change."

Now Wing returned with three beers.

In the minute between the time Wing left for the kitchen and the time he returned with three beers, one for each of them, Kal considered that he'd managed to calculate not only how long it took both Hank McGill and Wing Terrill (and Kal himself) to match Kal's lifetime total of beers consumed, but to acknowledge to himself he was all but in love with Wing Terrill's girlfriend, to mete out Julie Buck's psychology, and to ask her a question they both knew he already knew the answer to. Yet people called him a loafer. Barely left the house, according to some.

Two beers later Wing asked, "Do you think Tucker Mason knows Calla's in love with him?"

"He knows," Julie Buck said. "Half her friends have discussed the issue with him."

"Plus, she's asked him out two dozen times," Kal recalled.

Next thing Kal knew, Calla Dakos was staring at them from the hallway. He wondered if she'd been listening to them, as she'd listened two weeks ago when McGill announced Calla was crazy about Tucker Mason and everybody's world changed. That's how it seemed to Kal Norbert. As if she'd been the force of sexual energy that spun their world, and all they had to do was hang on for the ride. Something—sex, or the prospect of sex, no questions asked, or just something to talk about that everyone wanted to hear because you didn't know where it would take you, even if you'd best keep it to yourself—was always imminent around Calla Dakos, always implicit. Life was thick with subtext that you liked thinking about, instead of all the usual subtext that makes you wish you'd never bothered. It wasn't just that he was twenty-one—that's what the middle-aged Kal Norbert would think, looking back. Now here was Calla Dakos in the hallway, chastened, reduced, shriveled, as if she'd been sapped by the loins of a metaphysical virus. And City Hall, never around now, was in a free fall. Strumplater was gone for good, never to return. Wing Terrill and Julie Buck were snapping at each other, and Kal Norbert so missed the force that he was feeling its echo in his best friend's girl.

If their talking about her bothered Calla Dakos—that in itself a new peccadillo, the old Calla never frowned on attention, she *was* attention—she lacked the will now to bring her complaint to anybody's notice. Kal thought she looked helpless, limpid, looking at the three on the couch as if trying to figure who in the world they were, or who in the world was standing in the hallway watching them.

"Hi Calla. How was your day?" Kal asked.

Julie Buck laughed.

"Okay. Enough!" Wing Terrill stood up. He lifted his beer, finishing it in a flourish. Kal watched his friend for any physical resemblance to the Wing he knew a few years ago. The traces were vague. Wing looked like a lumberjack. Nothing unusual there—this was Oregon, where seemingly by municipal decree (as Wing once said) every guy had to look like a lumberjack, or else look like guys who looked like lumberjacks. Briefly Kal wondered if he looked like a lumberjack himself, or just like a guy who looked that way. "Come on, Kal, Julie, Calla," Wing was looking directly at Calla, who remained motionless in the hallway. "Let's go."

"I'm not going anywhere," Julie Buck said.

"Where are we going?" Kal wondered.

"We're going to see Tucker Mason," Wing Terrill announced to the group at the house.

Wing Terrill charged out the front door, Kal Norbert followed, Julie Buck, who seconds before wasn't going anywhere, nonetheless followed, as did Calla Dakos, who didn't so much agree to the mission as lack the will to resist. Kal figured Calla saw Tucker Mason in class, she saw him everywhere in her imagination, and now she was going to see Tucker Mason with the squad from the house. Maybe it really was fine with her. She didn't care about circumstance. She just wanted to see him.

Although this mission was entirely on Wing Terrill's initiative, the four cut a beeline to the station wagon, and soon Kal found himself behind the wheel. He noticed there was no discussion on the matter. And that he was a little tired and a little drunk from the four beers, that Wing Terrill had his own car, a Toyota, capable of seating four, and that none of them cared too much for Kal's driving anyway (that he'd arrived intact from New Mexico influenced them little on this count) never entered the equation. He didn't pay rent. The gas station lines were endless due to rationing since the oil embargo—and to a population in a blind panic that had to stop every two blocks to fill up. (This was Wing's observation, but it struck Kal as accurate.) Plus the price of gas was spiraling. It wasn't hard to compute. If they were going somewhere, Kal was driving.

"Left lane!" Wing Terrill barked from the passenger seat.

Kal jerked the steering wheel and swerved into the left lane. After half a mile he asked, "Am I supposed to turn left at some point?"

"Keep going straight," Calla Dakos said evenly.

"Do you know where Tucker Mason lives?" Julie Buck asked Wing Terrill. "Because if you don't, you don't have to give directions."

Kal glanced in the rearview mirror at Julie Buck in the back seat. He appreciated her rising to his defense, if that's what she was doing, though he noticed she was leaning backward, bracing her knees against the front seat, assuming the crash position.

THE PLANNING SESSION

"Here we are," Wing said after a while. If Kal wasn't mistaken, Wing slapped his knee. "En route to pay a courtesy call. Right Kal?"

"That's right," Kal said.

"Right Julie?"

Julie Buck didn't say.

"What do we do with him, Kal?" Wing Terrill said. "What form do you suggest our courtesy take?"

"I don't know," Kal Norbert said. "That's a good question."

"It's what I've been contemplating as well. Perhaps we'll pummel him. Bend an arm behind his back."

"And then pummel him," Kal said.

"Is this before or after we bring Calla in?" Wing wondered.

"Leave Calla out of this," Julie Buck snapped from the back seat.

"I see," Wing said to Kal. "We pay a courtesy call to Tucker Mason and leave Calla out of it. Brilliant! But if so, I fear our ministrations—our very point, Kal—might be lost on dear Tucker. Our efforts too subtle for efficacy."

"That's a consideration," Kal said.

"Have you ever seen two guys more full of shit?" Julie said to Calla Dakos in the back seat.

Julie may never have seen two guys more full of shit, Kal thought.

"We'll tie him up blindfolded, drive him to campus with his pants off," Kal Norbert proposed. "Then we'll drive him back."

"Yes," Wing nodded approvingly, "that will get him thinking."

"Then we'll tell him we're just getting started," Kal said.

"I hope you two aren't just getting started," Julie said. "Assholes," she muttered to Calla, who—as far as Kal Norbert could tell—was staring straight ahead at the back of Wing Terrill's neck.

"Guys like us," Wing said, "could take every bone in his body, grind them to fine powder, then not give the entire adventure another thought."

"Tough guys talking tough," Julie Buck said.

"Has she forgotten the scrimmage where we marched downfield on the first string?" Wing asked Kal.

"*Have you forgotten?*" Kal Norbert yelled back to Julie.

"Seriously Kal," Wing was saying, "Julie has a point. I don't want you taking a swing at Tucker. Agreed?"

"I don't know if I can agree to that."

"I understand. Such restraint goes against the very grain of your nature. Here's what we'll do. He'll be so afraid you'll take a swing at him that I'll take him aside. 'Look, Tucker,' I'll say, 'it's this or a knuckle sandwich. A double knuckle sandwich.' I'll say, 'See that girl over there?' Kal, do you think he'll play dumb?"

"There's a chance he'll act like he doesn't know who you're talking about."

"I'll say, 'See that girl over there.' That's all I'll need to say. No need to mention the cruel game he's been playing with her heart. His failure to look into her eyes and respond in kind. Should I mention that, Kal?"

"There's no need, Wing, but mention it anyway."

Kal expected Julie Buck to shout back with, 'Don't you dare,' but by now Julie Buck didn't seem to be paying any more attention than Calla Dakos to the planning session in the front seat.

"We'll say, 'You're playing a cruel game with her heart,'" Wing said. It appeared to Kal, watching Julie in the rearview, that she was staring into the back of *his* neck. "We'll say we don't appreciate it."

"We'll say we don't appreciate it, *Jackass*," Kal added.

Wing looked at Kal Norbert. "The Jackass'll get the idea."

"Agreed," Kal said.

"Agreed," Wing smiled.

Maybe things were falling apart. Maybe Julie Buck was snapping at Wing Terrill who, for all they'd been through, was as edgy as Kal ever saw him. Maybe Calla Dakos was a zombie, and Kal himself a handy guy to have around because nobody ever felt like driving or spending half the day in the gas lines, and Kal didn't have any choice, but they were a squad of housemates, official and unofficial, and they were going on a mission. Kal wondered if he'd know any of these people in ten years. He knew he'd always know Wing Terrill, though the time may come when they lived on opposite coasts—Kal Norbert could see himself following a woman anywhere, whereas a woman would follow Wing Terrill anywhere, that's as close an approximation as Kal ever got to the difference between them, but given the difference they were bound to drift apart—and were no longer best friends, that was possible, or even knew each other to speak of besides the memories of high school football and Sara Sherman and all Wing's girls and the six weeks Kal Norbert spent at the house in Portland, enchanted by Calla Dakos and Julie Buck and Carol Carter, if he ever got to know her; it wasn't hard to imagine never seeing Julie Buck again, if she split up with Wing, or never seeing Calla Dakos, though he was sure, once she was back on her feet, perhaps after this mission, he'd always sense her force somewhere, you couldn't ever entirely not know Calla Dakos once you'd lived in that house with her, though maybe someday—say in ten years—she'd be a housewife in Texas or a sociologist doing research or teaching at a small college somewhere, Kal liked that idea, perhaps raising a child, and her memories of these six weeks might not extend to her sleeker self crossing a semi-circle to French kiss you, or include the implicit standing offer. Kal wondered if they'd remember this moment—Wing Terrill and Kal Norbert and Julie Buck and Calla Dakos—when they rode in Kal Norbert's station wagon to Tucker Mason's house somewhere in the hills of north Portland, on a mission to recapture Calla Dakos's spirit.

Neither Wing Terrill nor Julie Buck said anything after Julie made it clear to Wing that he shouldn't give any directions if he didn't know the directions, then after the productive planning session in the front seat, and Calla Dakos wasn't talking much anyhow, so they drove on in peace and silence. There wasn't much traffic now. Tonight, Burnside could be any commercial street in any city. Kal wondered why it never occurred to him he could live here, parlay the visit into a long-term arrangement, maybe get to know Carol Carter—if she was *really* asking about him; Wing had a tendency to mistake common courtesy for genuine interest when it was directed toward Kal—and settle in with Carol Carter and see where it rides. He'd probably have to pay rent at the house, or eventually move someplace where he was expected to pay rent, assuming that Strumplater ever returned and resumed his rightful place in the alcove off the entranceway, and assuming that City Hall stemmed the free fall or hit bottom, returning to his attic room from Stan Dimstetter's couch, licking his wounds. And that Wing and Julie shifted back to the house from Julie's place. It occurred to Kal now that he'd never viewed anybody here, but Wing, as anything but tentative, temporary diversions; that when he took his walks through Sellwood imitating Wing with his hearty waves to the citizenry sitting on their porches, he was playing a role that never had much to do with him. He'd come to Portland not to lick his own wounds, but to step out of his life a while, and liked what he'd found better than he liked his life. But would he like it as much if it *was* his life, or was it mostly the safety net of being the Guest, the stranger from out of town, not so much a real person meeting real people but a plot device like those found in half the novels he was reading lately. Only in the novels, the stranger unsettled the mix, while here the mix unsettled the stranger. It occurred to Kal that he sold himself on an easy ride here because here had nothing to do with him, his real life was back in New Mexico for better or worse, and wondered if in a few months, if he was back in New Mexico, and nothing panned out again, he'd be telling himself that it didn't matter, his real life was back in Portland where he'd spent six weeks as a guest in a friend's house. Kal already knew he would.

This was the moment, driving down Burnside, finally turning when, with what seemed like more of a sigh of resignation than a helpful directive, Calla told him to turn left, that he understood Calla Dakos as much as he ever would. She was Assyrian, that's what she was and what she told herself. It wasn't completely a joke, not to Calla. She could take on the Magnificent Seven because she was Assyrian, that's what she was; she was Assyrian and not the girl who crossed semi-circles to French kiss strangers, and dropped her pants for every guy who'd shown half an interest in sampling the goods, seven in six weeks, according to Kal Norbert's casual calculations, but that wasn't who she was, not her real self; the authentic Calla Dakos was Assyrian. Kal wondered why she couldn't carry her Assyria with her anymore, once she'd focused on Tucker. Why did she lose that with him? Do you need to hurt as much as Calla hurt to find out who you're not?

"The Portland hills. A rich boy," Wing Terrill said as Kal followed the road. It wasn't raining tonight, Kal noticed for the first time. Which probably meant it would rain soon. As soon as you noticed it wasn't raining, it began. Perhaps that was why he'd never thought to parlay his visit to Portland into something longer.

"Don't be a jerk," Julie Buck redressed Wing.

"Why is that being a jerk?" Wing shot back.

The people who lived here never complained about the rain, Kal observed. At least not the people he knew. As if to live here you had to make your peace with the fact that it rained almost every day, except for the summer, when there was liable to be a drought. You could let it drive you crazy, or you could accept that it rained a lot here and not give it too much thought and actually enjoy the place, leaving the complaining up to guys like Kal, who—he had to admit—didn't really know or love the place. But he loved some people here, and you pretty much had to accept them too, and be happy about that, and not let them drive you nuts when they were having conversations like they were having now.

"It's your tone," Julie Buck was saying.

"My tone? Sweetheart, *please*. Why a rich boy? Because the truth is you have to have money to live in the hills," Wing Terrill was explaining, "And that goes for whether you're the owner of the Trailblazers"—Kal remembered the owner of the Blazers was rumored to live up here— "or a twenty-one-year-old collegian. And if you're a twenty-one-year-old collegian, chances are—though I won't say it's impossible, Julie. I won't rule it out—you didn't acquire that money working yourself to the bone each and every day of those twenty-one years. Chances are you got it by other means. Are criminal means a possibility, Kal?"

Kal looked at Julie Buck through the rearview and wondered what she was thinking. Her face was blank, as if to register the least emotion would merely serve to egg Wing on and she knew better than to fall into that trap. Of course, when they were getting along it wasn't falling into Wing's trap, it was Wing being a pretty funny guy. Julie Buck was a lot prettier when she emoted than when she imitated a rock face, Kal thought; he wondered if she'd be prettier on stage—rehearsals began next Thursday. Would he be around long enough to find out firsthand? For that matter, was the question moot—whether she was a lot prettier while emoting than in repose, where by most standards she wasn't pretty at all—because he still considered Julie Buck beyond pretty? He liked her more when they were knee-to-knee in the living room than when she was at Wing's throat. "Criminal means are always a possibility, yes," Kal allowed.

"Exactly," Wing said. "Only Tucker Mason is a famous straight arrow—witness his trembling fear of Miss Dakos, which we're going to remedy pronto—which leaves but one possibility, ladies and gentlemen: He got the money to live in these exclusive hills from Mommy and Daddy. Consider that! Hence, Julie, he's what's known as a Rich Kid. Further, this is confirmed by our knowledge that Tucker Mason Senior owns Chinaworks, Inc.!"

"Asshole, Inc.," Kal said, getting into the spirit.

"He doesn't," Calla Dakos said quietly.

It was rumored—even Kal heard it—that Tucker Mason's father owned Chinaworks, a large international corporation that, despite its name, had nothing to do with China, but manufactured expensive toys.

"Okay," Wing said to Kal, "he doesn't *own* Chinaworks. The stockholders do. He merely *runs* it. And who should happen to be the majority stockholder?"

"No, he doesn't!" Calla Dakos said, not with the vague murmur of resignation now, but as if she wanted to climb into the front seat and gag Wing Terrill.

"Calla Dakos," Wing said, "Welcome back."

THE RICH BOY'S LAIR

Tucker Mason may or may not have been a rich kid, at least by the standards of the college (Kal figured he was rich by most other standards), but he didn't live like a rich kid. His place was in the hills, a billion times nicer on the outside than the house in Sellwood, yet inside it was just another college hovel. If Tucker Mason wasn't such a famous straight arrow—which was news to Kal Norbert, though it fit as another explanation for his resistance to Calla Dakos—Kal could envision him lighting incense and passing around a bong.

Tucker wasn't snotty about the four of them showing up late in the evening at his rich kid's hovel in the hills unbidden. Tucker didn't look to Kal as if he was expecting them, but he didn't go out of his way to look like he wasn't expecting them, either. If Kal didn't know better, he would have thought Tucker Mason found their presence a pleasant surprise.

"Hi," Tucker Mason said when he opened the door, before the gang of four expressed salutations. He said their names one by one, as if taking attendance—"Cal Northridge" he said when he focused on Kal, which made Kal want to tackle him if Tucker Mason wasn't smiling pretty warmly at seeing him along on the visit, and if he wasn't a little touched Tucker Mason remembered him in the first place—and when it came to Calla Dakos, Tucker Mason not only said "Calla Dakos" but gave her a soft affectionate punch in the bicep.

"Thanks for stopping by," Tucker Mason said.

"Anytime," Wing Terrill said.

For a moment Kal wondered if Wing had taken Tucker aside earlier, possibly on campus, and delivered him a stern talking to, straightening him out on the issue of Calla Dakos. It was like Wing to do that sometimes—to step into what wasn't strictly his business and try to rearrange fate on behalf of his friends.

Calla Dakos, Julie Buck, and Kal Norbert sat on a couch, Wing Terrill in an easy chair and Tucker Mason in a chair he brought over from the table across the living room, after putting Dave Mason on the stereo. "No relation to *moi*," Tucker clarified as he hauled the chair over and sat down facing the three. Kal was curious if the Dave Mason album was one Tucker bought firsthand from a record store, or one he'd borrowed from somebody and never condescended to return. Could be City Hall was the original owner.

"Just because he wasn't an asshole this time," Wing Terrill said as they drove back to Sellwood, "doesn't mean he's never an asshole. Our central assumption remains intact."

Mainly Tucker Mason was exhausted. "I haven't slept in days," he revealed to the four on their visit.

"Me either," Calla Dakos said.

"Nightmares?" Wing Terrill inquired of Tucker.

Tucker Mason smiled indulgently, pointing at the wall behind the couch. "See that wall?"

Kal turned to look at the wall, then turned back.

"What wall?" Wing Terrill squinted. "There's no wall there."

Julie Buck glared at Wing.

"Behind that wall is my room. Every night Jay Reynolds sits on the same couch you're sitting on talking to Suzy Miller"—Reynolds was another guy from the school, Tucker's roommate, a delicate-looking, almost pretty guy known for always wearing khaki pants and a moth-eaten sweater. Suzy Miller was a pudgy, homely girl, acne-ridden, long brown hair, one of Calla Dakos's bosom friends, reputed to be a genius— "and they talk about their relationship. Every other word all night long is 'relationship.' *Relationship*," Tucker smiled. "If I hear that word again, I'll throw up."

"They have a *relationship*?" Wing Terrill asked.

Tucker Mason ignored Wing. "I'll pull two pillows over my head, but it doesn't do any good, I can still hear Jay Reynolds saying he's anxious—he actually uses that word—about their relationship. Finally, I'll doze off only to be awakened by Suzy Miller saying that the important thing is their *relationship*, yes, but it's not a strong *relationship* if Jay gets jealous every time she talks to other people. Then Jay says if she needs other people so much, they really don't have a strong *relationship*."

"And they go on like that all night?" Julie Buck asked earnestly.

"Every night," Tucker Mason nodded. Then he sighed, a little melodramatically, Kal Norbert thought, but in an ironic way he'd later recognize as postmodern, as if Tucker Mason, as far back as the early seventies, was simultaneously being melodramatic and making a subtle commentary on melodrama. In addition to commenting on relationships.

"It makes me wish I had a *relationship*," Kal Norbert said.

Wing Terrill laughed and smiled. Julie Buck glared at Wing again, whereupon Wing shrugged innocently: Kal's the one who made the crack. I just reacted.

"Have you asked them to have their conversation elsewhere?" Julie Buck asked.

Now Tucker smiled at the question. This smile, too, was ironic. There was a lot of history behind that smile, though whether it was a long history of exaggerating his annoyances with other people's intimate conversations, or else a reference to repeated futile requests that they conduct those intimacies elsewhere, Kal couldn't say. After all, these weren't any conversations. They were about *relationships*. You couldn't hold those just anywhere or take them elsewhere once you've begun. That was Tucker Mason's irony, communicated by his weary smile.

When the side of the album ended, the four stood up to leave.

They'd done what they could, taken their shot, rolled the dice.

Leaving took a while, generating several topics they probably should have covered while sitting down: their classes, plans even—Tucker included Kal in this—to take in a Blazers game. He fist bumped Wing and Kal and told Calla Dakos—who hadn't said a word the entire visit beyond "Me too"—that he'd call her tomorrow. And then Tucker Mason hugged Calla Dakos, until Kal and Wing and Julie turned away, as if they were intruding upon an intimate conversation.

"You see," Wing Terrill said from the front passenger seat—the death seat, as they called it—as Kal drove them back to Sellwood from their mission in the hills, "sometimes he pretends he's not an asshole. Unsuccessfully, I'll add."

Wing's pretty satisfied with himself, Kal thought. They'd gone over there to see Tucker Mason and set him straight, and it was Wing's brainchild, his idea, his initiative. Kal Norbert wasn't about to bounce up from the couch to take matters into his own hands. It wouldn't have occurred to Julie Buck, and Calla Dakos was too busy lying in bed listlessly. Otherwise, they might have sat up all night in their Sellwood living room snapping at each other, each wishing, for reasons of their own that came down to the same reason, that Calla Dakos would snap out of it. Now Julie Buck was glowering in the back seat and Calla Dakos was sitting as quietly as on the drive over, staring at the floor, still whipped, from what Kal could tell through the rearview mirror. If you didn't know better you'd think she'd been humiliated, that it was occurring to Calla Dakos the people she lived with, with whom she'd spent infinite hours talking, swapping intimacies, had taken advantage of her lethargy, hauling her over to the house of the guy she was obsessed with in reckless disregard of her feelings, all for an innocuous, muted showdown; a wiseass, half-assed, futile gesture which would always embarrass her, at best. (At worst, she'd have to leave town, assuming she ever snapped out of the lethargy sufficiently to summon the energy.) That would pretty much be Kal Norbert's view of the event years later; too many things would happen to Kal for him to remember, or at any rate credit, what he knew absolutely, with no turning back, as they drove back to Sellwood from Tucker Mason's college hovel in the hills, with Wing Terrill riffing that what they'd just seen wasn't Tucker the Decent Human but a misleading version of Tucker the Asshole on his surprising best behavior, and Julie Buck's asking him please, for the last time, to shut up, and Kal Norbert's glancing through the rearview at Calla Dakos, yet defeated, fixated on her knees: they wanted Calla Dakos to know they loved her.

"Thanks for the drive," Calla Dakos summoned the energy to tell Kal as she stalked through their door in Sellwood, then charged straight upstairs to her room. Julie, Wing, and Kal went back to their living room positions abandoned an hour before for their inspired mission.

"This calls for some beers," Wing announced, and left for the kitchen.

"That was interesting," Kal Norbert told Julie Buck. "Do you think it worked?"

"That was pure *shit*," Julie Buck shook her head tearfully. "Poor Calla. Did Wing ever stop to consider Calla?"

Well, Kal thought, why do you think we did it? But Julie's tears were surprising. He thought she was taking her view of the events mainly because it was Wing's idea to go on the mission; that, in fact, if somebody else came up with the idea—even Kal—and Wing insisted they not go, Julie would ridicule him about sitting on his *keister* and never taking a chance to help. 'Poor Calla,' she'd say then, too, though in this instance because nobody moved a finger on Calla's behalf, content to let their housemate suffer through the obsession with no significant group gesture. Kal wasn't absolutely convinced he wasn't right—that Julie wasn't taking the opposite stance from Wing's for the sake of their own subtext—but her tears told him something. Julie Buck knew she was a homely girl whether or not Wing Terrill glimpsed her idealized self. A homely girl. What would that be like? Kal himself figured he must be a homely guy, or the equivalent anyway, whereas City Hall, despite his recent free fall, probably wasn't. In fact, maybe that's why she was snapping at Wing all the time: that Calla's situation reminded her of every guy who'd shunted her, who'd fallen for the doe eyes and the pretty smile and the symmetrical face, leaving Julie in the wings, full of feeling and insight nobody she wanted wanted to hear. Kal supposed if he blurted this to Julie Buck—a la Wing Terrill—she wouldn't know what he was talking about, but

Kal knew: Calla's ordeal reminded her of how guys absolutely *were*: She knew Wing was lying from the moment he first reached across the couch and ran his hand through her hair. She wouldn't dispute he had his reasons, or that she had her reasons for believing him, but he was lying.

As usual in this house, the last person you wanted to overhear your conversation managed to burst into the room at the point you least wanted them to overhear. Wing came back with the beers. "That poor girl up there?" he asked. "Poor Calla Dakos?"

"How could you be so cavalier about her feelings?"

"I'm supposed to stand by and let her be miserable all day?"

"She's not a convenience for your amusement, Wing."

Wing looked across the couch at Kal and smiled. Kal thought the possibility that he had been using Calla Dakos as a convenience for his own amusement—that this is what their fieldtrip was about—hadn't occurred to Wing. Now that Wing thought of it, he wasn't one to dismiss the notion out of hand. "I see," Wing said. "Of course." He turned away a moment and leaned back into the couch, then turned toward Kal Norbert again—looking past Julie Buck—still smiling. "Is that what you think, Kal? Do you agree? We went over there so I could get my rocks off?"

Now they were both looking at Kal.

I don't want to get in the middle here, Kal thought. But he knew better. That's just what he wanted—to be caught in the middle, to decide between the two, to be in the mix, the center of the noise, the guy everyone wanted to enlist, the player crucial to their needs. Wasn't that what this six-week stint at the house in Sellwood was about? To step out of his life and feel that way? And why not? Wing was always the guy things were interesting around, the guy he thought he'd do well to be more like—who waved heartily to strangers and saw the idealized version of ugly girls and never forgot you were the guy who'd dated Sara Sherman—if only twice—and, what's more, the guy who'd summoned a carload in the middle of the evening to visit a rich kid he liked to riff about being an Asshole, on a mission to set the record straight on behalf of a nice girl he was the only guy who never slept with—and if Kal Norbert drove as an obligation to circumstance, in every other way he was the guy in the passenger seat.

He wished the three of them could sit there longer, remaining as they were; but you can't pretend forever, even when you don't know precisely what it is you're pretending.

Kal Norbert shrugged. "Sure," he said. "I don't know. Fuck, nobody's selfless, Wing. We all took Psychology 101. Skinner, you know."

They both kept staring at Kal until it became apparent that was his answer. Skinner.

"Okay," Wing Terrill said. "Skinner. Well, I'm a little beat." Wing nodded at Kal, stood up, smiled at Julie Buck. "Anybody coming with me?" Then he turned around and walked upstairs. Kal Norbert watched Wing Terrill ascend the stairwell from the couch next to Julie Buck.

Julie Buck didn't move to the other side of the couch where Wing had been before going upstairs, as the two sat on the living room couch for nearly an hour, arm brushing arm in the same positions. Was Julie Buck the girl he always wanted? As she looked at Kal now he thought there was a promise in her gaze. Or rather, Julie Buck's diffident gaze reminded Kal Norbert of a promise he'd made to himself. Was he supposed to touch her now? Or even kiss her? Guys like Hank McGill would. There were times he'd really thought he had more in common with Julie Buck than Wing Terrill did, that the greater coherence was theirs, though he wondered if he'd feel that way were she really available. Was she really available now? She talked about her play for nearly an hour—after ten minutes it was apparent to Kal that she was waiting out a suitable length of time; she wouldn't give Wing the satisfaction of following him immediately—and then Julie Buck smiled graciously at Kal Norbert—as if thanking him for all his help—and went upstairs to her lover.

NEW MEXICO

Later Wing Terrill would tell Kal Norbert that the hour upstairs waiting for Julie Buck had been the loneliest of his life. He didn't say this to remonstrate Kal—Kal couldn't imagine that—but because Kal seemed to like to talk about the events during his six weeks at the house, during the numerous phone calls he'd make once he'd returned to New Mexico and the rest of his life. Kal saw a significance Wing didn't but was willing to humor him about, if that's what Wing was doing. After all, Wing was the one stuff actually happened to—for one thing, splitting up with Julie Buck about a week later, which was six days after Kal Norbert loaded his station wagon and drove back to New Mexico. "The loneliest hour of my life," Wing would say. Kal would sense him restraining from bursting into laughter, though Wing sounded serious. And then Kal would move on to some other nuance. Once Kal said to Wing over the phone, "Look, about the Skinner stuff I said that night—I think I was missing the point. If people refused to do things on the grounds it could be misconstrued by somebody—looking for a motive, maybe—that there was something in it for them, nothing would ever get done. Nobody would do anything. That's the other side of the Skinner argument."

Wing was quick to agree, though they both knew that Kal really was missing the point. Kal made a choice that night, and there was no pretending otherwise, though Kal tried, and Wing let him.

Julie Buck's Ophelia was a large success, according to Wing, and Kal called her to congratulate her. She seemed pleased to hear from Kal. She'd split up with Wing just three weeks before—officially it was Julie's idea; in her reasoning, she had her play to concentrate on; a clear break was preferable to dragging on with interminable negotiations through rehearsals. Kal congratulated her on her triumph. Anyway, he just wanted to keep in touch, that's what he told her, and Julie Buck agreed it was a good idea. Kal had heard already—through Calla Dakos, whom he also called occasionally—that Julie Buck was seeing somebody else. He wondered if this somebody else was a guy she'd been eyeing while still with Wing, when Kal himself was convinced if she had a somebody else it would be him. Kal never talked to her again, though he'd expected to see her—and Calla Dakos as well, and even City Hall—at Wing Terrill's funeral two years later. But the house had dispersed by then, for good, and they may well have not heard until too late.

Kal liked calling Calla Dakos the several times he did in the few months after he'd packed his station wagon and returned to New Mexico. She managed to shake her lethargy and—to everybody's surprise, most of all her own—became involved with Tucker Mason. Later Kal heard third- or fourth-hand that they'd split up, but for years, when he thought of her, he liked the idea of Tucker and Calla still being together, of her dream not only coming true but being worthy of the time and emotional torture she'd spent dreaming it. He wondered if their mission had anything to do with Tucker finally falling into place for Calla, and liked to think it did—in fact, he liked to think the mission was essential, the *sine qua non* of Calla Dakos's pursuit of Tucker Mason—and maybe it did play a role, realistically, though it wasn't for several months that Tucker Mason saw the light and crossed his own semi-circle toward Calla Dakos. Before then, though—while Kal was still in touch—she was back on her feet, Wing reported, probably not (Kal imagined) compiling a new version of the Magnificent Seven, but putting all that far enough behind her that Tucker Mason could take another look and accept the baggage—an interesting term, Kal would think, with baggage of his own, for radiating enough sexual energy that rooms vibrated long after she left—as who Calla Dakos was once, but not the current state-of-the-art girl he awakened to most mornings.

She'd tell people she was Assyrian. According to Kal Norbert's resource books, the Assyrians ruled Mesopotamia, the cradle of civilization. They were known for their extreme cruelty and fighting prowess, as well as their monumental building projects. Their architecture was magnificent, they excelled in the arts, and nobody knows exactly why they disappeared from civilization. Perhaps they self-destructed, weakened enough by civil strife that an opportunistic enemy walked in.

And who didn't self-destruct? Wing Terrill missed the turnoff ramp to a highway in Bend, Oregon, and slammed into a concrete bridge support at a speed well beyond the posted limit. There was speculation he was racing another car, a Jeep, which sped away after the crash. That Kal Norbert couldn't imagine. Wing was in Bend with a woman he'd met at the bank where he worked in Portland after graduating from college. It was said they were serious, though Kal Norbert didn't hear firsthand from Wing. (It had been months since they'd last talked. Nothing personal, no estrangement, just the rhythm of their lives.) At the funeral he couldn't help but notice that the woman, grief-stricken, wasn't one of Wing's homelies; she was beautiful, and Kal liked to think that Wing had found his idealized version.

So Wing must have been relaxed, on vacation, a beautiful woman waiting back at the hotel. Kal never knew—there were different stories afloat—why or where he was driving by himself. Some people make mistakes day and night—story of Kal Norbert's life, he'd often think—and then there's Wing

Terrill, who lets up once, for a second, and pays a price so far out of proportion that nobody who loved him, like Kal, could ever really be happy again. That's what Kal thought for a few months after the funeral, anyway, though within a couple of years Wing was mostly a story he'd trot out occasionally when he wanted to impress women that there was more to him than met the eye, that he'd had experiences that moved him and marked him, that there were bruises Kal Norbert wouldn't show just anybody.

Calla Dakos—whom Kal Norbert eventually equated so often with Wing Terrill and the house that after several years he was hard put to have a truly independent thought of either—wanted to be Assyrian. Cruel, merciless, beautiful, vanished without a trace. To be that essential, that feared, that worshipped, that pretty—who wouldn't want to be like that, at least to have been that way, for a while? It might drive somebody to take on the Magnificent Seven. Almost twenty years later Kal Norbert thought of her. Where is she? Is she back to crossing semi-circles? Is Tucker Mason still in the picture, with far greater rights than Kal to these thoughts? Of course, it was hard to imagine she was back to her old tricks, or that she was anything like she was standing in the kitchen at the house. Still, were people thinking that's Calla Dakos, that's how she is, that's how you have to take her? That it's worth it to have been there at maybe the one sustained moment that her youth and her longings converged in such a way that she was extraordinary? Was her spirit intact? Was she still breaking hearts?

Kal knew.

The night Kal thought of Calla again, he was at a party in Santa Fe, talking to a woman he'd just met, who was telling him that she'd never been to Paris, though she'd always wanted to go. In a rare moment of instantaneously saying the perfect thing, Kal told her she carried Paris with her. And the woman was charmed to pieces. For a moment Kal thought this woman, who was far more beautiful than he'd ever seen Calla Dakos twenty years before, was going to cross their own semi-circle to embrace him and to kiss him. He hadn't thought of Calla Dakos in years, but in that moment Kal Norbert knew. Absolutely.

THE LEGEND OF ELK AVENUE

THE LEGENDARY SAGE RABBI Akiba, known as the genius of the Oral Law, was at forty no closer to making his mark than was Dan Bluestone, the would-be sandwich impresario of Elk Avenue. Upon hearing the sage's saga, the sandwichman found that fact relevant to everything. It made him feel virile—he could now imagine a new life where the smile of the twenty-five-year-old clerk behind the counter at Dawson & Sons, Drycleaners, was meaningful—and nearly obsolete, for the beginning of Akiba's new life implied a life discarded, and there was much about himself Dan Bluestone didn't want consigned to the dross. That in his new life he might assimilate the richness and wisdom of the old while releasing the anger and pain, Bluestone found unlikely. Such neat maneuverings had never been his way. Bluestone's scars never altogether healed over. And though this was not a quality acquaintances would have recognized in the stocky sandwichman—he fancied himself unflappable to the naked eye—it's what Bluestone liked best about himself. Though unflappable to the casual observer watching him fill their lunchtime order behind the counter at his shop, a look of contentment—complacency, even, to the offhand study—singing across his blunt gray eyes, you could make your mark on him, you could take this man. You could make him better.

What did Rabbi Akiba like best about himself? The truth's impossible to arrive at, of course, by any route other than coincidence. Nor could a notion, even the most implausible, be disproved if consistent with the known facts of the sage's life. That was enough for Bluestone as he contemplated the question while making a corned beef Reuben for Laurel Pinkstein one overcast afternoon in the winter of 1999, two millennia after the Rabbi's execution during the Bar Kochba Revolt. Laurel Pinkstein was a first timer at the store. The distinction—first timer vs. repeater—was more important to many of Bluestone's customers than to the sandwichman himself, for they considered the shop on Elk Avenue a well-kept secret and themselves to be members of the secret club. That a more prosperous sandwich joint, famous among tourists, was two blocks over on Main only added to the cachet. Bluestone was famous among the members of the club ('Have you tried his pastrami?' 'He gives extra sauerkraut.' 'Bluestone's finger's heavy, his touch golden with the pumpernickel.' 'It's Paradise there.'), but that few others ventured the two blocks from Main to Elk was part of the reason he found himself reduced almost to tears by Akiba, who'd been a failure at forty as well.

Or perhaps it was Laurel Pinkstein. Because the shop was empty that afternoon, he could concentrate on her rather than swap sallies with the regular clientele (Bluestone's Beefers, as they called themselves), though it occurred to him if he was swapping sallies—rather than fastidiously applying the Thousand Island potion to rye in silent consideration of Akiba's humiliations—Laurel Pinkstein might snicker at a crack, might guffaw at a quip Bluestone delivered ('Oh I get it' flashing from her ovals). If such were the case, he would take it from there. She was medium height, medium build, her hair long and curly in black ringlets and thick waves that seemed out of place framing her thin, pale face. To the sandwichman, she looked winded.

The amazing thing to Bluestone, the heart-ripping stunner, the knee-knocker, is that she didn't recognize him beyond being the Deli guy. Would she remember him even if he pressed the story upon her? Would it move her beyond the momentary novelty? They'd been tykes together over thirty years ago at the Rabbi Akiba Hebrew School in Copake Lake, New York. Actors, even, in the annual Purim play. Laurel was Queen Esther, Bluestone a courier who silently attended the King. For some reason, in his capacity as courier he held a sword and a shield, which he brandished out of boredom during the King's soliloquies. Laurel's Queen Esther was a freckle-faced little girl with long curly brown hair, beyond which he couldn't now remember her with any precision other than her name. When Esther told the King she was a Jew herself, born and bred, so tear the heart from her breast and hang her raging husk in testament, there wasn't a dry eye in the house. Even Bluestone's cardboard shield tremored at the spectacle. But it wasn't—Bluestone knew this even then—the selfless pronouncement of a martyr's faith that rocked the boy so much as the grandeur of a girl his age standing under the Copake Sunday School lights pronouncing words Bluestone himself knew and reducing—enlarging—a roomful of adults to the caverns of their souls. At six Bluestone knew he wanted to be like that. It must be a kind of Paradise to look out from under the lights and see the tears of strangers—if you call the Jews of Copake you knew by name but never actually spoke to strangers—emboldened by something you spoke. Such power shook the crying boy's heart. His shoulder and sword fluttered.

After the show, after the procession of strangers and friends heralded Laurel Pinkstein, as Bluestone played hide-the-tefillin with the other tykes, he ran up to the girl to whom he now, over thirty years later, couldn't recall ever having spoken to before (she was in the class behind him), and asked if she would be his girlfriend. In that moment he loved her hopelessly, deliriously. Queen Esther wrinkled her nose. Baffled, she looked at the courier, not quite as if he'd beshat himself, but as if the courier had left his rightful station to stray into the lights and deliver lines from the wrong play. Well, if he learned something in that moment about what was possible and about who he wasn't, he wasn't about to blabber it to Laurel Pinkstein now, when they were meeting in early middle-age.

"What's up?" she asked Bluestone pensively before placing her order.

"It's this, Ms. Pinkstein. When I came up in the business, all the top sandwichmen, great as they were, were even better womanizers. Inveterate. Insatiable. Hell-bent to raise a ruckus. People would come from miles around to sample their roast beef confections, their hot mustards, and they'd be pleased, of course, by the appreciation, but what they really wanted was to glimpse a slip as the pretty gal from Dubuque reached for her water glass. Ever met a gal from Dubuque, Ms. Pinkstein? The way these guys talked! You'd think they were judging the Miss America pageant, nude version. And it wasn't just talk. Sheesh. Customers were chattel. Beef for beef, they'd snicker. Their art was their hustle. It was deflating, Laurel. I promised myself I wouldn't be like that. Yet here I am, looking at you," Bluestone didn't say.

"I'm glad you are," Laurel Pinkstein didn't reply after the briefest of hesitations, not reaching across the counter to touch the sandwichman's magical hand.

She was a sweet girl, mid-thirties, never married. He wondered if he placed a personal in the hip weekly for a Jewish girl (Once Queen Esther? From Copake?) would Laurel answer. "I don't usually make a Reuben with corned beef," is what Bluestone said as he passed the enormous sandwich, a dapple of potato salad included as a side, across the counter.

"Pretentious ass," said Laurel Pinkstein.

A shepherd, a sandwichman, what's the diff? Not apples and oranges but Macintoshes and Grannys. A distinction without a difference, to Bluestone that's what it was.

Akiba was an illiterate shepherd until he met Rachel, a sweet, dark-eyed gal. Perhaps she spotted Akiba in the field and ushered him over. 'What's a guy like you doing in a place like this?' 'Huh? Whazzat? I'm seeing that the sheep don't light out for Disneyland, Miss. Also, there's the big bad wolf and his boys.' Yes, Akiba liked what he saw with this dark-eyed potato. Maybe he couldn't read Torah but he could read her eyes. There was—perhaps Bluestone was pressing it here—something in the way she moved.

Here's what Akiba learned about her when he asked a few questions around town: Rachel was not only beautiful but also the daughter of a big shot. A legitimate scholar. A talmid chacham. As for what he thought about scholars, it was the shepherd's practice to throw stones at the luftmenschen when they wandered by his sheep field lost in thought. Jealousy? That's what Akiba thought in later years, by then a great scholar himself looking back, the codifier of the Oral Law, but the attribution struck Bluestone, who lately considered such matters, as a quarter-shade too convenient. (How nice it would be to spin his own youthful folly as justification for a life spent slapping cold cuts and sauces on rye or wheat.) Still, young, beautiful, the daughter of a macher, Rachel was out of Akiba's league.

But Akiba had a card up his sleeve. That's what Bluestone found inspiring as he contemplated the legend. So when the sandwichman confronted the various hijinks in the saga, all the supernatural bubbamyses that came with the legend, burnishing its core like yards of wrapping paper inside an oversized package, Bluestone could take all that with a grain of salt. This was a folk legend found in a folklore book a Beefer left in the shop, after all, not a physics test. Because Akiba, from nothing, from sheep dust and thornbush, held a card, Bluestone could look it in the eye and see his own broad sandwichman's mug beaming back. The girl was a beauty, young, wellborn, hot ideas, sass, down-to-earth. And Akiba? An illiterate. Already forty years old.

What was forty then? How old in today's years? The question bore consideration. Bluestone figured they didn't have actuarial tables in Akiba's day, given the havoc of flood and pestilence, to say nothing of polio, uncured meats, you name it. Forty then wasn't the same as forty now; it wasn't easing into your prime, plotting your move; it was nearing the end of the line, placing an order for the marble. To get a reliable equivalence you had to add—what? Bluestone wondered—say half. So in today's years Akiba would be more like sixty to Bluestone's own green forty. On the other hand—though this was none too convenient to consider (who wouldn't like the idea of another twenty years to toy with before playing your hand?)—by similar tabulations Moses was reported to be 120 when he died. That's what the same folk book said. That this was a guy who spent forty years in the desert—he wasn't weaned on yogurt cultures and medicinal grains in Soviet Georgia, after all—weighed heavily. You had to figure they weren't too punctilious with chronological reckonings back then. Who was counting? Who wasn't? Well, Bluestone figured Moses's 120, realistically, was more like eighty. Which meant Akiba's forty (assuming similar fast and loose eyeball calculations, or perhaps haphazard carvings in a tree he got back to none-too-often, given his range of sheepherding), reduced the full, realistic third, was a raw twenty-seven when he encountered Rachel in the field and was moved to venture a few discrete inquiries back in town. Twenty-seven? Sheesh. So twenty-seven years old changed the program, righted the boat, got the girl—who cares? That's what you do at twenty-seven. Combine that possibility with a melatonin and a physics text—or the actual writings of Akiba—throw in a glass of red, and Bluestone could go a full eight hours plus change on his futon. You didn't need Akiba to be twenty-seven.

If they said forty in the books, then Akiba was forty. Who was the sandwichman, himself no talmid chacham, to suggest otherwise? Also, it wouldn't surprise Bluestone if the books provided for the old-style calculations, furnishing the figures already adjusted.

So Akiba was a bona fide forty, illiterate, a journeyman shepherd (good or bad at the trade, who can say?) scraping by, one imagines he didn't pack an extra bar of soap on his sheeptendings, morose, jealous, but he had an ace up his sleeve. There were no depths to which he could descend but that he had an angle to play; such was his Akibian inspiration, his get-up-and-go in the face of love.

He'd change his life!

If Rachel couldn't brook no illiterate sheep guy, no sheep maven even, for a spouse, to spend bountiful nights sleeping graybeard to spring bosom—no cachet there, no status, no razz-ma-tazz, no yeah-I-knew-him-when—well then, he won't be a sheep guy, thanks for asking. He'd become a rabbi, a sage. Akiba would right the boat. He'd be the genius of the Oral Law!

If it was almost too much for Bluestone, he had his reasons. Her name was Laurel Pinkstein.

When the sandwichman closed shop he closed shop. There were no two ways about it. You were in or you were out. That was his way. The closed door was the closed door. So after his friend Heidi Cohnbinder told him her stories about shopping after hours, Bluestone was in on the game. At 6:10 (not 6:01, 6:02, 6:03) she'd knock on the window of the shoe shop or the dress store. The proprietors—working stiffs like Bluestone, for whom the office was the office but away from the office was Paradise—would point to their watches and shake their heads efficiently: 'Sorry sister, we open on the morrow at 8 sharp.' But Heidi Cohnbinder was Heidi Cohnbinder, and her smile a twist of Paradise, and the way she raised her brows in utter comprehension of the proprietor's bind but going him one better—she was Heidi Cohnbinder—resulted in the doors being opened, closing time or no closing time—this when Heidi Cohnbinder was merely browsing, no intent to buy. Well, she was a pretty girl, the sandwichman would grant you that. It was possible some guys hadn't heard the Cohnbinder stories of flapping her lashes at hapless working stiffs wanting nothing more than to call it a day at the shop, but what can you do? She was Heidi Cohnbinder. And what would Bluestone do in their shoes, not knowing they were pawns in the Cohnbinder game, meat on her dish, targets to be throttled for what they were, guys beholding a pretty gal? Well, he was onto her, he knew her tricks, Heidi Cohnbinder couldn't smile at Bluestone but that he'd smile back in good-natured mirth, not with heart aflutter but as at a joke. They were pals. He knew her ways. He loved her but, since they were pals, could take her or leave her. He was in the know. He wasn't going to open up at 6:01 or 6:02 (much less 6:10) 'cause a gal knocked at the pane and smiled her dazzler, sizing up the sandwichman as a weak-knee, a gaper, an open-mouther. The closed door was the closed door. That was policy.

But as Heidi Cohnbinder was to strangers, the young woman knocking on the pane—recently turned closed sign facing her unobstructed—was to Bluestone, and a few days after Laurel Pinkstein walked out of his shop with her corned beef half-Reuben, Bluestone found himself opening the locked door, 6:07 or no 6:07.

She was petite, dark-haired, dark-eyed, pointed face. "We're closed," Bluestone told her halfheartedly.

"All I want's a sandwich," the woman said.

"But a guy's got to go home and read his Akiba!" Bluestone didn't protest.

The shop had six tables, four of which now had chairs upturned on their surfaces so Bluestone could get the floors. The woman took her coat off and sat at a corner table away from the counter, as if to signify to Bluestone he could continue his cleanup duties if desired, she just wanted her roast beef and special mustard.

"You want vegetable soup?" Bluestone shouted over the counter.

"How much is the vegetable?"

"Ordinarily $1.75 and a steal at that, but you qualify for our take-it-home or throw-it-out post 6:05 doozy. Whadya say you take it off our hands for free?"

"I couldn't do that."

No Heidi Cohnbinder she, Bluestone thought.

"Okay."

"How about for a dollar?" the woman said.

As Bluestone worked her order the petite, dark-haired gal introduced herself. Amy Weintraub, she said. She'd long heard the sandwichman's legend, she said. Pastrami wasn't pastrami without Bluestone's sauce. The aficionados reported his black ryes were the freshest, his seasoned beefs smooth and crisp. Even the baloney—not featured—sold big. And nobody got shortchanged in price at Bluestone's. What do you do ten minutes before the apocalypse? You order a Reuben from Bluestone's, then you make love, that's what they say around town. Plus McCovery's two blocks over on Main closed at 6:00, a policy hard and fast, so she'd made her way over.

Bluestone, who'd heard it all before, listened with half an ear, preparing Amy Weintraub's tray. He gave her extra on the roast beef—extra by McCovery's standards two blocks over, typical for Bluestone. He checked the potato salad for freshness—affirmatory—and twisted a dapple with extra English. Potato chips, too. She didn't mention a beverage and the sandwichman didn't want to get her going, so he tossed in an egg cream. McCovery's or no McCovery's, Bluestone had his pride. He went the extra lap. If you were nice to the sandwichman he was nice to you, and if you walked into his shop that was plenty nice, was the word among the aficionados.

He didn't want to mop while Ms. Amy Weintraub cooed over her delectable roast beef on sauteed sourdough, nor was it his place—or desire, especially—to initiate the swapping of commonplaces. What's more, four times out of five Bluestone wasn't a shopkeeper to make conversation to unravel the silence. He liked the silence. He liked sitting at an unstacked table in the silence while across the shop floor a petite, dark-eyed young woman who'd smiled through the door pane at 6:07 (and if it was Al Weintraub, it went without saying, or Dick Weintraub, or Bobby, there would be no special soup rate, no sandwich with the potato side scooped with extra English; Al Weintraub, in fact, would be halfway across town by now, or have found another place to eat) and whom he'd let in because not even Akiba, the most tendentious of moralists, could resist a naked woman in a palm tree (saved from sin only because it was decreed), because—Bluestone pushing here—policy was the backdrop against which you define who you are, singing—even if by implication—your lurking desires and muffled cravings to the world, which the world didn't want to hear, thank you, was across the tables with their chair legs upside down, on the other side of the floor, oblivious to the sandwichman, he'd bet, and numbed to the crisis at work, and the fate of the Rockies, and what her boyfriend said and what she said back, and the nursing home a thousand miles away where her father sat in his chair thinking of her, because there she was cooing in her concentrated silence at the food he made.

Oh, Bluestone considered her life.

He didn't want to mock. He wouldn't mock. That Bluestone's own life was the stuff of mockery, such was the sandwichman's lot. There'd be no carryover, no half-baked residual impact, no shading of perspective just because you could always mock him in a pinch. He wouldn't mock her. After all, he had his defenses, and she might not. She'd never smiled in mirth at Heidi Cohnbinder's dazzler. She'd never inspired a cadre of Beefers. She'd never—to the best of Bluestone's knowledge—fallen in love with Laurel Pinkstein because at a time Laurel would barely remember he'd seen her in the lights reduce an audience of adults to tears, and there she was over thirty years later walking into a sandwich shop at the very instant the proprietor was contemplating the great Rabbi Akiba's falling for a gal named Rachel.

Once a failure now a sage, what brutal satisfaction it must have been, wandering through the hills of Palestine he knew so well from his sheepherding, leading his disciples through their paces. And all he could think about was Rachel! They were wedded—a man of honor, he'd made his promise and followed through—but his thoughts became impure. The pearly tones of her flesh, yes. Her black eyes gleaming incandescent, that, too, taunted the Rabbi's imagination. But what he pictured over and over again was her muff. Mornings discussing nuances of dietary laws with the boys, there was her muff as if smeared on a tree. (But that was no tree.) Afternoons reading the Torah he'd have to shake his head, then read again. Nights he was with her.

They'd do the beast with two backs. He was doing okay, a reader now talking up scripture with Rabbi Eliezer, Rachel liked the new man he'd become fine, he was the luckiest guy around, but mornings after she kissed him goodbye and sent him off in his smart robes with his satchel of scrolls, but afternoons, there was that image everywhere: Her muff.

It was driving him nuts. Sicko. Addled. What could a guy do? When the very thought of her thrust him toward sin? It was tricky, defying resolution. Well, there was one. To be the man she wanted, a scholar worthy of resting his graybeard by her delectable bosom all their earthly days, he'd need to leave. Scram. Bolt to the blue. Sheesh. Around her he was hard put to finish his shemas. So he leaves. 'Dear Rachel....' (That note Bluestone would like to read.)

Away from Rachel's distraction the Torah itself became sexual to Akiba. What joy and zealotry there was to be had resided there in contemplation. When you leave a pretty gal to study, you don't slough off unless you're a shmuck. This was no shmuck. Akiba obsessed on the words of Torah, feasted on their penumbras, saw shades of illumination no sage had glimpsed before.

Since it was all written by Adonoi it was all relevant, all legally laden. Even grammatical inconsistencies, even the twirls of penmanship were applicable to everything on the sexual glade. He fomented approaches to the oral law, set up guidelines of interpretation. Akiba, now a genius, a sage, advised the Sanhedrin, emerged as the prime mover behind the Halacha, argued for the Song of Songs' inclusion. (You could write a book, Bluestone thought.)

After twelve years away from the distractions of his good woman, Akiba—once an illiterate shepherd into middle age—was already a legend. His followers numbered 12,000. When some were tempted away from study by thoughts impure and profane (for boys will be boys) the sage, who'd given up so much to the altar of study, mocked them mercilessly for their weakness. After twelve years he returned to Rachel, ready for her at last, the sage and genius worthy of her yearnings.

Rachel stood at the door as Akiba approached. Perhaps she shook her head dismally at the spectacle. One imagines his beard shocked white by now, and the 12,000 chachams cloaked in rags lined up behind him as he walks pensively through the sheep grazing yard toward the vestibule and the woman who had made it all possible, whom he'd abandoned in the name of grace and light twelve years before.

"Another twelve would be better," Rachel says.

Akiba spins around to leave without uttering a single word.

One imagines the twelve grand turning in their tracks, on cue.

The brutal satisfaction Akiba must have felt through the twelve more years. His disciples doubled. Word spread. Well, you could mock him. You could mock the sun for its regularity, too. Bluestone regarded Amy Weintraub finishing her roast beef on sourdough at the table across the floor.

Here's what he saw: Amy Weintraub was a gal who wanted to be a waitress. Not a high-pressure, big-ticket, move-'em-out, clear-your-station, 'Hi-I'm-Amy-I'll-be-your-server-tonight' joint. And not, Bluestone sensed as well, with a slap of disappointment that surprised him enough he almost stopped contemplating Ms. Weintraub, the origin of the slap unknown, for he was thinking about her mostly to pass the time, and maybe—this was possible—to test out his Akiba on this just-another-customer, this petite, dark-eyed specimen of the human race, not in a sandwich joint either did her dreams settle; the big-ticket joints too crass, the sandwich shops with their Bluestones and their local hype small potatoes. She wanted a breakfast joint/coffee shop, hopping, lines out the door for the tables (the counter usually available with a seat on the swivel chairs), taking their orders, johnny-on-her-toes with the coffee and decaf, cracking wise with the truckers and students and brokers and attorneys and artisans (not that she'd known one to get up before the joint closed at 1:00), the builders and clerks, you name it; the occasional celeb, too, in town incognito, over whom she'd make a fuss ('More joe, honey? Like hashbrowns with that, doll?'), but the same fuss, the identical to-do she'd make over everyone. Even Bluestone, should he take the busman's holiday and stand in line twenty minutes to wait for his omelet and joe. That was Amy Weintraub. Of course—this was Amy Weintraub too, as the sandwichman considered her—she'd never filled out an application. The wish real, yes, but never inquired within.

"You want a job?" he asked across the shop floor. Not that he could afford her.

She looked up from the last bites of her seasoned sourdough—plate cleaned but for that and half-a-dapple of potato salad—quizzically, her dark eyes widening, as if the sandwichman read her mind, even anticipated thoughts by a good half-step she hadn't quite taken herself until he bothered to speak up and shed light on her true desire. (Bluestone carried away here, but wasn't that how it must have been for Akiba when he nailed down a disciple to the practice? It couldn't always be—even accounting for contemporary distractions such as everything—that they liked his way with a Talmudic interpretation, so they kissed their honeys goodbye to follow the ragged sage through the hills of Palestine the rest of their wandering days. Here and there he must have sized them up one-on-one and customized a desire, delivered the bull readymade so they looked back across a room—a thatched hut, maybe, with deer hide strung across the door hole—and thought, 'Man, this guy's uncanny, he sees through the smoke and the fog and the pretense and names my very heart.')

"Thanks for asking," Amy Weintraub looked up from the remains of her roast beef and sourdough, "but I have a job."

Bluestone nodded. No harm no foul. "You ever wanted to be a waitress?"

"Mister, I never wanted to be a waitress."

Amy Weintraub glumly looked down at her potato salad and finished the half-dapple, then reached over to slurp the egg cream.

According to Rabbi Akiba the most important thing for a Jew is to study, because study leads to practice. Probably he wasn't talking about Amy Weintraub's thighs. But Bluestone thought the principle held.

Because Amy Weintraub ordered another egg cream, insisted the sandwichman 'do what he had to do' so she wouldn't be any bother, the sandwichman sponged and mopped and balanced the register as she worked her egg cream with petite, dark-eyed deliberation. An hour later, he'd not only offered to walk her home (she'd lingered as he locked up) but she'd accepted the offer, and he found himself beside a naked Amy Weintraub in Amy Weintraub's bed. "Why me?" the sandwichman asked.

"Pshaw. You're a sandwichman. You're Bluestone, the Legend of Elk Avenue. You get all the girls."

"Why you?" the sandwichman said, reaching for her bosom.

A while later they sat up in bed sipping tall glasses of lemon water.

"Tell me a story," Amy Weintraub said.

"Rabbi Akiba would mock the rank and file for their earthly longings. After all, he'd left his lovely bride then returned after twelve years and left her for another dozen—such was the measure of his diligence. To Akiba, given all that, those disciples whining about their impure thoughts and profane temptations were pussies. Toddlers, really, pure and simple. They may as well be Goyim! Well, maybe his condemnations and demands got out of hand. The guy could be rough as he mocked the weenies, and the very force of his weenie-mocking ribaldry grated the powers-that-be. They set up a trap. One day in the woods—get it?— he woke up from a nap to behold a beautiful naked woman smiling at him from the top of a palm tree. Even the sun itself stopped in its tracks, enveloping her in golden rays. That was part of the trick. Akiba wasn't in the Torah frame of mind. No, he wasn't steeling himself for a test. He just woke up and this golden-locked, big-bosomed, smooth-skinned, long-legged, tanned beauty called to him in a voice like milk and honey and spread her legs."

"She sounds like Heidi Cohnbinder," Amy Weintraub said, not unpleasantly.

In fact, it occurred to the sandwichman, that's whom he envisioned.

"Guess what happened? Akiba strips and charges up the tree like his train pulled into Paradise. Halfway up the tree he comes to his senses, slinks down, cries bitterly, gets the lesson, if you follow me. He could have sinned, been exposed for a phony, a sham, a flim-flam, a Torah-spouting huckster, a con, except it was decreed by the powers-that-be that he be spared. No harm no foul. This was merely a lesson for the sage in human fallibility. After that, when a disciple groused about yearnings of the flesh, Akiba bit his tongue. His comments came back watered down. That's right."

"Do you like my hair this way?" Amy Weintraub said.

After Amy Weintraub, it seemed to the sandwichman that the dam broke. While it wasn't always identical, it was always similar. He'd change his line of patter with one gal, alter his approach with another. It didn't matter what he said as much as who was saying it and—he guessed—whom he was saying it to. Sometimes he'd feel like a phony, but who's to say that's true? And who's to say who Bluestone is? It's not like he never stood behind a counter in his shop contemplating Akiba and just passed himself off that way. And if the Legend of Elk Avenue razz-ma-tazz struck the interior Bluestone as farfetched, most likely wistful mocking on Amy Weintraub's part (Bluestone and Akiba were by no means exclusive members of that club), it's not as if the sandwichman didn't have a gang of Beefers talking him up, spreading the good word. Sometimes he entered a room, and when he left the room, he imagined strangers wondering who he was—that's the way he projected himself. Not that the legend meant anything to him, but if it gave pleasure to a roomful of strangers? If it quickened the heart of a lovelorn shayna? One gal he never even mentioned Akiba to. Nor was she aware of his own Elk Avenue legend. (When she asked him what he did, the sandwichman shrugged, idly quipping, "I'd tell you, but I'd have to kill you if I did!") He encountered her on the street looking for a kitten; just as the sandwichman was offering to join the search he heard a faint hiss—undetectable to the frantic woman—under a neighbor's dilapidated porch, where the two soon found the kitty crouching mournfully. Hot is hot, as the Beefers liked to say about Bluestone's onion vegetable. Momentum is momentum. Nor does momentum discriminate. The woman's name was Whitney Payne, and if Bluestone wasn't mistaken, she was a shiksa.

With Laurel Pinkstein, whom he called a few days after sleeping with Amy Weintraub (and who agreed, after some hesitation, to see a movie with the sandwichman), he told the classic Akiba. "A disciple asked the rabbi to sum up the crux of Jewish learning while standing on one leg. I'm not sure, Laurel, exactly what leverage the disciple had. Talk about cheeky! Did he hold a gun to his head? A knife? What was in it for Akiba?

Here the tales are hazy. But the old sage assumed the one-legged position. The crux? It was the golden rule. 'Do unto others as you'd have others do unto you. The rest is commentary,' said Akiba. I love that: 'The rest is commentary'! And then he lowered his leg, I guess."

Here Laurel could roll her eyes and discount the sandwichman as a fanatic. Or she could take the ball and run to him. "You always seemed so pretentious. You can make a sandwich, Bluestone, but it's not the end all and the be all."

After the movie he asked her to his shop. Music from his boom box, splitting a real Reuben—which Bluestone made as he never made a Reuben before. Who knows what it meant to her? She had that brittle look he saw on some women who never married, as if they were on the verge of slipping out of graciousness to levy a bitter judgment. Without intending to, he told her about the tiny Queen Esther he'd seen in Copake so many years before, who had—this he knew she wouldn't swallow, but still he told her, because how often would he find himself face-to-face in his shop with Laurel Pinkstein, the boom box waxing classical?—to his six-year-old mind (but even now, thinking back, in ways in which he'd never gotten over), transfigured his concept of the possible. He handed her a Diet Coke and she took the sandwichman in her arms.

Now they were entwined on Laurel's couch. Laurel's black ringlets fanned across Bluestone's cheek. Could he do this forever? "Typhoid raged through Kalvaria, worse than any Cossack. My grandma told me this story. She was a little girl, but day and night for two weeks she helped the others work. They weren't really sandwiches as we know them—as I make them—just black bread dipped in broth—a puny gob of chicken breast sunk into the damp yeast. My granny did the deliveries. Sometimes she'd enter rooms and see friends already dead, but sometimes not. See? Sometimes not. They thought my granny was immune to the typhoid. Who can say why she never caught it? For two weeks day and night she delivered the tiny sandwiches as the fevers raged. She didn't sleep, she didn't eat, and as she entered the rooms, the living sang out for joy and praised God's mercy. That's the glory of the pursuit, Laurel. Food's life, but you can't carry a steak in your pocket. Later Granny came over to America and worked as a seamstress. When I was a tyke, she'd hold me on her knee and tell me the story about when she was a girl and the looks on the faces of the living when she'd enter their room with her basket of black bread dipped in broth."

"Shit, Bluestone. I'm sorry."

"But you're right, Laurel. How could you see? Sometimes I get lost in the drum rolls and forget what counts," the putative Legend admitted, surprising even himself.

As for Heidi Cohnbinder, he never forgot—even in the weeks after (re?)discovering Akiba when his fortune turned—that she was really just a pal, providing insider's glimpses for the sandwichman into the workings of beauty. Bluestone never really knew what was in the bargain for Ms. Cohnbinder. Though according to some he was the Legend of Elk Avenue, there were plenty of bigger streets with bigger legends, better looking than Bluestone, richer most certainly, who could make their own mean sandwiches, and all looking at Heidi Cohnbinder with the same eyes. What's beauty? She was Paradise made palpable in the flesh; whether she was the signature of the heart and soul as well, the flesh was plenty. You couldn't ask too much of any one person, Bluestone knew that much. The girl in the tree with the voice of milk and honey, the golden-locked big-bosomed visage enveloped in golden rays probably didn't juggle and play chess too. Or if she did, nobody asked. Perhaps that's where he came in with the Cohnbinder girl? Face to face with her dazzler most guys turned supplicant, falling into line, beseeching beauty from knees and palms. But the sandwichman, as a bud privy to her dodges, laughed in her face.

So while he was in bed with the Cohnbinder gal—notwithstanding he was lovers with Ms. Weintraub and Laurel Pinkstein and once even with the shiksa Payne (and a few others, too, who frequented his shop in the weeks since he heard the story of the forty-year-old Akiba changing his life; one day an illiterate, the next a sage—a certain Ms. Feld, a discreet Molly Tannenbaum, attorney-at-law, and a Ms. Esther Miller, the haberdasher's divorced second wife)—it was atop the embroidered bedspread where they lay, not beneath, fully clothed, untouching save for comradely knocks and brushes as one or the other freely tossed arms or legs as vehicles of emphasis.

He'd gone there thinking he'd marry Laurel Pinkstein and left knowing he'd marry Laurel Pinkstein.

But it was when he was talking to Heidi Cohnbinder about Akiba's execution in the Bar Kochba revolt that he understood why Akiba came to him in the middle of his own life. (It wasn't just that as a boy he'd attended for one year—and there saw Laurel—the Rabbi Akiba Hebrew School in Copake Lake, New York, and assumed Akiba was the bearded, jolly administrator with the lisp and the loudly embroidered yarmulke, who'd welcome the classes from the pulpit, "Hello boils and goils!" Or so Bluestone remembered. The paperback book of folktales the Beefer left behind at the shop was surprising.) Heidi told the sandwichman that she remembered the story of the revolt. Was she just getting him to change the subject? On the other hand, Ms. Cohnbinder spent a month on a kibbutz the year after college, before Bluestone knew her—Bluestone remembering now, though he'd forgotten until he began the story and she interrupted to remind him, grabbing his arm as it swung in the air for emphasis, "Bluestone!" She had a jones for this kind of stuff. How could he not be nuts about her? Heidi Cohnbinder was a pretty girl but not just a pretty girl unless that's what she wanted you to think. Though if you got too caught up in thinking she was more than a pretty girl, and it didn't suit Heidi Cohnbinder, she'd lower the boom on that, too. Maybe Bluestone was a cool cucumber in his current guise, a legend, but he knew both of them knew, as they lay on her bed discussing Akiba and the Bar Kochba revolt, that she could cut him to strips if she wanted. For a moment he thought this was why he embraced the sage. He knew he'd marry Laurel Pinkstein (not exactly chopped liver herself), but the Heidi Cohnbinders would always beckon, and though he'd see the dodge and never touch them, in lust or hope, that's not to say he'd resist now or then if he opened his eyes and Heidi Cohnbinder sang to him, naked beside the sandwichman in her bed.

Akiba thought Bar Kochba was the messiah. Perhaps you had to believe you're following the messiah if you're rebelling against the Romans, who in their reign of repression went so far as to outlaw Judaism. Perhaps Bluestone himself would bite off his finger to demonstrate the ferocity of his loyalty and rage—that's what the Jews did, signing up to fight beside Bar Kochba, pledging their signatures in blood. And for several years the Jews recaptured Jerusalem. Finally—so the sandwichman read in the folk book—Hadrian sent his most vicious general, Severus, to smoke out and starve the Jews by surrounding Jerusalem. 580,000 Jews—including Bar Kochba, the false messiah, as it turned out—were slaughtered by the Romans. Thus ended the rule of Judea for 2,000 years, until May 5, 1948, when the British left Palestine and the state of Israel, a phrase Bluestone distinctly recalled, when he thought of it after thirty years, the presumptive jokey Akiba invoking from the podium at the Akiba Hebrew School in Copake. ('Boils and goils, the birth of the state of Is-rye-el thirteen years ago today...') In 1978 Heidi Cohnbinder, according to Heidi Cohnbinder, spent six months on a kibbutz, chasing after, for the one and only time in her life, a guy she liked.

After throwing his support behind Bar Kochba, the putative messiah, Akiba was hanged by the Romans for teaching Judaism, which was outlawed, to the Jews, who were outlawed.

Why did he believe Bar Kochba was the messiah? Heidi couldn't say, and none of the other girls he courted in the three months between the time he found the folk book and the time he'd return it—Bob Pruskin, the Beefer who left it, accepted it back from the sandwichman without comment—and go on to other obsessions or, more precisely, he'd return to a life without obsession other than to make the best pastrami-on-rye Elk Avenue ever saw, and to make it day in and day out for years—as many as twelve perhaps, and then another twelve, if necessary, if that could get him what he wanted, even if what he'd wanted really—as it would turn out—was the twelve more years paying the bills by dressing up corned beef on sourdough. The other girls in those three months—the Amy Weintraubs, the Laurel Pinksteins—never heard of Akiba other than the stories the sandwichman told and didn't offer commentary.

But the best story Bluestone knew is that Akiba had glimpsed Paradise and returned in peace. Once you've seen Paradise, went one version, you had to believe the Messiah has come.

On the embroidered bedspread next to the golden-haired, jumbo-bosomed, milk- and-honey-voiced (Bluestone pressing here, though her voice, moderately shrill, was not unpleasant once you stopped expecting the milk and honey to pour through those dazzling teeth), kibbutz-seasoned Ms. Cohnbinder, Bluestone contemplated Akiba in Paradise. "Facts are scarce," he told her.

Like Laurel Pinkstein, Heidi Cohnbinder didn't roll her eyes. Not exactly.

"Yes," she said. "The *facts* about the guy's trip to Paradise 2,000 years ago are scarce."

"There are plenty of different stories." According to one in the Beefer's folk book, Akiba traveled with three other sages to the cave of Machpelah, where they followed the scent of cedar that evoked Paradise, the very route the souls of the just took to the Garden of Eden. According to some, the gates open for a flash every hundred years. "There was luck involved in timing it right, but the four sages were prepared. They'd calculated that the time was approaching. Fortuitously, Akiba was watching that very instant, and the four squeezed into the earthly Paradise. Inside the gates one sage looked and died. One went insane at what he saw. One couldn't reconcile what he saw with the Torah and knew instantly his Torah-worshipping life was a pack of lies. Bubbamagumba. In the blink of an eye, in the flash of eternity, he turned heretic. Akiba alone returned in peace."

But what was Paradise? What did Akiba see? There was no record of Akiba mentioning it to anyone, not even—given that *facts* are scarce—to Rachel or his disciples. The legends grew, until there were almost as many stories as there were people.

What was Paradise to Heidi Cohnbinder? To Amy Weintraub? To the Beefers (to hear them tell it, a full Reuben at Bluestone's Deli would do)? There were times in Bluestone's life—he understood this now, lying beside her, wondering if he should marry Laurel Pinkstein, who was willing—when Paradise was Heidi Cohnbinder.

Did he want Laurel Pinkstein? Thirty years before she gave him a glimpse of Paradise, until the lights dimmed, and the adults lined up to herald the young Queen Esther, and Bluestone played hide-the-tefillin. Well, in an hour he'd meet Laurel Pinkstein. Whatever he told her, nothing was binding. He knew he could go back on his word, though she'd hate him. If so, he'd find a way to live with himself, he wouldn't die or go nuts, or walk around spouting from one leg in recompense, but he knew he'd never again be able to think of that moment in the lights in exactly the same way.

Akiba came back. That's what got to the sandwichman. He'd seen Paradise, but that was enough. You didn't have to die or go crazy or turn everything you valued topsy-turvy. Paradise was cool, groovy, mazel, neato, but it wasn't someplace you had to stay. Was it something worth knowing? You betcha. Yes sirree, Bob. Affirmatory. That's right. It could make you think the Messiah was near. But Akiba reopened the gate from the inside and returned to Jerusalem and the Talmud.

Bluestone lay beside Heidi Cohnbinder on her bed, thinking of Laurel, who was waiting for the sandwichman's decision.

Had he been to Paradise himself? There were times these last few weeks, after he slipped into Queen Esther's bed, when he thought so. But who can know? And whom could you ask, in so many words? And who, worth listening to, would venture commentary?

Was Laurel Pinkstein what he found when he got to the Garden, or when he returned?

MISGUIDED MISSILES

E LLEN CALLED TO TELL me that Sid the Kid didn't get into the college of his choice, which was approximately a dozen rungs down the ladder from his choice two years ago, when he began doing methamphetamine. Crystal meth, as they call it. If that's what he was doing—it's hard to get an entirely trustworthy report from Sid the Kid about his drug chronicle. He's caught between telling the truth and sounding like an absolute moron, and lying to his mother to spare her feelings—interesting the degrees of solicitousness one discovers when they hit bottom—and therefore *being* an absolute moron. Not that Ellen would be inclined to believe him. She's not moronic, anyway—plus, you only get so many shots at the credulity game before they take your quarters away. Even with your mom (which, I suspect, is one of the few things my ex-stepson has learned in his seventeen years). Still, she's more inclined to give the boy a break than anybody else the boy knows.

It's ruined his mother. There's no other way to put it. Her health has fallen apart. She's put on weight. Wrecked by worry. She doesn't sleep but stays up most nights crying. Adjusts her Prozac. Even her long red hair—her pride and joy—has lost its luster. She obsesses on the phone—off the phone, too, though I never see her off the phone, so to speak. You get a dozen kids doing the stuff and maybe four can't handle it, make catastrophic choices, compromise their future should they have one. For the other eight it's all bullshit—more evidence of adult hypocrisy, as if more evidence was necessary. (Ellen herself had a major history back when.) Of the four, Sid the Kid wouldn't be at the top of the class, but a close second. Not only mostly F's for two years at school, but a few jackass misdemeanors—he's made a fetish of stealing Snickers bars from the 7-11 at Heiling and Yale—totaled his car, gained a couple hundred pounds, lost about three hundred. A young drunk, too, practicing to be an old drunk. If kids—I'm generalizing, of course—knew how selfish they were, they'd kill themselves. I'm absolutely convinced if Sid the Kid could glimpse his true selfish moronic depths he'd kill himself in an inspired moment of rectitude. So maybe it's a good thing he's clueless. That's the bright side.

My sister called when I was thinking about Sid the Kid, so I shared the rumination.

"Poor Ellen," Rachel said.

"That's right."

"It just goes to show you."

Actually, Rachel has heard the Sid the Kid story in regular installments over the last two years, and probably thinks it's becoming a broken record by now—and songs you didn't want to hear in the first place, before the fissure. Rachel and I are something of a broken record about it too. How many times can she say Poor Ellen? How many times can one adult commiserate with another that it just goes to show you? In fact, I'm no longer clear that it does go to show you, or about what, exactly, it shows you more clearly than before it showed you.

"Why don't you call her, Rachel?"

She hesitated for a moment. I could envision her for that moment lying on the couch, maybe in the flannel shirt I gave her which rises over her distended stomach as if she's pregnant. Which, as she knows too well, she'll never be. Maybe that's why she'll never call Ellen—or why Ellen is never liable to call Rachel, though in many ways they've always loved talking to each other and were often inseparable back in the days when they were sisters-in-law. The marriage era, as we sometimes refer to it. Rachel was married then, too. The irony would be unbearable. And though Rachel's bitterness, for lack of a better term, plays out far more frequently as compassion than as grousing, there's still the spectacle of Ellen complaining over and over about Sid the Kid—like all true obsessives, she can't help herself—and Rachel on the other end, the good empathic listener, offering the occasional well-intended, usually charming observation, letting her vent. But in the end things are what they are. Rachel can't get away from that, and after twenty minutes of Ellen venting, Rachel probably couldn't help herself from letting Ellen know. Nobody needs that, needless to say.

"He'll be okay, Bart."

"Thanks, Rachel."

Her voice is pretty much the same, a little hoarse, but over the phone it's easy to imagine I'm talking to the same Rachel looking as she has most of her adult life. Long black hair, very pretty, green eyes that always look like she's just found the last clue to the puzzle. It's only in her adult years that we've been friends, really. Mom told me a couple of years ago that Rachel never complained about me— "What could she say?" as Mom, ever my cheerleader, put it—which put me to shame, in that for years a good portion of my conversations with my mother consisted exclusively of my complaining about Rachel. Still, as adults we've been friends. As kids she hated me. I'm convinced of that. She knew that as her baby brother I'd warrant a certain amount of attention and was philosophical about it in her big sister way, but I was a sickly child, and the attentions necessary to nurse me to normalcy went above and beyond. Way beyond, as far as Rachel was concerned. In fact, once in high school, where Rachel was a couple of years ahead of me, I passed her in the hallway and Rachel said hello. I looked over my shoulder, not as postmodern commentary on sibling relationships but because I was curious about who she was speaking to. I knew, of course, it wasn't me. It was, though, for the hallway was clear; the one time in that school, in that era, I can remember her conceding—even begrudgingly, in empty hallways—public acknowledgment, though as adults we can't walk two feet without her introducing me to somebody as her brother. She's thirty-nine years old now, and until a few months ago looked a good decade younger.

"Crack any cases today?" Rachel asked.

The question was rhetorical, Rachel's way of saying goodbye without actually saying goodbye. Saying goodbye, as far as I could tell as her brother, was Rachel's last superstition. I laughed and we hung up.

Though, too, if I'd cracked a case, I assume she'd be happy to hear about it.

As it happens, though I was in my office, where I've known myself to go about the business of cracking cases, I changed into my jogging shorts and took off. I've cracked cases while running, too—the solution that oddly enough never occurred to me before jogging into my consciousness as I tear up the Blake Street hill. Though later, back at the office, staring at the case files, it turns out there was a pretty good reason it never occurred to me before, as the cracked case snaps open under further scrutiny. So usually when I feel myself on the verge of a case-breaking inspiration, I turn up my headphones and fantasize that I'm a rock star. Today's the best day of the early spring—sunny, low sixties, snow melting, half the town in shorts or sleeveless shirts. (Though in my days teaching at the U, I'd noticed there wasn't an inevitable correlation between weather and apparel. A good quarter of the guys, for example, wore shorts year-round. Below freezing, you could count on it. There they'd sit with their raspy knees. Perhaps it was a fraternity ritual.) I'm surprised today so many people drive convertibles. It's the kind of thing you never notice in the summer, as if spring is the acclimation phase of acute sensitivity, before the nerves blunt as one labors through the dog days of summer. Acute sensitivity? I suppose Ellen would laugh at that—and perhaps I should call and reveal the insight; she could stand a laugh what with Sid the Kid. Rachel would chuckle, too. It's well known within the family that I'm pretty opaque—which is to say I don't always take the concerns of others as seriously as they deem appropriate. Nobody does, of course. But I betray it more quickly than most. Evidently. Though since Rachel's been sick, I'm sure she'd say I've been pretty attentive. And I probably talk to Ellen—really talk to her—a lot more now than when we were married, though I suppose she'd say now that we're no longer married it matters a lot less.

I'm certainly not opaque to the girl jogging half a block ahead of me. Winter has left her bottom a bit bulkier than she desires—her butt tremors almost imperceptibly, an event that likely would pass you by unless you applied intense concentration to the matter—and her long brown hair is tied back. When the wind jostles her hair it's like a long furry animal rides uncomfortably down her neck. For a moment I wish I could keep following her like this. There are observations about her thighs my consciousness has yet to articulate. I wonder if she'd love me if she gave herself the chance to really know me but, alas, we're just two running bodies passing in broad daylight. Before I'm ready I'm half-a-block beyond her.

That's the problem with being in shape—if not quite in condition—when everybody else is peeling their eyes open in lethargy from the winter's hibernation. You're forced to keep your reveries brief.

This is my easy run today. Strictly optional. More a tour of the jogging trails that skirt our city and curve toward the hills than a training run. Three soft miles. My training run is in the morning, 5:30, six hard miles through the blustery cold. Not that it matters much. I wear my headphones on the training run, too, but can't sustain the rock star fantasy for more than a few seconds, and when I pass a beautiful woman—which happens more often than you might imagine at 6AM—I don't have the physiological luxury of sustained observation. It's more like an elusive whiff of cherry pipe tobacco.

I cheat a little on days I work the upper body during my weight sessions, don't push the throttle down quite so hard on the training run. I don't know why. Or I do know why, but the explanation—I want to save myself a little for the benches, curls, presses, lateral lifts—is never quite satisfactory. For some reason, when I work the legs Tuesdays and Thursdays, I have no such compunctions. I can run myself into the ground on my run, then later the legs respond in the weight room. Or perhaps I'm merely less vain about the lower body.

Not that it truly matters. For me the game is emotional—always was, always will be. I really mean that. A matter of convincing myself it's truly possible, then relaxing enough—emotionally—so the possible falls into place with the considerable help of a vicious crossface half nelson I'm relaxed enough to throw. Full-tilt boogie. Full intensity. And I don't care if I win. That's what I convince myself of. Though I do care, of course. Care enough to knock myself out every day at 6AM, to work my hands and biceps and lats and delts beyond the point of dizziness and nausea, beyond muscle collapse, care enough to be a thirty-seven-year-old semi-adult who spends half his waking hours visualizing single leg takedowns and slipping in the half. But if I think I care—really care—things get complicated then. You can ask Ellen about that.

I'm not suggesting everything is a question of mind over matter, though this admission may surprise a few people who've made the mistake of buttonholing me at parties when we're both a few sheets to the wind. That's when I'm liable to lapse into my Jaycee inspirational number. ("If I didn't believe I could tear this house apart brick by brick and squeeze it back together I wouldn't bother to walk through the door. Because you know why? Because I can!") Or some such riff that inspires them to buttonhole somebody else: Mission accomplished. That's just a number I whistle, a con I'm working that the truth is I'd do quite well to believe myself. That's the best kind of con going. (It got me married to Ellen, and it got me divorced.) Mind over matter? Whenever I'm working that line, half-believing it, I want to run into the brick wall to remind myself I can't run through it, no matter what dreams I whisper to myself in the night.

I mean people feed that shit to my sister all the time. Rachel nods and smiles. She's charming, she's gracious, she knows they don't know what they're saying, that their denial of death—to paraphrase Ernest Becker from my college textbooks—has kicked in so deeply they're as clueless in their way as Sid the Kid. They're insensitive and blind to their insensitivity, that sums it up in Rachel's view. Needless to say, not an attractive combination. So she pities them and cuts them a few billion miles of slack. Though what she says to herself I don't know. Whereas I want to throw them through the brick wall.

Actual conversation:

Them: I know somebody who was given two months to live. They ______ and they __________. They willed themselves to live, they wouldn't take no for an answer, and now they're healthy as she-goats. Mind over matter. (One friend, in our facsimile of this conversation, actually tapped her finger to her temple at this final insight.)

Me: Sure. That's great.

Because Rachel's not going to survive this. Because someday—it won't be more than a month or two—her organs aren't going to function, squeezed to death by the berserk cells which enclose them like plums to their seed. And her will doesn't have too much to do with it in the end. But don't tell me she's weak. Don't imply she wasn't up for the fight, or that Madame She-Goat wanted to live more convincingly, with greater fervor, more absolute intensity, than Rachel. And don't tell yourself, either.

That's the kind of stuff I end up thinking about on my runs if I'm not careful. It gets me fired up a bit, too, but it's pointless, empty. That's why I visualize the thick arm moving across the circle. I clamp the wrist, snap the elbow, swing him by me in a classic textbook—lo, immaculate—arm drag.

Back at the office I shower in the restroom down the hall, towel down, and call Ellen. I want to tell her Sid the Kid's college rejection is for the best—not the best of all circumstances in the best of all possible worlds, but the best under these circumstances in this world. I mean it. If ever a kid's not ready for the rigors of serious intellectual pursuit, it's Sid the Kid. Not to confuse serious intellectual pursuit with college. Kids go to college, even motivated kids, fired up, they're carrying the family flag, and they'll do the crest proud, nothing's going to stop them, mind over matter, and within two weeks they figure out this college crap is a lot of fun. There are girls here. If you open your dorm door, you're liable to see one walking down the hall.

There are guys here, too, who get high and drink all day and are none the worse for wear as far as anybody can tell—Christ, the girls like guys like that. They're loose. They're fun.

I saw this happen too many times to mention in the five years I taught freshman comp at the U, and I consider it one of the subtle tragedies of contemporary life. These kids want to do well, they know what's at stake, but they're eighteen, and eighteen ain't what it used to be. That's what we tell ourselves who've survived being eighteen, or—like me—breezed through without noticing. The tragedy is subtle because to many kids it doesn't matter—perhaps most of those drinking and getting high all day, cutting classes, none the worse for wear to the naked eye, understand the distinction. Anybody can go to college and flunk out, or even go to college and register a 2.3. Half the professors these days are so cowed by the student evaluations they'll give you a B just for showing up, goes the campus legend, though I never met one who admitted it. But if you want to go to med school or harbor fantasies of a career in clinical psychology or the hard sciences—as Sid claims to, though the intensity of his conviction is unverifiable—you can't blow that first year before wising up. You can't take the view there are other guys here getting high and drinking and they're none the worse for wear to the naked eye. Because they're not you. And it seems highly unlikely that Sid the Kid is prepared for much in the way of enlightened perspective.

I want to tell Ellen to keep him out until he's ready—that because he's not ready, those rejection letters are blessings in disguise—but she's not home, or not answering her phone anyway. Not that it hasn't occurred to her dozens of times before without my counsel. I leave a message telling her I just got an idea. Which makes her more likely to call back than if I just ask her to please call back. That's the way it is with Ellen. She may call me five times a day or she may not call for a week. But she seldom returns my calls. And as frustrating as that can be, if I have something specific to tell her—'Hold the kid out of college, Ellen'—or just feel like talking, in the long run I suppose I'm happy she doesn't return the calls. It gives me that much more ammunition or makes me feel that much better that we did the right thing when we split.

I'm about to call it a day when a heavyset, late middle-aged man walks into my office. For a second, I don't know what to make of him—I don't get much walk-by business and he doesn't look the way I've imagined the voices I've talked to lately looking. In fact, with his jutting jaw and bulbous nose—the nose looks almost rubbery, like a very authentic-looking costume store nose—sneering eyes, and clownish cowlick, he reminds me of the way a lot of guys used to look back in the days before no-fault divorce. Or the way I imagine a lot of them looking back then, which was before I quit teaching and went into the business. Hell, it was *before* I began teaching. But a lot of private detectives stayed in business because of guys that look like this. Their wives would hire us—note the *us*—to play our surveillance game, tailing these guys for evidence of what in polite society, were there such a thing, they'd call 'marital indiscretion.' Dicks would take comprehensive photography—entering and leaving the building, later the woman entering and leaving, entries in logbooks recording times, possibly—this would happen more often than you might imagine, given the furtive nature of the enterprise—long range shots taken with the zoom lens through wide open windows. For some guys who are indiscreet, drawing the blinds would be cheating. And it was always bulbous-nosed fat guys like this one—at least in my imagination—who manage to attract surprisingly presentable younger women to salve their cheating hearts. Why these pretty women go for gauche blobs like this guy I can't say. Maybe they don't.

Sometimes in old movies you see the shamus bursting through the door, flashbulbs popping as the entwined actors wiggle in stunned if momentary incomprehension on the cheesy bed. You'll notice the actress always manages to pull up the covers rather faster than the man in his boxers can reach for his pants. That's the cliché, and probably almost as accurate as the urban myth about the alligator crawling up through the toilet, or the sadistic killer calling the babysitter from the upstairs line. Still, an elderly gentleman who worked the trade for half a century once told me he used to do just that. I was skeptical, and not just because these old dicks are known to tell more stories than Scheherazade. You had to cultivate talents to keep the mind occupied on the eternal stakeouts. Here's why: Every year I pay a lot more money than I'd like to for a private detective's license that gives me the right to do absolutely everything a private citizen is entitled to do on his own. But nothing more—that's the catch. Breaking and entering has been on the statutes for a long time, and the pictures you take with the flashing bulbs are tantamount to a signed confession. Of course, the elderly gentleman would point out—should I be so brazen as to voice my reservations—that the shamus isn't the only one being incriminated by the action photos, and that the gauche blobs—like the one sitting in the chair across my desk now—are more preoccupied with their own legal dilemma, which is about to become a thousand times worse than it was the instant before they winked at the buxom lass hiding her goods under the covers. ("It's a bluff, Bart," the old gent would say. "That's the game. Nobody bluffs a private dick. These fat creeps lookin' to shoot their wad in a lady of the evening? C'mon Bart, be serious. Think like a shamus. You don't shit a shitter. You don't bluff a bluffer. They're pussies.") Lady of the evening? It's not that the elderly gentleman was curiously circumspect, but that it's useful to see the world in blacks and whites if you're going to burst through the door taking pictures. These weren't tender hearts yearning for solace and connection in the crass universe, this was a fat creep—a pussy—sealing a coldhearted shady business transaction with a downtrodden gal who deserved better. To hear the elderly gentleman tell it, we're the ones—note my identification—wearing the white hats.

This is all theoretical, though. I never voiced too many reservations around the old gent. When these old shamuses start talking, you wish you weren't brought up to be so polite and respectful and you could just tell them to cut the bullshit, you're not buying, thanks. But after they talk for a while, you never want them to stop.

"I see you're licensed," the fat guy said, pointing at the framed document on my wall after we exchanged pleasantries.

"Does that surprise you?" I said. I'm not sure why. A simple 'yes' would do to address his observation.

He began to say something but didn't. That told me he probably wasn't here to threaten me. That happens once in a while—once, in my case, a few years before, not long after I first got my license, now that the fat guy brought it up. Somebody thought I was getting too close to some information they—or the guy who hired them—didn't want me to circulate to the guy who hired me. The information I'd found wasn't incriminating or even compromising in any context I could imagine, though you'd be surprised at the kinds of things people would prefer to have kept to themselves. Their age, their army record, their college major. One guy went into a tizzy because I'd found out he'd spent a year at Southern Illinois University before transferring to Colorado twenty years before; he was apoplectic at the prospect of word getting out. I suppose what so infuriated him wasn't the information itself and the dire consequences of its revelation—it didn't make much difference to me, anyway—but his understanding now that he couldn't hide. He couldn't invent the past. He couldn't remake himself, despite the great American myth that many of us do it every day, that liberation is just around the corner and a few lies away. He'd had the year he wanted to forget about—maybe a low GPA, or he was disciplined for a college prank—but it turns out you can't run away completely, you can't erase a year of your life and pretend it never happened, not forever, inconvenient though it may be to the current script. You're never home free, that's what angered him, not when there are guys out there hiring guys like me to be industrious, and guys like me getting a little lucky. If the notion weren't so grandiose, given the smallness of the revelation, I'd say when he threw his fit he was crying over the loss of his illusions. Another one bites the dust, I guess, and we never have quite enough to begin with.

By the way, I played dumb with the guy who threatened me—acting only slightly more oblivious to what the guy who hired him was so afraid of than I actually was—and finished the job I was hired to do no more and no less fastidiously than I would have pre-galoot in my office. I did watch my back, though, for a couple of months. I never heard from either again, though I have seen the guy who hired the guy around town a few times. He doesn't appear to know who I am, needless to say.

"It's nice to put on my wall next to my master's degree," I said about my license when the fat man didn't respond, at least not verbally.

"Yes, you're the Scholar."

I didn't look too closely—it's not polite—but I was sure the bulbous, possibly costume, nose shook when he talked.

"Plus I'm less likely to run a scam on the client. The license is a kind of collateral, you could say."

"The Scholar," the heavyset man repeated, "tore up the mat in Cheyenne."

"A bit of an exaggeration," I allowed, "considering the competition. Not that I wasn't pretty pleased."

"With cause," the fat man winked.

He was getting less threatening by the minute.

"Do I know you?"

"Never forget a face, do you, Scholar? Myron Gruber." He leaned forward as if to shake my hand but pulled a business card out of his pocket instead. I took it but didn't glance at it, other than to see the moniker *Gruber & Gruber* emblazoned across the top.

"Which one are you?" I wondered.

"Enough with the charm," Myron Gruber said. He had a way of talking out of the side of his mouth, as if he had a toothache, which would throw you if his enunciation weren't so immaculate. When he talked, you had the impression he was practicing scales for the Gruber Institute of Locution. I'd never seen anyone talk like Myron Gruber outside of faculty meetings back when I was teaching at the U, or I'd never bothered to notice. And I would have noticed. "Got this brother, Ron. Ron, you see, is a monster, Scholar, of both temperament and physique. You think I'm big? I'm junior scale next to Ron, trimmed down, lean, lithe, reduced budget, quick as the blur of a terrified hummingbird's wings. Well not that quick. No. Not greased lightning, Scholar, but you should know I'm talking figuratively. In relation to Ron, I'm approximately the speed of lightning halved, though to others I'm slow, ponderous. Cumbersome. We've always been close, Bart. Brothers are brothers. Brothers to the teeth. When he yawns, I scratch my nuts. When he barks, I fart—not always in perfect synch. You get the idea?"

I admitted I did; not that I wanted to.

"Big Ron's the Gruber on the business card you astutely observed. I'm not surprised. You're a scholar, a quick study."

"Okay, okay," I said.

"Here's the problem, Detective," Myron Gruber said. He paused a moment to see if I was still following him. I nodded, but mostly I was wondering if he was toying with me. I mean I know he was toying with me, but toying above and beyond the toying he did with everyone. A million laughs was Myron with the locution. Maybe he found the entire concept of a private detective agency amusing, saw the shingle, connected the name to the story in the paper last week after I won my weight class in Cheyenne (I've gotten more grief from the article than admiration), and walked in to indulge a few laughs. Or maybe he came in for a legitimate purpose, but once face-to-face couldn't help himself.

"We all have problems, Mr. Gruber," I said. "That's why I'm here."

"We're at odds, Scholar. I don't see eye to eye with Ron. Brothers to the teeth but we're seldom *simpatico* outside the office. We never chew the fat as in our days of innocence. To Ron, I engender each and every calamity that befalls him, and they're plentiful in their multitude. Our wives, too, are at each other's throats. Why the barbarity? Why the aversion between two born breast-to-bosom? Here's the scoop: *We don't like each other!*" Myron Gruber laughed suddenly and ferociously, his enormous body breaking in waves over his chair until the explosion halted just as abruptly, and he looked at me placidly across the desk. "I'm taking the high road on this one, Detective. I want to bury the hatchet. I want to apologize, say I'm sorry, though Ron's a monster of temperament, a doofus, a jerkwad, a shtunk, a shmendrick, a shmegegge, a shmuck."

Myron shut up for a moment and eyed me under his heavy droopy lids for my reaction. I really didn't have one, other than to marvel at how he could get so much out of the side of his mouth. "Oh, I get it," I said finally.

Myron laughed again, this time modestly, agreeably, more of a wink than a chortle. "I'm putting you on, Bart. I'm spoofing you."

"You don't say?"

"You don't gotta go running to Ron sending my heartfelt regrets. I'm just a tease. But I would like to apologize to you if you took it wrong. I'd like to say I'm sorry for my," here he treated me with another deep bursting laugh, "misguided missile!"

After he caught his breath I said, "I get the joke, if that's what you're wondering." A part of me, a small part, was wondering why I didn't scuff him by the collar and toss him out of my office. Here's what I was thinking as he apologized—sincerity undetermined—for his riff: Were he standing, I'd possibly duck under and drive him out with his arm bent behind his back; or I'd execute a fireman's if he came at me with his arms flapping loose, and dump-and-roll him out the door before he was quite aware. The closed door might present an obstacle. I wouldn't want to ram him through—it was my door, after all—and it seemed unlikely I'd be able to stop in mid-fireman's to open the door before following through with the execution of the dump-and-roll. It's the sort of thing you can't stop in the middle of when the bulbous-nosed gentleman thrown across your shoulders is well over three hundred pounds. Oh well. That was my thought.

I suppose I wasn't being quite literal about the fireman's either, but I think in these terms quite a bit. It's part of my visualization practice. Even when I'm walking down the street for a newspaper, I'll notice somebody walking toward me presenting an angle with their carriage and I'll find myself—or make a point of it, sometimes—visualizing what moves I'd use given that angle for a quick takedown or—I try to avoid this because it's less productive, less realistic, but this is visualization, after all, not reality, and one does what they must to stay interested—slamming them to their backs for a quick fall. Not just ruffians and frat boys, but grandmothers, toddlers. Perhaps it's not a socially adaptive form of fantasy, but I thought it paid off last month in Cheyenne—my moves were automatic, considering the fifteen years of rust. It's part of the deal I have with Rachel. She does her visualization—probably missiles firing away at cancer cells—and I do mine. That's our game. Anyway, it makes me feel less hopeless. Still, I suspect she's not entirely convinced that I follow through with it the way I like to tell her I do. She doesn't ask too many questions.

Mostly, though, I don't throw him out, either in fantasy or reality, because I want him in my office. Not all evening, maybe, but another half hour or so. I want him to have an interesting proposition for me. I want him to have something amusing I can tell Rachel about and tell Ellen about. (As for confidentiality, I don't think too much about confidentiality. They know they're not supposed to tell anyone this stuff.) As for me, it wouldn't be the worst thing to have something to occupy myself with other than my visualization and working out four hours a day and Ellen's various disasters—Sid the Kid's merely the latest—and my sister's dying. I need him so I don't have to go home just yet. Myron Gruber across the desk may have his own agenda, he may think he's working me a bit with his bizarre laugh routine, but I have my own agenda working here, too.

And Myron Gruber did not disappoint me.

"Yes," he repeated. "That's my misguided missile!"

"Clever of you, Mr. Gruber."

"But Ron's proud, Scholar. Sometimes to the point of paranoia. Be careful with the apology. He may *insult* you!" Ha ha.

I may have found Myron Gruber more amusing if he found himself less amusing. No, deadpan wasn't his style. I wasn't even sure if he was laughing at me because he found the concept of Misguided Missiles sort of funny with its cornball implications, or if he was laughing because he understood it really was a joke. The reporter for the *Bugle* didn't get the joke when she reported the concept at face value in the feature article that came out last month after I swept my weight class—and won the trophy for Outstanding Wrestler, though I imagine that was more a monument to age and novelty—in Cheyenne. She was a nice enough gal who took her job awfully seriously, and I'm afraid I wasn't too much help. She'd ask questions and take her glasses off as she awaited the answers and I found myself pausing contemplatively before delivering the answers because she looked so much better with her glasses off. The way she wrinkled her nose suggested she was either baffled by the answers or was considering what her next question might be to turn the interview into more promising directions. She didn't know sports, that was obvious, and most writers who know sports don't know wrestling all that well anyway, but I could tell she was desperate for an angle. It wasn't a sports story, as she made clear, but a general interest feature article for the local page.

Even if I could have told her at the time what this was all about, it was personal, a can of worms I didn't want opened on the local page. So I began playing up the private detective angle—at least the business might get something out of the coverage. She reminded me of a lot of pudgy, vivacious blondes back in school who had great personalities and took the world seriously. That was Ms. Suswhite, except for the personality. Proving, I guess, that nobody's a complete cliché. The private detective business is deathly dull for the most part, all the venue surveying, skip tracing, reeling in of runaway adolescents, security checks demanding hours on the horn getting through to abrupt people for whom your interests are the lowest priority imaginable, accident and criminal investigations which may sound flashy but almost always lead to portraits of stupidity (and that's putting it charitably), all resulting in the endless writing of reports nearly as stupefying to read as they are to compose. But she didn't want to hear that any more than I wanted to tell her. The closest parallel I can think of with my old life back in academia would be the role of the bibliographer, tracking down each and every obscure reference and summarizing, bearing in mind, amidst the mountainous minutiae, the mountains. In most cases, of course, there is no big picture beyond what the client wants, but I was pretty sure this particular irony would confuse her even more, if that were possible. It didn't seem so judging from the obsessive wrinkling of Ms. Suswhite's nose. I was torn, I guess, between wanting to impress the pudgy blonde and wanting to rescue her, a combination, I know, that has led more than a few blindly adrift. For all I know that was the angle she was playing. What male alpha could resist? Plus there's something about somebody interviewing you because you've done something interesting, and having them find you uninteresting, something which I didn't need at the moment given the state of my life. So I didn't mention the tracking down each and every obscure reference, thank you. ("You're a private detective?" she managed. Her lids looked heavy from across the desk. "What's that like?") It's the doing something extra, the making a difference, the easing of their burden, the setting the record straight, the playing fair. It's the making up for what can't be made up because nobody will. The doing the dirty work so you don't even know there is dirty work. That kind of stuff. It's doing the job the guy who hired you could do himself if he had a clue and the time. "There's Misguided Missiles," I told her.

Ms. Suswhite lifted an eye now. "Misguided Missiles?"

"That's right. Did you ever go the one step too far and break the friendship? Perhaps you knew better all along but were truly inspired by the momentum of the moment? And you wanted the friendship fixed but knew you weren't the one to fix it. Anyway, your friend won't talk to you or take the breath and make the move to patch it up. Your lovers found other lovers. Or they've complained too often to their friends so there's no turning back without losing face. Did you ever hurt somebody's pride, Ms. Suswhite, and have too much pride yourself to walk to them hat-in-hand to eat the humble pie? Or they've hurt yours and have too much pride to come to you hat-in-hand, and you couldn't do it yourself, go to them, because you shouldn't have to? Because it wasn't your place to? See, Carla," which was the pudgy blonde's name, though I'd been calling her Ms.

Suswhite, "that's Misguided Missiles. Because shit happens and we shouldn't have to torture ourselves over the little stuff. Because people say things they don't mean to and it's not always the matter of the ambiguous remark taken the wrong way—though I handle those too—it's stuff they meant at the time but meant unwisely. The stand they took informed by misunderstanding and false premise. The calling a spade a spade when it turns out it wasn't a spade, it was only the light. Or the calling a spade a spade before you understood there was gardening to be done."

Carla's brow was still raised. I think she was trying to follow my metaphors. Still, it was the longest speech I'd given since I'd stood in front of a freshman class five years ago to lecture on the laxity of the *ad hominem* argument. I wouldn't have minded some response. I guess that's what the published article was for.

"I see what the client wants, Ms. Suswhite. I lay the groundwork if they want. I run as the middleman, make the call, pay the visit, sing their lament."

She looked doubtful now, wrinkling her nose again. Why not? It's not as if I wasn't winging it. "And you get paid for this?"

"Not always. Sometimes they talk to me and decide it's cheaper to do it themselves. I give them free estimates, you could say, hear them out, talk to them straight until they know what's involved. If they decide at that point to paint the barn themselves, that's cool."

I think she was contemplating the latest metaphor, losing the battle to reel it in, so I couldn't resist adding, "It pays in the long run to play your cards straight up on the table."

"Interesting karma," Ms. Suswhite said.

Considering what I gave her, the article came out okay. Light on the wrestling, a little less light on Misguided Missiles (though it gave Rachel and Ellen a laugh), heavy on the comeback angle. Made-for-TV movie material from a writer reared on made-for-TV sagas. And if she made my triumph at Cheyenne a little more Herculean than warranted by the event itself, what's that they say about newspapers? Fish wrap. There was a nice picture of me sitting at my office desk, staring into the void, not blankly but as if I was challenging the void, even the hint of a smirk as if I was holding a card the void didn't know about. Laying the works for a sucker punch. Was the void ever in for a rude awakening–there was a hint of that about the mouth. A handful of people read the article, or anyway were moved to mention it to me in the days afterward. Nobody at the supermarket said anything. I told a couple of friends about it, broaching the issue indirectly when they didn't bring it up themselves. ("Seen the *Bugle* today? Fish wrap!" "Why do you ask?" they inquire.) I could have played it straight, I guess, for all anybody cared. You worry over how you'll come across, you do the pudgy blonde a favor to help her out, why bother? If a tree falls in the forest, etc. Sure, it might make something nice for the scrapbook nobody's ever going to look at. More people mentioned it to Ellen and Rachel than to me, though, and that made me feel okay. And ever since, I've been thinking of calling up Ms. Suswhite to thank her. Should she be up for more confusion, to be conducted at a local eatery, well, there's no telling how the conversation could turn. Would it be so terrible? And then there was Myron Gruber, chuckling to himself across my desk.

"Mr. Gruber," I said, in case he still wasn't catching on, "there is no Misguided Missiles. It was a joke. But I'll talk to Ron if you want."

That got Myron going again. That I intended it as a joke he found even more amusing than the concept itself. "It's just a sham?" he finally managed.

Look who's talking. "Not a sham, a joke. I had my reasons. I do apologize if you were taken in." As if I'll see the day when I could take in Myron Gruber.

"You'll talk to Ron anyway?" To my surprise he managed not to erupt into paroxysms as he delivered the question.

"An idea's an idea."

"Ah," Myron Gruber was sitting up in his chair across the desk now, leaning forward, sober, composed. Was the laugh riot all an act? Why not? He winked at me. This wasn't Myron the Elegant Aggrieved anymore. Wasn't Myron the Goof. This was Uncle Myron. "Exactly. Ideas don't sit in judgment over other ideas, do they, Scholar? We who articulate the ideas perform that office. I was reading the other day that some people—scholars like yourself—find Freud to be something of a sham, the whole notion of repression to be theory, not fact. But does that make it a sham by itself? Or is it a sham because twentieth century psychoanalysis climbed aboard its theoretical back, and now teeters precariously? Why should it be more questionable now than it was in Vienna? Ideas are ideas, sir. If we're taken in by them, is it the fault of the idea? Nazism, there was an idea too. The lure of the crooked sign to the vulnerable and the weak of weeny. Ah yes, Scholar, there were only good Germans seduced. It's not their fault. There's an idea too."

Well, the man was a crackpot. "Fine, Mr. Gruber."

"Scholar, here's the idea. Who is it, exactly, that we serve up to the average Joe? The *Chaim Yankel*, if you will? Who do we offer for the shmo in the street—the shmo at home, watching in his living room—the shmo at the turnstile, ticket in hand—to identify with? Yes, that's right. The outlandish, the oversized, the mighty magnificent of body, beyond our reach. The easier to love, the easier to hate. They're like us but they're not like us. When they win we win—we share the glorious triumph. When they lose we lose—but not completely, Scholar. Not utterly. No. Because though they're like us, they're not like us. You're a bright guy, Scholar. A quick study. You see where I'm going? This ain't no *pilpul*."

"I haven't a clue," I admitted.

"Maybe some small thing about them catches our eye. It reminds us of us. That's right, *nous*. Their hair is like ours. Or the beautiful actress is like the girl we botched it with long ago, only more so! She's magnificent, she's oversized, she's out of reach. That girl we botched it with long ago? There was a reason. She was the actress, yes, but the actress reduced, the actress halved, the actress shriveled to miniature scale—but you know what, Scholar? Miniature scale is real. And real ain't what we see in our dreams, it's why we left in the first place."

"Gee, this is interesting," I said. As for why Myron Gruber was here, I wasn't so interested anymore. The half-hour of diversion was up. Maybe he really had taken Misguided Missiles seriously. But people stop being amusing—or even articulate, for that matter—when they pontificate. They become boring. (And I was in school long enough to know, taking it and dishing it out both.) Even when, like Myron, they pontificate out of the sides of their mouths. It was a neat parlor trick, I'll give him that, but only in moderation.

"I do go on, Scholar," Myron said. "Forgive me. Here's my point—"

"Your point?"

"Cheeky, cheeky, Bart. But you'll do well to pay attention. We were quite impressed"—I took it by 'we' he meant *Gruber and Gruber,* but maybe not. He was big enough by himself to seat two— "with your performance in Cheyenne. And don't kid yourself, it was just that, a performance. *Mano a mano*. Playing to the clamorous throngs. But it wasn't just anyone out there shooting those takedowns. It was the Scholar, the Professor, the kind-hearted Detective, thirty-seven years old, embarking upon his mythic adventure: *The Big Comeback*. That's why your name was pasted across the headlines. That's why I'm sitting in your office now, Scholar. But what kind of effect do you desire? How big? How wide? Do you seek to move our imaginations the way other men seek to move molehills?" For a second Myron paused.

I don't think he expected me to say anything at this point. Not even that I didn't see where he was going—that much I assume was understood. I'm not too sure Myron knew where he was going either, but he was enjoying the ride. He was pleased with himself, Myron. If he had a hat, he'd flip the hat in the air.

"Nobody remembers Cheyenne, Scholar. It's gone. It's over. *Finis. Kaput.*"

"Thank you," I said.

"I know, you have your little amateur circuit. The freestyle meet in Fargo. The Greco-Roman Open in St. Paul. Maybe a crack at Midlands. A year down the road there's the Regional Qualifier. Then, if you're lucky, a low seed at the Olympic Trials, early elimination to the guy who finishes sixth, but a great story to tell the grandkids. Is that what's happening, Mister? Are those your sights?"

"An interesting scenario, Myron," I began, and would have continued—you don't teach comp five years at the U if you can't take the ball and run—but it turns out Myron didn't especially care if these were my sights.

"You ain't gonna make it, Detective. Try as you might, cry as you might. Those boys are too young, they're too quick, too good. The rules they play—the rules of sport, the rules of competition—favor the younger boys, play to their young boy dreams. But who cares, right? You'll still get the great story for the pishers with a few mat burns to spare. Nobody knows, nobody cares. How many more Cheyennes, Bubkes? How many times can the *Bugle* run the story? Not a dry eye in the house, but no moist eyes either. You see now? Nobody's watching. You think you're going to make the Olympics? You think you'll thrill the masses? Win the precious gold? A thousand more Ms. Suswhites mining your dreams? I'll be candid, Bart. That's dreck. That's *shtus.* That's—and here's a word I don't use often, but you've got me worked up—that's *farblondget.*"

"Thank you again, Myron."

"Oh, that's clever. But I know you're not one to shy away from the candid assessment, Scholar. Unless it's the tax assessor!" Now Myron guffawed. I'm not sure he planned to guffaw—and he was nothing if not calculating—but his last crack was too much for him.

"That too, Myron," I said. "It's been great chatting."

"So. Nu. Here's the point: Theater. That's correct, sir. The matrix of entertainment and performance doubled. The show, but without the proclivity of true sport to demystify. The hero in tatters, yes, but only to rise again. Myth, yes, but myth come alive. You want life? You want the Comeback Kid to emerge from Regionals, to make the Olympics? That ain't life, kid. That's fairy tale. Life's the inevitable fall of the stud from Okie State half again your age. Life's falling apart in the prelims, nursing our torn discs, dreaming what might have been in stories to our grandkids. Them apples the rules. *Nu?*"

"If I still had a granny I'd introduce you, Myron. She spoke Yiddish, too." This was the best I could do as riposte.

"Professional wrestling."

"Hmm?"

"The mid-size circuit. That's my pitch. You're the Star. The Scholar. The Hombre. The Macher. The macho soap opera of the dream made palpable in the flesh, played out on the mat. But not by the overfed and the outrageous of body. Not by double jumbos and the hoarse throated with their sinister transparent baby shticks! We're talking wholesale identification here, not just the realm of farm boys and rural tyros, the juvenile of emotion and intellect. Not our dreams grown grotesque and distorted, but something true for the guy in the street to relate to. When I read the article in the *Bugle* I knew. Scholar, you were too much to be true, but you were true. Are you interested yet? How's $20,000 to start?"

I told Myron I'd get back to him.

So that was the scam. Pro wrestling for sophisticates, featuring Bart Coldecker as Sophisticate Incarnate. I didn't tell Myron that when I was teaching at the U, I was considered something of a lowlife. Perhaps he could figure that out for himself: This wasn't reality, after all, but image. Anyway, he'd hired—here's irony—a private detective to see if the basic facts as represented in the story corresponded with reality. What's reality? I came out clean as a whistle, Myron told me. The genuine item. The authentic thing. (Unless you press too hard, it wasn't necessary to tell Myron.) He might have done better—and saved a few sawbucks in the process—to hire me to write up the report.

Pro wrestling for regular-sized guys, so regular-sized guys in the audience wouldn't have to project quite so hard to envision themselves in the ring. Perhaps the lifelong jocks would hit the weights a little harder, add a mile or two to the run, try out some material at open mike night to refine their bit, and—who knows?—in a few months, maybe, call up The Grubers for a tryout. That possibility could loom in the air for years. (I was no *boychik* myself, as Myron might say.) And the regular-sized gals watching the regular-sized guys wouldn't have to project quite so hard either.

There were plenty of counterarguments to the concept, of course. Here's one I tried on Ellen, when I called her the night after Myron Gruber stopped by the office. "We like seeing the big guys sound like morons. It makes us feel superior. That won't work so well with regular-sized guys. It won't be so important."

"That's right," Ellen said. "Nobody likes to feel superior to regular guys."

I saw her point.

"I was married to the Scholar," Ellen added in a mock wistful tone she perfected so well that sometimes she could fool herself.

Did I mention Myron threw in 10% ownership of the franchise?

2.

"Without illusions we cannot live"— Otto Rank

I played up the notion for a few days. Told Rachel. Told Ellen. Went so far as to call back Myron Gruber a few times for clarifications—that's when he threw in the 10% ownership of the franchise. No additional obligations, though we never quite covered what the original obligations were. He wouldn't—or couldn't—clarify too much with his elaborate circumlocutions, but he had a way of eventually getting around to the point.

And what was the point? I played that question up for a few days too. The axis shifted beneath my feet, I waxed philosophical, and the axis shifted a few feet more. It wasn't a crisis, Myron's proposal, but it engendered a crisis, if not in reality then in the telling. For conversation's sake with Ellen and Rachel—and at a party or two with some people I barely knew, who exchanged confidential looks as I waxed: Blowhard on the rampage—I entertained some large questions. What am I doing here? What do I want? What's the good life? Is it courage to take the risk and jump ship, or is it courage to stay the course? What does it all matter in the end? Rachel would listen earnestly.

She'd ask the cogent question to advance the soliloquy. I'm sure it wasn't lost on either of us that if Bart Coldecker, Scholar Incarnate, came to fruition on *Gruber and Gruber's* Regular Guy Wrestling Circuit, Rachel wouldn't be around to see the fruits. Why was I doing it? Why was I raising the issue, begging Rachel's indulgence? Sometimes I'd wax existential on the ins and outs and see her watching me, curled up on the sofa under her blanket (by now she was almost always cold), wool socks on her feet I'd sometimes stop and massage, watching me with such a blank look on her face it was as if she was counting to a thousand. But still she'd encourage me. "It sounds like a good idea if that's what you want to do." And: "My brother, the show biz impresario."

"I hope I amuse her," I said to Ellen once after going on and on to Rachel about the glorious possibilities, in the process suggesting that if I didn't go pro on the Gruber circuit I thought I had a pretty good shot at the Olympics (more nonsense even than the pro circuit—Gruber had been right about that, at least). "What's the point? Why am I torturing her? Why am I so insensitive?"

Luckily this was the phone. I don't like to imagine what Ellen's face must have registered, not just at the melodramatic pyrotechnics, but the thought that similar melodramatic posturing on my part might have served our marriage well. "She likes to stay involved," Ellen said finally, when I shut up.

"But aren't I being cruel?"

"It's a legitimate business proposition," Ellen said. Again I was happy I couldn't see her face as she dished out the solace. As if either of us would know a legitimate business proposition from a pie in the sky. Buy high sell low was the formula for our few joint investments, to say nothing of our marriage. But she knew I had a $20,000 escrow check in my pocket. "If it happens, you'll always like to think you included Rachel. And you do amuse her sometimes," Ellen added.

Here: I enter the ring through the ropes, bounce around on my toes, stare out at the crowd. Rachel's there, as is Sid the Kid (*"Daddy!"* he shouts at the ring) and Ellen ("You're hot, sweets!"). A discreet distance apart sits Carla Suswhite. As a concession to theater, I wink at the camera, remove my cap and gown, wave to the Phi Beta Kappa section of the gallery. Do I go too far? I'm forty years old, wrestling again for the *Gruber* World Championship, and my knee is killing me. "Ladies and Gentlemen, straight from the halls of academe, the Prince of the Ivory Tower, the King of the Campus Bucolic, the Scholar Incarnate... Bart Coldecker!"

Oddly enough my opponent is Wendle Mosby. Wendle Mosby, my nemesis from back in high school. I don't think of Wendle Mosby for fifteen years and then there he is ducking through the ropes, flexing his mammoth black biceps to the crowd, the body beautiful whirling a backflip in the ring, my opponent for the *Gruber* World Title. He wrestled for Waukegan High back then. At every turn, especially when I thought I was good, as fate would pose the lesson, there was Wendle Mosby lying in wait, indestructible. I'd pin five guys in a row and there was Mosby taking me 6-2 in the dual meet. I couldn't get a grip on him where he didn't grip me harder. I couldn't throw a move where he wouldn't block and counter. I'd pin another five and there was Wendle Mosby to take me 7-1 in Sectionals. Senior year more of the same. Six times in two years we went to the mat and it was never close. I was twice as strong as anyone else in high school and Wendle Mosby was twice as strong as I. Coach Wapholder thought I was intimidated by Black guys, though Mosby was the only one I didn't beat and—I neglected to point out at the time—Coach Wapholder never wrestled Mosby himself, never shot in for the deep double only to be flattened. In addition to the strength factor there was a quickness deficit. I may have been beaten before I stepped on the mat—that was the corollary to Coach Wapholder's theory—but I was always beaten before I stepped on the mat, and that didn't stop me from winning big against everyone else. I was a baby in high school, I tried but didn't try full-tilt, I left a little in the reserve tank, never left my heart on the mat, those guys I pinned I pinned with one arm, that's what I tell myself when Wendle Mosby climbs through the ropes. I went further Downstate than he did, losing in the semis when he lost in the quarters. He was ten times as good as the guy who beat me and a hundred times as good as the guy who beat him. I heard he'd wrestled at State with a broken arm—that he might have broken it against me at Sectionals gave me some moments of baseless satisfaction and many hours of remorse at the injustice. I did have a chance to ask him about it a couple of years later. Six times we wrestled and six times he muttered "good match" as he obligatorily shook my hand after the thorough thrashing. Wendle Mosby. He signed with Northern Illinois, wrestled a couple of years, mixed results (arm problems? Maybe, though college was a different game), then faded from sight.

Once home from college I saw Wendle Mosby at Northbrook Days, a summer carnival where every kid on the North Shore put in an appearance, though Northbrook was far afield from Waukegan. But it was him. He was standing outside the Ferris wheel line with his huge arm around a gorgeous white girl. He had a neat mustache, a trim afro. In his free hand he held a giant teddy bear. Maybe he was feeling lucky that night? I introduced myself, and Wendle Mosby smiled distantly. Not unfriendly, but there were a lot of guys he beat six times, that's what the inscrutable smile said. He may not have even altogether taken me in a couple of years before in high school—the smile said that, too. Or maybe he was a lot more interested in the eerily beautiful girl snuggling against him as the Ferris wheel behind them spun to shrieks of laughter. It didn't exactly encourage conversation. ('Ya wrestled me, Pal? Cantcha see I'm busy. Scram.') At that moment I had already wrestled first string a year in college, beaten a lot of state high school champs—they were a dime a dozen at that level—and Wendle Mosby was already a washout. But there was the gorgeous girl melting under his gaze. There were the six matches. I'd be hard put to say he was the loser.

Some guys have your number. You put them behind you by knowing you'll never see them again. If you think of them, you tell yourself you've beaten a lot of guys a thousand times as good as they were back then, that in high school you'd been immature emotionally and always left something in reserve, that you're the one who went on to make the mark while they washed out. But that still doesn't mean twenty years later you want to see them climb through the ropes when you're up for the *Gruber* World Title. The world doesn't turn *that* fast.

"Where do you get these punks?" you yell to Myron Gruber beaming in the front row, smiling out of the side of his mouth. "Waukegan?"

He can't grip me but that my grip is stronger. He's quick, but this is Bart Coldecker he's up against. The trunk of a tree. Greased lightning.

Otto Rank, what's it say that Rachel is dying, my ex-wife's falling apart, and my reveries make quick work of Wendle Mosby?

I take Rachel to the grocery store.

She has good days and bad days, and on the good days sometimes we'll go out. Not for long, but to the store or a drive. Sometimes a movie, a cup of coffee. Just to remind her—or myself—there's a world beyond her living room that isn't entirely beyond her. What she mostly likes on her good days is to stay home and have her friends visit. There have been times we've been halfway out the door and immediately abandoned our plans when friends dropped by. I wish I could say I was always above being irritated at such turns. Usually I am. Rachel's idea is to have the wake before she dies, not to write her off yet. Of course, not everybody feels comfortable around somebody who's dying, and though Rachel's quick to put visitors at ease there's no mistaking that she's lost twenty-five pounds she didn't need to lose, that her stomach's distended, that she looks twenty years older, that her hair's ratty (though it hasn't fallen out, as everybody told her it would), swamped with gray, her skin's sallow. As of a few days ago her beautiful voice is always hoarse, and it's as painful as anything to know already I'll never hear that voice again. She's thirty-nine years old and she still doesn't have a mark on her face. I think that's how she measures beauty these days.

Some friends haven't come by since the diagnosis. I've seen them in town, suggested Rachel might like a visit. They say—I'm generalizing; the stories do vary in particulars, but they always come down to the same thing, which they're willing to tell me now that I've caught them in the act of continuing their own lives as if they didn't have a friend named Rachel—that they can't handle it, that her illness reminds them of too much they don't want, or can't afford right now, to be reminded of, that there are things they don't want to relive, perhaps the death of somebody they loved—or perhaps not, perhaps the sight of Rachel would just make them unhappy and depressed. Uncomfortable. (Which they can't afford, at the moment.) Well, Rachel's dying and would like a courtesy visit and they don't want to be uncomfortable. Too fucking bad! That's my view and it may even be Rachel's view—I'm sure she's subject to those feelings at times, it would be natural anyway—but she's never talked to me about it. Verboten. Rachel dying is not big on sounding bitter. She may not have any choice on whether she does this or not, but she can choose to do it graciously.

But it certainly does have its effect. And if somebody drops by—on a good day—you can bet Rachel's going to drop everything and spend all the time with them she can. So sometimes our plans to go for the drive or to the grocery falls apart on the way out the door if a friend shows up and wants to chat. So the bunch of us all turn around and trudge back to the living room.

Almost always they want me around. Rachel's friends have never shown so much interest in me as since she's been sick. Some she's spoken to nearly every day for ten years—in one of our numerous fights years ago she revealed that her friends were more of a family than her family, that's how close they'd been (that she was also looking to score points at my expense wasn't lost on me, either)—but now they needed a buffer. Already she's transfigured into not quite Rachel, and if a situation emerges, it's better I be there to supervise. They love her dearly, but they're leery too. The speed at which they've already let Rachel go is startling.

If you suspect I'm being unfair, you're right. The worst of them treat her like she's radioactive when they come by—but at least they come by, unlike a lot of others, and for that I'll assign them due credit come the reckoning. The best of them—three or four—are closer to Rachel than they've ever been. Her best friend, Shari, is over two hours a day when she gets off work, and I suspect they talk about things Rachel could never talk about with me. That she's scared, and angry, that this is all so unfair. (I don't know what Shari says in return, but she listens well and isn't obsessed with making points of her own. I used to think it's because she didn't have any, but now I see her reticence as tact and wisdom.) That's on the good days. On bad days—Rachel did tell me this once—she hurts too much to draw a bead on how she feels about it all.

Someday I think I'll focus on all those who rose to the occasion and were nice to Rachel when she needed them. I'll forget those who didn't answer the call, or forgive them their own accommodations. Sometimes I look forward to that day, far enough in the future that I won't have to face what I'll be facing soon, which will be past me, the healing (as they say) begun. I'll fall in love with Shari. We'll remember how gracious Rachel was, and congratulate ourselves for being there, for allowing her an audience she could radiate to in the most dreadful circumstance. Though I suppose—I hope—when that day comes, I'll be intensely jealous of days like today, or every day of my life until now, when Rachel was alive.

So I know we'll drop our plans if somebody comes over. The good thing about her current chemo regimen, though, is that you can make plans. For several days she's nauseous and sore—blistery sore—to the pit of her organs, but then she'll have a good day, still sore but not so drained, always followed by a bad day, like an evil twin, good day, bad day, good day, bad day, and on for a week—the second week—before her next treatment. You can count on the rotation, you can make plans. Unless she overdoes it.

In the grocery—a superstore large enough that we're not liable to notice anybody we know (whether they notice us is their call)—she grips my arm. We walk very slowly, she breathes heavily, like a horse, and we never stop talking, though I'm sure anybody watching—nobody does, of course—would notice mostly the silences. There are motorized carts by the entranceway outside the automatic doors, and wheelchairs are available too, but Rachel says she'd rather walk. So we walk. She's wearing the same brown raincoat she wears almost every time we go out in public now. She's had it since college, but before her illness, before the months of symptoms while they prodded her and ran tests and grasped for a diagnosis, she hadn't worn the raincoat in many years. "I always had a hunch about that coat," she said after she came across it in the closet. For all its lack of use it's none the worse for wear. Brown leather, elegant, chic but casual, large enough to be comfortable without looking like she's wearing a tent, the raincoat cloaks her withered body. But she still looks twenty years older than she did a few months ago. I know she's afraid people will think she's my mother.

We're back to our familiar topic. New angle. "I'm not sure, you see, about this Olympic stuff. It's fun to contemplate, but it may not be realistic."

"Do you need some onions?"

I assume Rachel's talking literally—though I won't put anything past her—and wheel the cart by the onions. 59 cents.

"You ever notice that onions never go on sale?"

"No. Did you start training again because it was realistic?" Rachel rasps.

"I'm not sure what I was thinking," I admitted. "I guess I wanted a change."

Rachel breathed heavily. I noticed a little girl—she couldn't be more than five—staring at us from the corner by the meats. She tugged at her mother's dress and asked her a question. The mother looked at us, smiled, looked away. I assume she answered the question, though the tyke tugged at her dress again, to which the mother whispered harshly then glanced at us again, less indulgently now. "You said you're better now than you were in college," Rachel said.

College. That's the huge family myth, that I was this superstar wrestler in college who fell a nose-hair short of the Olympics. If luck had smiled on me, I might have been a household name for a few days back in the seventies, thanks to the coverage on

ABC. Etc. I certainly wouldn't have minded luck smiling on me, it might even have made a difference, but you could just as easily say luck did smile on me and that accounted in part for the small success I did have. I was an above-average college wrestler, which is a lot more than you might expect from somebody who wasn't much better than an above-average high school wrestler. I never placed at Nationals, but I did qualify for the Olympic Trials—I was one of about sixteen in my weight class, most of whom didn't have a prayer, and some of those who didn't have a prayer, I didn't have much more than a prayer against myself. But that was enough for the family. Nobody in the family ever had the least interest in sports, so context was missing. They didn't fully appreciate gradations. Wrestling has a million levels, but increments didn't concern them. I still hear it whispered at family gatherings that I missed the Olympics 'by a whisker.' Maybe one of Rip Van Winkle's. But who's to say over the years I didn't buy into it a little myself?

Some in the family think I never got over coming so close, that it wrenched my soul and made me into the obsessive Nut who at thirty-seven came out of retirement to chase the ever-so-elusive dream. That's family. Why confuse them with reality?

Half of Ellen's family, by the way, are under the impression I won the Olympics.

"I didn't say I was better. I'm better emotionally, though, and that can go a long way. I beat a couple of guys in Cheyenne who might have given me trouble in college."

I wheeled over to the Romaine lettuce. One thing I liked about Rachel, she never jumped all over me for getting the pre-washed, hermetically sealed bagged Romaine. Ellen didn't either. Some women I've known you'd think I told them I voted Republican, or lived out of my car.

"Is it that important to be realistic?"

"No, Rachel, but is it so awful?"

Rachel didn't say anything as she steered me toward the Bing cherries. I packed as many as I could into a plastic sack without feeling gluttonous, though this was mostly for Rachel's benefit. A few years ago, I came down with gout. According to Rachel's book of folk remedies, an abundance of Bings in the diet is known to dilute uric acid before it can accumulate into a crystal in the big toe—you'll know what I mean if you've had it. If you haven't, no amount of explaining is adequate. As far as I can tell, it works, too. Unfortunately, the Bings are out of season about ten months a year. For *that* the folk book offers no remedy. But it was nice of Rachel to remember. I think I mentioned it to her once but there it was, encoded: Bing cherries for Bart's gout. I probably mentioned it to a few other people too, and they might remember or they might not. Ellen—who lived with it—wouldn't forget, though she tries. With Rachel, even now when I'd excuse her being off her game, it's not just information, it's pertinent. Because I whined and moaned for a few days several years ago, it's real for her. And it's all I can do not to tell her I'll miss that.

"Should I get apples?" I asked.

"One thing I liked about you is that you weren't realistic," Rachel said. She'd always had a tendency to refer to people in the past tense, but lately it was eerie in her raspy voice. She stopped now, gripping my arm, staring ahead, lost in thought. "You went into teaching when there were no jobs teaching college."

"Now you tell me," I said.

Rachel glared at me before smiling. If she was paying me a compliment, she was probably thinking of taking it back. But she had a point to make. "You got out of teaching the second you had some security and became a private detective. Who ever heard of that? I don't know anybody who has a brother who's a private detective."

"With some of these guys it is hard to imagine," I admitted.

"You didn't care what anyone thought," Rachel said. "You didn't care about the objective view. You knew what you wanted. You wanted what you weren't getting in teaching. You made a comeback in wrestling fifteen years after nobody knew you left in the first place, and already you've won a tournament. Is that realistic?"

"I divorced Ellen," I said.

"I didn't say you were perfect, Bart."

"Well, all that stuff I did, sometimes I think I wouldn't have to change course in midstream with the big dramatic gesture if I thought for a second and made the right choice in the first place. It wouldn't have hurt to be a little more realistic at the outset, Rachel. Want some granola?"

"Maybe you won't make the Olympics," Rachel said, "but I don't know what that has to do with anything."

"What does that mean?"

Rachel turned to look at me. It may have bothered her that I wasn't getting it. She'd always been that way. And she never doubted for a second whose fault it was. "It means if your goal is to make the Olympics then you're right, it's probably not realistic."

"You know that's not what I mean. I never really had that in mind until after Cheyenne."

"Keep talking," Rachel said.

"I wanted to compete, I think. I must have wanted not to embarrass myself. Yeah, I wanted to beat guys half my age, that kind of crap. I wanted guys to call me Pops, and guys who were conference champs to curse under their breath when they saw my name in the brackets one round ahead. I wanted a reason to work out five hours a day that wasn't totally narcissistic. I mean, it sounds better to say you're in training."

"I don't want to have this conversation," Rachel said.

"After Cheyenne everything changed. Now I'm this Olympic contender supposedly, at least among people who don't have a clue as to what's involved. Rachel, you do something you think is interesting, work at it like crazy, and suddenly what you get is a lot of people setting you up for failure."

"Who are these people?" Rachel asked. I was just pushing the cart now, with Rachel holding my arm. We weren't putting anything in the cart anymore, and if people didn't magically clear a path when they saw Rachel, I'm sure we would have knocked a few over.

"Well, there's me," I said.

"Exactly."

I really didn't know where this stuff was coming from. I wasn't too sure I meant it, either, and wasn't just contriving a mini-crisis so Rachel could ride to the rescue. The better to have another good memory. One more triumph for the archives. At the memorial service I could tell people, 'There she was, dishing out advice, taking care of others right until the end. But who was there for Rachel?' perhaps melodramatically—and everybody would forgive me, of course, given the occasion.

I think what bothers me is the quickness with which I accept that nobody especially cares. I know I make some noise about it, but it hasn't been a discovery, I think, so much as an assumption. Which has proven true, I may add. Self-fulfilling prophecy? You can't discount that, but I still expected it. Ten years ago, longer—who knows?—I might have bloodied a few noses. I might have actualized my visualization, thrown fits, grabbed some collars when somebody didn't fall to their knees, broken by her plight. If Rachel was going to die, the least they could do was move away from town. Because it's over here, it's over. At what point did I figure out my sister's dying, nobody cares, but that's okay, they've got their own problems to tussle with, how much can you expect from people anyway? That this was something I could take the longer view about? And what did I lose—what was the price of figuring that out? One day you're the center of the universe, the next day you're a speck of dirt among the billion specks each with their own dirty concerns, and not a ripple of consciousness noted the transition from one view to the other. It's too pat to say I got back into the game—began wrestling again—to prove to myself I still had some fire in my belly—or to see if I did?—but it's not something I could overlook if the question bears any importance at all. If I'm not a speck of dirt. Still, it would be a lot easier on the shoulder and knee if I'd just grabbed a few collars when people told me they're sorry, but they couldn't make it over to visit Rachel.

"Mostly I think I'm wrestling again because I'm upset about your illness," I blurted.

She stopped the cart. I'm surprised she had the strength. With her hoarse voice, even talking may have been hard for her, but she tried. We were about ten feet from the checkout line, and as we stood there, I noticed half-a-dozen people wheel their carts ahead of us. I wish I could have appreciated the moment a little more as we stood transfixed and Rachel poured over what she wanted to say because she knew I thought it was important, rather than find myself vaguely annoyed, suddenly impatient that the wait in line would be that much longer, altogether losing sight of our project here as if this was just one more day at the grocery.

As for Rachel, I think she was oscillating between thanking me but telling me I was being silly, and that she already knew my returning to wrestling after fifteen years, my burying myself in working out and visualization and whistling about the Olympics might have something to do with her diagnosis. After all, one day she gets the news, the next I'm up at 5AM for roadwork and mailing in my entrance fees. But she doesn't want to tell me I'm being silly—not only do such proclamations have a way of aggravating matters, but she's touched I'd go to the trouble—or that she already knows why.

Or maybe she's not thinking that at all. Human motivation's so complicated. There are reasons we do things, culled after the fact to make sense of the act, and sometimes we're satisfied with the explanations; but we tend to like our explanations neat 'n' tidy and our actions imbued with meaning, so in the end there's the distortion, with our explanations bearing about the same relationship as to why we do what we do as Ms. Suswhite does to a Barbie doll.

An elderly man stepped behind us and paused, as if this was the checkout line. "You don't have to wrestle," Rachel said finally. "It's okay. You tried hard."

It was an outing I would savor for a while. A good outing with my sister. Those last words I'd turn over and over.

It occurred to me later that night, when I got back from my run, that the entire shopping trip passed and we never mentioned Myron Gruber or his offer, not directly anyway. I called him within a minute—before I could think about it again and change my mind—and left a message on his machine thanking him for his interest and the opportunity, but that I had to pass. I'd get the check back to him soon.

The next day there was a message from Myron on my machine, asking me to sleep on it. He had patience, Myron. I'll give him that.

Two days later Rachel was back in the hospital. A pain in her side was unbearable—had been for days, even, I guess, as we rolled down the aisle at Safeway. She told Shari, who immediately drove her to the emergency room. Her liver it was, though the cells and fluid smothered her spleen and heart and lungs, in no particular order. Within twenty-four hours she couldn't eat, couldn't really take in who was visiting in the hospital though she was conscious still. She'd peer at people as if she was watching them underwater through cheap goggles. I'm not sure she even identified me. Ellen started showing up, too late to have that conversation they were always meaning to have, though I think Rachel took her in through the underwater murk. Even Sid the Kid came by a couple of times. He didn't stay long, I didn't take him aside for a stern talking to, but he showed up, more than once. He'd always liked Rachel back when she was the Aunt, and it couldn't have been easy for him to see her emaciated, hanging on, battling for what must have struck him as so little. By now it was clear even if Rachel pulled through this time, her organs were so compromised that the next crisis wasn't more than a few days around the corner. But he'd liked her, so he made his stand in that last week, for Rachel, and for me, I think, and because he knew his mother would appreciate it. I told Ellen I thought he couldn't have done that six months ago when he was stuck on crystal meth, but she shrugged. Not that she didn't agree, but I think Ellen's given up on interpreting Sid the Kid's few unambiguous gestures as unambiguous signs of maturity.

Dr. McLean, who lifted weights almost every hour he wasn't on call, whom I often saw down at the gym tugging at his bulky security belt on his bulky stomach, Rachel's primary care physician, as we say in these days of managed health, told me it could be two hours, two days, or a week before Rachel gives out.

We were at the Club, two sweaty middle-aged guys in muscle shirts staring each other down. "If you were a betting man, Doctor, which would it be?"

He stared at me briefly. Here we go again, I could imagine him thinking. When the news wasn't good, families had a way of looking at him as if they were accusing him of something. And why not?, I could see myself complaining to Ellen after Rachel died. These guys think they're gods, why can't they perform miracles? At the moment, though, if we were two sweaty middle-aged guys in muscle shirts, one of us was nuts, he must have thought. And training for the Olympics. He could tell I was too tired, and exasperated, and short, ready to lunge, maybe at him. I'm sure he saw guys like me all the time, though perhaps not staring him down in the gym. "You know," he said, still breathing heavily from his last set of benches, "this is hard for me, too."

"But if you were a betting man, Doc," I insisted. Note the emphasis on Doc.

He told me a week.

At the hospital nobody was visiting. I told Rachel I'd be back in a couple of days. I talked to her for a long time, said the kinds of things which were just between us that I won't go into, except to say that I did tell her I wish it was me instead. If somebody overheard that, I know they'd say I was lying—to myself anyway—but I know I meant it, and Rachel knew I meant it, though she looked at me through her tepid murky glaze as if I was nuts. "You tried so hard," I said to my sister.

Ellen came in as I was leaving. I told her I was going to Rapid City. "Don't," Ellen said. "You can't!" Tears suddenly stung her face. Betrayed but not surprised, that's how I thought she looked as I walked down the corridor; though exactly whom I was betraying—Rachel, or myself, or even Ellen, the good image of myself she still enjoyed—was less clear cut. "She won't be here when you get back! Bart, *please*. Bart...."

It took all night to get there.

Whenever I drive all night to some place I've never been, I think of the passage in *All the King's Men* where Jack Burden pieces it all together after he figures out Ann Stanton, whom he's loved since his youth, has become—has been—Willy Stark's mistress. It's a magnificent passage. He ends up in Long Beach for one of his Great Sleeps, as I like to think of it, though Robert Penn Warren doesn't explicitly acknowledge this entry as one—there are others he does—in the novel. This Great Sleep just lasts for a day, but the day matters, and when it's over he drives back. The idea, of course, is that he's changed, coarsened to butt-headed reality, ready to engage the sour world with his new understanding, but I've always wondered if Jack Burden was changed all that much by his night journey. Or was he changed because he learned something about himself by the way he reacted, that this compelled him to slide behind the wheel; so he slid behind the wheel and drove all night and slept through a week of his life so he could try to become somebody else (a lesser man, perhaps, but equal to what lay ahead), that it meant that much, but that the drive itself, that the Great Sleep, was just the prism through which he learned who he was.

I kept playing back, as I passed through the hills and fields and infinite small towns that light the highway like dying stars burning themselves out through the force of their own energy, what Rachel told me in the supermarket. "You don't have to wrestle. It's okay. You tried hard." The more I turned it, the less clear it was. I tried hard? She's the one for whom every day was an ordeal beyond imagining, for whom the good days were promises that won't be kept, for whom the bad days were siren calls through which she didn't have the luxury of caring if the promises were kept. Promises? Maybe on the bad days she welcomed death, though she wouldn't say that to me. Maybe she had to struggle mightily with welcoming death, fighting for the long view—to have a long view—when she knew there wasn't any long view, not for her. No, the levels on which Rachel tries I can't begin to guess. For me it was a run in the park compared to that—that's what I thought when I passed Medicine Bow and stopped for a midnight snack of two bran muffins and coffee, with a plate of pasta as an afterthought. Ellen tried so hard too. She had the child who was torturing her, the ex who didn't stick it out for reasons which were clear to both of us, though the question which may haunt both of us until the day we're in Rachel's spot is whether the reasons, though clear, were good enough. At some point you need to shrug and say they were, or else you never would have left each other. That's what I was thinking as I passed Gillette.

It was a clear spring night, bone-chilling. The roads weren't wet, but you had to think of black ice. Every mile it seemed there were signs warning of deer crossing, and every mile at least I saw roadkill in my headlights. I wondered if the signs hastened or slowed the detritus? After Gillette I turned up the stereo. By now I couldn't have told you who was playing.

"You think you do things for no reason but there's always a reason, isn't that so?" I remember postulating to a crestfallen kid in my office, back when I was teaching. The kid hadn't turned in an assignment for weeks and didn't know why (that's what I surmised after he offered a few tepid excuses). Because I was the teacher, he was quick to defer to my interpretation. Yes, he didn't know why. It's the perfect question for a college kid, both because it answers itself and it has no answer, such is the precision of its circuitry. Sometimes people just do things, and the detritus mounts.

It's okay, you tried hard, you don't have to wrestle—well, of course I tried hard, but I didn't try at all. You have to appreciate the precision of the circuitry. It only depends on what you're talking about.

Who was Rachel talking to in the supermarket? She'd still be alive when I got back at this time tomorrow, that's what I told myself as I crossed into South Dakota, but we'd never talk again. That was over. Was she giving herself permission to let go, as she gave me permission? We could quit. We'd fought the good fight, we'd discharged our obligation. We were everything we wanted each other to be, given our limitations of nature and temperament. It was okay now. It was okay.

It wasn't Cheyenne Redux, but considering I wrestled up a weight after driving all night on a whim, Rapid City was okay. The mats were spread across the high school gym. As often happens with freestyle meets there were more wrestlers than spectators, a point I'm sure wouldn't escape Myron Gruber's attention. I doubt there was anybody off the mats who wasn't related—loosely by friendship, forever by blood—to somebody on the mat. A lot of the wrestlers were local. They'd lumber to the stands after their match to huddle with their parents or girlfriends. 'Thought you had him on that takedown.' 'Your shoulders were up.' 'Fucker's got a mean arm drag.' The last was said to me by a short heavyweight who plopped down beside me in the third row as I leaned back in contemplation of the lights, taking in the yells and thumps, the words of solace and effusions of thanks. I looked over at him. He was still breathing hard, and his fat face was flushed as he eyed me and tried to pull a T-shirt over his fat, sweating shoulders. I wanted to tell him to dry off before slipping on the T-shirt. At first I was touched that this kid thought I'd been paying attention to his match and might have a few things to say to ease the sting of his defeat. Defeat? I had no idea. He reminded me a bit of Sid the Kid before he took off weight on his latest meth binge, and I remembered again how touched I was that Sid showed up to see Rachel. I was lying back in the third row in my wrestling togs, a few minutes from warming up for my own match. I was old enough to be this fat kid's father, older than he could realistically imagine being himself. Briefly I wondered what the fat kid thought his life would be like when he was my age. What visions were rolling around? Of course, he was clueless, but who'd want the kid to be right, to nail it on the head? Nobody envisions happiness itself, in the abstract, but the particulars that represent happiness: Beautiful women, sex, money, Olympic gold medals. Who knew what it meant to this kid now? Though you can bet if any of those particulars saunter his way—and they might—they'd add up to something a lot more complicated than the vague abstraction he now envisions. You discover a lot on your way to finding out you were wrong. Or you discover you were right, but for the wrong reasons. And they're not the same thing, that's what you can't get over, wanting the difference to mean something, knowing it does not.

There you are anyway, leaning back in the third row, still in your togs, almost ready to warm up. Yes, the fucker has a mean arm drag.

I beat a couple of locals in it mostly for the workout, then won a shaky 7-6 in the final over a Division II All-American from South Dakota State. The last guy, Murdoch, could have taken me. I got him early on a full back suplay, and knew I was in trouble when I didn't get the stick. I was dizzy and lethargic after that, holding on but busy enough the kid didn't know it. He was wary of another throw—at least some guy in the stands, probably his father or coach, kept yelling for Murdoch to watch for it after I landed the first suplay. ("Timmy, watch for the suplay! Watch out for the throw, Tim!" He had to be leery.) Murdoch was intimidated by my age, I think; that I must have by now an arsenal of secret weapons; and that I'd come so far obviously I meant business. Word was out about Cheyenne, too. People were respectful and curious. So I was able to squeeze by playing the kind of defense where you keep the other guy on the defensive, insinuating a throw here, setting up a tilt, tying up a leg. All cat and mouse stuff. The guy wasn't too good, not in terms of what I'd be up against, but he dominated after that.

I had plenty of excuses—I was wrestling up a weight, I'd driven all night, my sister was dying, I hadn't planned to enter but took off for Rapid City because I needed a long drive and the excuse to take it—but everyone wrestles hurt. There were guys who'd driven here from California. It bothered me immensely that after I became dizzy early, I relied on savvy to get by. I didn't work through the lethargy but accommodated it as if I knew nothing would work. I was licked. I told myself to tough it out, to steel myself, this was my new life, to roar on through the other side, mind over matter. I told myself to channel the ferocity of my rage over Rachel, that I hadn't gone to all the trouble just to be dazed on my feet at a second-rate meet in South Dakota. Faking an arm bar, I had my little man-to-man with my interior defeatist. But it's all a little much to take seriously, wouldn't you say?

So much for the Olympics.

I laughed out loud.

For a moment the kid Murdoch stopped and looked at the ref, who looked at me and then back at the kid: "Wrestle," he barked.

Perhaps he was mulling over blowing the whistle. I could have turned the kid at the moment—he'd let up when I laughed, and I had the half in and saw an angle—but I didn't. Give me credit for that, though perhaps the credit's due to my exhaustion. I needed the blow myself. So much for full-tilt boogie. I was still thinking cat and mouse. The poor kid wasn't fully apprised of the irony. If Murdoch wasn't losing, he might have asked if I was okay. You don't get that too often in college meets, I guess. Guys don't burst into laughter as they slip in the half. Perhaps that's because college meets are wrestled by college kids. Well, the sportsmanship was questionable. Did he think I was laughing at him? Did I insult the boy? Of course, Murdoch must have taken it as commentary about himself from a guy who'd been around, who had a magic arsenal.

It wasn't until I was out of Rapid City that it occurred to me that I could have mentioned something to the Murdoch kid when we shook hands after the match. But what can you say? Isn't that what it always comes back to—what swallows the generous impulse? Maybe this: 'Good work, kid, keep at it. And nothing personal there with the laughter bit. (If you think that was something, Murdoch, I'll introduce you to Myron Gruber.) You see, it really had nothing to do with you. There are things you're not liable to be aware of. Take my sister, who's dying while I'm a thousand miles away. There was something she told me and I wanted to see if it was true. Still, I should be by her bed. She'd understand, you can bet on that, but is that good enough? I went nuts for a while.' Maybe not.

You can say something.

I was past Gillette when it all became clear again.

Angles. That's all you need for leverage. You can force one or find one. You do it with muscle or guile. And when the door is open you walk through.

Even when you're dizzy, like I was against Murdoch. Even when stars blink before you like you're taking a peripheral vision exam. I do what I do to stay alert. I grab the leg, swing around, kick out. But now when we hit the mat Murdoch yelps and I'm quick with the hammerlock before he knows.

The cloud lifts, the stars blink. I'm in with the headlock, I rock back with the guillotine, I squeeze a key lock, a twisting knee, a scissors, a chicken wing. Even as I throw the series, I know it's impossible. That's the beauty. I'm ready for anything. It's not the original angle that matters, not against guys better than Murdoch, but what opens up after they respond to the original move, or the move after, or the one after that. You work it by muscle or guile and when the door opens you walk through. Nothing else matters. You find the angle, you move.

A full back suplay? A hammerlock? Against better guys than the kid I just beat, I'll keep the arsenal basic: leg drops, arm drags, work the two-on-one, hook a leg, try some misdirection. Most moves are hybrids I couldn't name. A kelly but not a kelly, the arm too low, too high. Technique is everything but the target is elusive.

And better guys than Murdoch are always working a con to get an angle. You have to be aware of that. I promise myself I will be. Yet it doesn't matter what they do—that's the beauty too, the fleck of purity it's worth driving all night to remember. There are constructs—rules, boundaries—but within the circle none of that is applicable, not with the guys I'll have to beat. Within the circle he'll have his will, his con, his dreams, and then there's me, so full of my will, my con, my dreams, but none of

that matters either because I work it by muscle and guile, that's all the truth I need, and when the door opens, I walk through.
 Now it's clear.

for Joni Eron Hobson (1951-1990)

About Author

Don Eron lives in Boulder, Colorado. *And Go to Innisfree* is his first published book.